f-2021

A Captain for
Caroline Gray

PROPER ROMANCE

A Captain for Caroline Gray

Julie Wright

THORNDIKE PRESS
A part of Gale, a Cengage Company

LIBRARY OF CONGRESS CIP DATA ON FILE.
CATALOGUING IN PUBLICATION FOR THIS BOOK
IS AVAILABLE FROM THE LIBRARY OF CONGRESS.

ISBN-13: 978-1-4328-8868-8 (hardcover alk. paper)

Published in 2021 by arrangement with Shadow Mountain

Printed in Mexico
Print Number: 01   Print Year: 2021

For Scott
Du är min alltid.

CHAPTER ONE

The ball had been a disaster.

Certainly, Caroline Gray's dance card had been filled respectably, if not entirely, and the conversation had not been dull. And the food — oh, the food. Caroline had loved every creamy morsel. The entire neighborhood admired the Prescotts' cook.

In truth, Caroline hadn't even realized how disastrous the ball had actually been until the next morning when her mother entered her bedchamber before the maid had even arrived to light the fire.

"Get up," her mother said, pulling down the coverlet that Caroline had embroidered herself.

"What is it, Mother?" Caroline saw the wild, desperate look in her mother's eyes, and sat upright in bed. "Is something wrong? Is someone injured? Are you ill? Is the house on fire?"

Her mother schooled herself, fixing her

7

features with a calm Caroline recognized as a lie. "Nothing's wrong, Caroline. I simply cannot have you lolling about in bed all day when plans must be made and futures must be discussed. I've already called for your maid. It's a disgrace that I arrived in your rooms before her. Really, Caroline, you are far too relaxed in your relationships with your servants."

So, it was "Caroline" and not "dearest" or "sweet pea" this morning. Mama must have been truly worried to have adopted such formality. That was quite unlike her.

Futures? Plans? Of course. Mama wanted to discuss the lack of any proposal or offer made for Caroline's hand in marriage.

Caroline had tried this season — really, she had — but to no avail.

She touched her forehead, feeling a headache coming on. There was nothing to be done for it, however. Her mother wasn't the sort to be dissuaded. The woman was the very best mother any girl could ask for, but she had the steel backbone that any proper English lady required for survival.

Caroline swung her legs over the side of the bed and ignored the violent chill that swept through her as soon as her toes touched the floorboards. She wished the fire had already been set.

8

Her maid arrived only a moment later, but that moment had been enough. Nita nearly dropped the kindling for the fire when she came face-to-face with Mother's disapproving glare.

Her mother did not scold — not out loud. Rather, her disapproval was voiced in the pursed tightening of her lips and the wrinkle of irritation that appeared above her brow.

Poor Nita. Caroline would have to figure out a way to make up for her mother's mood this morning. Perhaps she would have Cook make some of Nita's favorite tarts.

Her mother's gaze fell on the open sketchbook at the window seat. Her eyes softened for a moment as she saw what Caroline knew to be the drawing of Lady Romania Brown dancing with her husband, Sir Walter. The elderly couple had the most beautiful, soft wrinkles in their faces, and Caroline felt compelled to capture the moment as soon as possible. She'd stayed up quite late after the ball to recreate as much as memory allowed.

The softness in her mother's eyes hardened as she whispered, "I wish you'd have spent your time at that ball making your own attachments instead of merely recording the attachments of others." Her mother turned away from the sketchbook, and

Caroline hid her pencil-smudged hands behind her back. "When you're done dressing, Caroline, meet me in the drawing room."

"Will we be long in the drawing room?"

Her mother gave no response.

Once her mother had left, and the sound of her footfalls proved that she'd gone down the stairs, Caroline turned to Nita. "I'll dress myself if you would be willing to go to the kitchens and fetch me a breakfast that I can eat quickly."

Nita shook her head. "Your mother is in an awful mood. Is poking her further such a good idea?"

The casual comment made Caroline think her mother might be right about her being too relaxed with her servants, but she preferred them disrespectful and honest. "It is precisely because of her awful mood that I require this. Clearly a scolding is in my future, and the chances of me being trapped in that drawing room until dinner are extremely high. Please, Nita. I will need my strength to face whatever is coming."

Nita swallowed hard and took a last, desperate look toward the door before giving a sharp nod and leaving.

Things had been strained regarding the staff after Caroline's father had died. They

10

worried over the future, which made sense. The estate was entailed on Caroline's cousin — a pleasant man who allowed her family to remain at the family home in spite of her father's passing. In spite of the fact that the home was now his.

But Caroline's cousin was not an old man. She had met him several times during the course of her seasons in London and found him to be handsome, intelligent, and agreeable. In truth, Mr. Moore's youth and charm and newfound wealth of property that came to him by way of her father's passing meant he was in a position where marriage was an amiable notion.

His marrying would necessitate him taking possession of his inheritance.

His taking over his inheritance meant Caroline and her mother would be displaced.

So, yes, the household servants were worried. Would the new master keep them on? Would the new master be as good to them as her father and mother had been? For even though Caroline's mother occasionally indulged in moody tempers, she was a practical woman and treated those in her employment with respect and fairness.

But they all had time. Mr. Moore had not

declared a preference for any young lady, as of yet.

Her mother had once hoped Caroline and Mr. Moore might find a compatibility with one another beyond mutual respect, but being agreeable and being compatible were not the same thing. Mr. Moore preferred pretty ladies with pretty smiles — pretty smiles on mouths that remained closed.

Caroline knew she was pretty with her dark hair and fair face, but keeping her mouth closed proved to be a struggle for her on most occasions. Though her cousin laughed alongside Caroline as they debated the finer points of politics, and he'd seemed to enjoy hearing her opinion on the state of the world, he did not ask her to dance at many of the balls.

Once dressed, and the rolls spread with marmalade Nita had smuggled out of the kitchen had been devoured, Caroline squared her shoulders, lifted her skirts, and descended the stairs. When she entered the drawing room, she hesitated at the sight of her mother bent over needlework.

Her mother never did needlework unless she wanted to think. She felt it a waste of her time, and she didn't much care for the way her fingers cramped from the tedious, repetitive motion.

Caroline didn't care much for needlework either, but her mother insisted she maintain the skill. "Once you're mistress of your own home, you can choose to quit the endeavor altogether, but not until then," her mother often said.

Her father had laughed when her mother said such things. He'd taken great pride in his two daughters, their only children due to her mother's poor health in childbearing, and they had raised the girls to be inquisitive and expressive.

Her parents had expanded their daughters' education to include politics, science, and literature — fields of study more often reserved for gentlemen — which meant that Caroline and her sister, Josephine, were well-read and knowledgeable enough to make discussion in a room full of ladies quite difficult.

Josephine had been lucky enough to make a match with a man who loved his wife's wit and intelligence. He wasn't wealthy, but the living he provided his wife was comfortable since Josephine knew how to run her household efficiently.

Caroline had yet to find such a man. Most of them were put off by her strong opinions.

Most ladies were put off by those opinions as well.

And though her mother had encouraged the very science lessons that had led to Caroline's failure to find a man in her first, second, third, and fourth season, her mother still scolded her as if the fault fell entirely at Caroline's own feet.

But her mother doing needlepoint?

Something more severe than a scolding awaited.

"Sit," her mother said without looking up from her work.

Caroline sat.

Her mother finally laid her hoop and needle to the side on the settee and looked up. "It was the last ball of the season, Caroline."

"Yes. I am aware, Mama."

"And was there anything, any flicker, any hope in a match?"

Shamed that she had not accomplished the task which had been placed before her, Caroline pressed her lips together and looked down at her skirt. "No, Mama."

"What of that young man Mr. Moore introduced you to when he invited you to dine with him and his mother?"

Caroline winced. "Mr. Alton? He sucked his food through his teeth while he ate. Is it so much to ask that a gentleman chew his food without getting it stuck in his teeth so

14

consistently? And he picked at his nails then flicked away his findings in my direction. Do you know how often I had to wipe away his nail debris from my napkin and skirts?"

"Those are small habits a wife can correct, not reasons to refuse his interest. He liked you," her mother said, sounding quite desperate.

"Did he? How could he? He argued the most preposterous ideas with me. He tried to convince me that the world is, indeed, flat. He kept saying how His Majesty's fleets will someday reach the edge and then where will our great country be?" Caroline shook her head.

"And when I mentioned William Herschel's telescope and his discovery of a new planet and how lovely and poetic such a discovery was to me, he said the strangest things about our world and other planets. It was hard to tell if he'd been drinking too much or if he actually believes his ridiculous outdated ideas. So even if he professes to like me, Mama, can you imagine discussing Volta's battery or Dalton's atomic theory with such a man?"

Instead of agreeing, her mother became agitated. "You don't have time to nitpick at the men who might choose you, dearest."

"But, Mama, I know comparative little of

15

discoveries and science. How am I to discover more if I do not have a man at my side who is educated enough to discuss them with me? How will I ever teach my children? You would not have accepted such a man."

"My options were of a different sort than yours. You know that." Her mother dabbed at her forehead with a handkerchief.

"I do know I need to marry," Caroline said. "And I am trying. I'll do better. We're not yet desperate."

Her mother's gaze flicked up in a storm of heat and fear. "But we are!"

Caroline startled, and her mother lowered her voice.

"We *are* that desperate, dearest. Your cousin, Mr. Moore, is engaged."

The words struck the terrible reality to Caroline's heart.

"Are you certain?" Caroline asked.

Her mother's shoulders slumped as if the burden of sharing this news had proved to be too great for her. "Quite certain. They have not made the news public, but his mother informed me of the engagement last night as we were bidding farewell. I think she meant the relaying of this information to be a kindness, to give me the soonest notice possible. And far better to hear it from her than from the neighborhood gossips."

"Engaged." Caroline wished she hadn't convinced Nita to fetch the rolls; they felt like sickening lumps in her stomach. "What will happen to us?"

Her mother closed her eyes, took a slow breath, and opened her eyes again. "My brother has offered me space in his home. But there is not room enough for us both. There is not room for you at your sister's either."

Caroline felt real panic rising and crashing over her. This possibility had become reality so much sooner than she had ever expected.

"Then what am I to do?" she asked, hating how small and afraid she sounded, hating how brutish the economics of her situation really were. "Mr. Alton truly did not like me, Mama. If he had, he would have made an offer."

Her mother squared her shoulders in a way Caroline knew meant that there would be no argument. "I spoke with a friend last night — Mrs. Barritt. We visited her when we were in town last."

Caroline nodded. She hadn't exactly liked the cold, priggish woman, but she remembered her.

17

"She mentioned she has a son in India. He's a third son, you know, and wanted to make his own fortune. He's quite established now, as his father purchased him a commission as a captain in the army, and he has become quite engrossed in his duties. He has no inclination to return home.

"Mrs. Barritt mentioned how he is very much in need of an English wife. She saw you dancing last night and mentioned what a pretty girl you were. She asked after your prospects."

Caroline's hands, which had been smoothing her skirts, stilled. "Of all the impertinence!"

Her mother sighed in exasperation. "The question was not an insult, but rather an inquiry as to your desires for a future match. She made you an offer."

Caroline sucked in a sharp breath, sharp enough she felt it cut her all the way down to her lungs. She stood and began pacing. "She made an offer? To me? That's absurd. I'm not about to accept an offer made from a woman I've only met once, on behalf of her son, whom I've never met at all."

"Listen to me!" Her mother's voice rose as she stood as well. "No one expects you to accept an offer of marriage from Mrs. Barritt. The offer she made was to pay half

18

the cost of your passage to India. In exchange, you will accept an invitation to her son's home for dinner, meet him, get to know him, and see if you two will like each other well enough to want to form your own agreement. She has asked that you agree to accompany him on three separate occasions of his choosing, aside from the initial dinner."

Caroline processed the information, visualizing each sentence, forming an understanding of every word. After a long moment, she shook her head. "No. I cannot go." She moved to the door as if to end the interview.

Her mother grasped her arm. "Do you think you have any choice? Sit down, child. Sit and listen to me rather than keeping your own counsel."

Caroline sat, sick with terror and angry at the insult.

"Do you wish to see yourself passed around your relations like an unwanted parcel?" her mother asked. "Do you wish to see yourself as the nursemaid to your aging uncles or aunts? Or as a caregiver when your sister delivers her children? Do you not wish to have children of your own?"

"Of course I wish to have children, Mama, but this? India? To be cut off from those

19

same aunts and uncles and cousins? To be cut off from *you*? From Josephine? To have no relations at all? Would that not be far worse than caring for those same relations?"

"Do you think I like this?" her mother demanded. "That I want this? I take no joy in the thought of my child on the other side of continents that are wholly unknown to me. I fully accept my own fault in this terrible business. Your father and I may have given you certain advantages, but we failed to make you and your sister the sort of women who would attract favorable marriages. I felt myself above teaching you the importance of flirtations and silliness, and now I am the one who must take blame for your inability to find a husband.

"Josephine inherited her gentleness from your father, that kindness he exhibited in all his days. But you? You are a mirror of me — and my temperament — and for that I'm truly sorry." She fell back to the settee with her head in her hands.

Caroline could not allow her mother to take the blame. Caroline could have flirted her way to a husband, but she hadn't. Her punishment for that failure would see her exiled from the only home she'd known and cut off from her entire family.

The blame was hers. The terrible burden

was also hers.

She saw the sag of her mother's shoulders and wondered if maybe her mother's burden was worse than her own.

She loved her mother dearly. They had all felt the loss of her father, but her mother had frayed in ways Caroline had not expected from the strong woman. What would it take to see her snap altogether?

Caroline could not — *would not* — be the one to force the color from her mother's face and the smile from her mother's lips.

But going to India? Were things really so desperate that she had no other choice?

She sat by her mother a long time and considered her options, discarding each one as it proved itself impossible. All of them. All of her prospects hinged on marrying. Without marrying, she had no possibilities. No prospects. No choices.

Caroline had spent her choices in the public lecture courses learning about physics and at dinner parties discussing politics.

Each one of those choices had led her to this moment where only two choices remained: to be childless and husbandless — an option that tore her heart to shreds to even consider, or to leave for India — an option which still tore at her heart, but one which offered at least a glimmer of hope for her future.

Caroline wanted to be a mother. She wanted to be a wife.

If she stayed, she would be neither.

If she went, she had the possibility of both.

It was the only choice that made any kind of logical *and* emotional sense.

Caroline briefly closed her eyes, then said, "And I do not have to marry him if I do not wish? There is no obligation that I am under to accept her son in particular?"

Her mother's nod was slow.

Caroline took several breaths to clear her mind as well as her lungs. She forced some brightness into her voice. "Well, then, if it doesn't work out, I can return home. Consider all the lovely adventures we'll have to discuss over tea." She gave her mother what she hoped to be an encouraging smile.

Her mother did not return the smile. Instead, tears filled her mother's eyes. "I will not have enough money to bring you home. The price of your passage is . . . considerable. My income without the estate is scarcely enough to live on. I will barely have enough to pay my part of sending you."

Caroline said nothing to this new information. What was there to say?

Why had she not flirted and flounced and pouted prettily to the boys of the *ton*? She could have. Her features were fine enough that many men had thought to court her during her first season. They all liked her well enough before she opened her mouth. Conversation with her led them from interest to wariness. And when they'd discovered that she was often found at public lecture courses on physics, their wariness turned to outright disdain.

The invitations to social gatherings became fewer. She held out hope, over and over, that a man would value her thoughts. How wrong she'd been.

If only she would have pretended . . .

But Caroline had not pretended.

She had done as her mother had done and silently looked down on the frivolities of society. Just not silently enough. They must have felt her censure weighted in her every word. She hardly did anything to hide it. Surely, they would not have judged her so harshly had she not judged them first.

She had created her own trouble. But she would not continue to be a trouble to her mother. She could do that much. Because her mother was right. What options were left to them aside from a spinsterhood that would only be bearable to one rich enough to not care if she married or not?

Caroline wanted to marry. She simply realized too late that the business of marrying was more multifaceted than she'd suspected.

But she could pretend for her mother that all was well and that the idea of India wasn't so bad.

It *was* bad, of course, but she would pretend otherwise. She would pretend she felt some excitement. She would pretend to thrill at the adventure of it all. She would pretend that her heart was not breaking at the thought of leaving her family and her beloved England.

No.

Not merely breaking.

Her heart was already irreparably shattered.

CHAPTER TWO

Caroline watched her two steamer trunks be loaded onto the ship named *Persistence*. *How fitting,* she thought.

The trunks held all the earthly possessions she was allowed to take with her on a trip from which she might not return. True, there were more books, paper, and pencils than anything else in those trunks, the weight of which was likely why the porter tossed her a rather impertinent glance.

She had said her goodbyes to Josephine and to her mother. Caroline had not wanted a public display of her sorrow, so she made her other farewells in private.

Her mother had embraced her so tightly Caroline imagined she could feel her mother's fingerprints on her shoulders.

"Find love, dearest," her mother had said through wracking sobs.

Find love.

Caroline had to look away quickly.

Mr. Moore had offered to see Caroline to the ship, and their ride together had been full of Caroline explaining all of the delightful reasons to travel to India. By the time they'd arrived, she'd almost convinced herself that the entire adventure had been her idea.

"I'm truly sorry, cousin, for being the reason you have found yourself with a need to travel," Mr. Moore said, his voice low and full of sincerity as he stood by her on the dock. "I had not been looking for love, but it found me anyway. I did try to put it off for as long as I could in the hopes that it might have found you too."

Caroline thought it brave of him to enter such a discussion with her. It showed a mark of his character that he felt capable of saying the uncomfortable things. It made Caroline mourn her inability to have been more flexible regarding her compatibility. He would have made an excellent companion — in time. After he'd grown used to her being *her.*

But instead, he would make another woman an excellent companion. And that was for the best. Did she truly want to cheat some man out of genuine happiness by making him believe her to be what she was not?

26

Caroline held out her hand, and Mr. Moore took it. "Do not worry yourself," she said. "Love is a business best not put off to the last moment. Take this advice from someone who knows."

He smiled at her. "I only wish there was something more I could do than convey you to this place."

"There is. Keep an eye out for my mother every now and again. I do worry for her welfare."

"I will be certain to check in on her as often as I am able. You have my word." He nodded but then looked above her head and squinted as if confused by what he saw.

"What is it?" Caroline asked, turning around. Behind her cousin's carriage, a man and a woman hurried up and made as if to call her attention.

"Do you know these people?" Mr. Moore asked.

As the couple grew closer, Caroline recognized Mr. and Mrs. Barritt. She had become well acquainted with them over the past few weeks. It felt strange to be under the scrutiny of a woman who already considered Caroline to be her daughter-in-law. The mortification of having them survey her from every angle and murmuring things to themselves made her feel like a horse at auction.

But why had they traveled so far when she had said goodbye to them just days before?

"Yes," she murmured to her cousin. "They are Mr. and Mrs. Barritt." She didn't explain the particulars and hoped she wouldn't have to. Mr. Moore had already expressed guilt for his role in her situation. How much worse would her pitiable state be if he knew the whole of it?

"Thank you for seeing me to the docks, Mr. Moore." She gave a quick curtsy in the hopes that he would leave, but he stayed, making her cheeks flush hot with the knowledge that she could not do this odious, mercenary task in private.

"Miss Gray!" Mrs. Barritt raised a gloved hand in greeting.

Caroline smiled and prayed there was warmth in the gesture since she felt no warmth in her veins. She curtsied again. "Mrs. Barritt. Mr. Barritt. May I introduce my cousin, Mr. Moore?"

Formalities observed, they turned back to Caroline. "We wanted to give you this." Mrs. Barritt nudged Mr. Barritt, who was startled into remembering the package in his hands. He moved to hand it to her, thought better of handing such a bulk to a lady, and mumbled something about making certain the package was placed in her cabin by one of the crewmen. Caroline looked at the bundle, remembering her mother's words asking her if she wanted to be nothing more than a spinster passed between family members like an unwanted parcel.

"I'm sorry?" she said, realizing she'd missed part of the conversation.

"We felt so silly for forgetting to send this with you when you last saw us in London. We immediately struck out after you in hopes of catching you in time. Please tell our dear Nicholas how much we love him, how we think of him every day and pray for his safekeeping." Mrs. Barritt looked like she might cry.

Mr. Barritt looked at the ship and the bustle on the docks as if he had no part to play in the conversation. Caroline felt better knowing she wasn't the only one who had wandered off mentally.

"Nicholas Barritt?" Mr. Moore asked.

"Yes." Mrs. Barritt looked delighted to have someone say her son's name. "Do you know him, sir?"

"Only a little, ma'am."

"He's been gone to India these last two years. We've missed him a great deal. But

29

how delighted we are to send a little present from home."

Mr. Moore looked at the package in Mr. Barritt's hand, but Caroline's cheeks burned, knowing that *she* was the "little present" meant by Mrs. Barritt. She had the peace of knowing that Mr. Moore misunderstood the situation for all of one moment before Mrs. Barritt spoke again.

"When I saw Miss Gray dancing at the Prescotts' ball, I thought how sad it was that my Nicholas was not there to see her, not there to meet her. I knew at once that I must allow him that honor. And here we all are!"

Caroline was incapable of stopping Mrs. Barritt's words — not without being rude. That she had to smile at having a woman who was virtually a stranger pay for Caroline's passage to India so that her son might have a shot of gaining an English bride made Caroline sick.

She knew all about seasickness but now wondered if perhaps it wasn't the voyage that made people ill. Perhaps illness stemmed from the reasons that necessitated the voyage.

Mr. Moore's face registered surprise. He'd not known his cousin had agreed to such terms. He'd only known that she'd decided to travel and find her own way in life. But now he knew the truth of it.

Caroline felt the heat of shame rise to the tips of her ears as his gaze fell on her and refused to leave.

Mrs. Barritt reached out and hugged Caroline hard. "Make sure you tell our Nicholas how beloved he is for us. I'm sure the two of you will get on quite well. His prospects are full and rich."

Unlike mine, Caroline thought as she offered a thin smile to Mr. and Mrs. Barritt, who departed to find someone who could see their package safely delivered to Caroline's cabin.

She did not dare look at Mr. Moore's face.

"I am sorry, cousin," he said again, only this time the soft pity in his voice made Caroline's eyes sting with tears. There would be gossip enough in the *ton* now that she knew Mrs. Barritt had no intention of keeping silent on the agreement.

"It's an adventure I'm glad to take. Please do not make yourself uneasy over the matter."

He stepped closer to her and whispered, "But you haven't agreed to marry Nicholas Barritt, have you? No arrangement has actually been made, has it?"

She finally met his eye. "No. Of course

31

not. I would never agree to marry a man I've never met."

He looked relieved. "Good. Miss Gray, it isn't too late to change your mind. I would be happy to pay for whatever the Barritts have invested in your passage. I'm sure I could introduce you to —"

"Please do not worry for me. I've made my choice." Would her pride allow her to be a charity case for her cousin? Even if her pride could withstand such mortification, Mr. Moore's friends knew her already — or at least they knew of her reputation as a know-all.

He didn't look convinced, but also seemed uncertain how to handle the situation. "If you're sure. But . . ."

"What is it?" she asked when he hesitated.

"It is probably nothing. Just be careful with him. I heard something once, and . . . well, be careful."

"Thank you for the warning. I will, indeed, be quite careful. Thank you. Truly. But I should be boarding. Goodbye, Mr. Moore." She bobbed a quick curtsy and turned so he would not see the tears on her lashes. The *ton* might be able to gossip over her desperate circumstances, but no one would be able to say she had shed tears over it.

Just like the name of the ship, she would persist.

CHAPTER THREE

Captain Thomas Scott surveyed the strange man and woman who had boarded his ship.

"It would mean ever so much to us," the lady continued, "if you would be so kind as to place this package in the cabin of one of your passengers. She's going to India as a bride for our son. Isn't that ever so lovely?"

Thomas tried to mask his disdain as the man attempted to hand him a parcel. "I am sorry," Thomas said. "But I have crewmen who will do well enough to make deliveries for you. Surely you're aware that captains do not fetch and carry like dogs."

The man looked uncomfortable as he tucked the parcel back under his arm. He glanced at his wife, as if for support.

"We insisted on speaking to you personally," the woman said. "It is a matter of great importance to us that you keep an eye out for the lady in question as we do not want her to become timid during the voyage."

Though he raised his eyebrows at her, he understood her meaning perfectly. They did not want her unchaperoned. "I assure you, madam, we keep a woman to serve as chaperone."

It was true enough in spirit, if not in law. Clara watched after the girls who boarded his ship, but she didn't follow behind them at every moment. He found that the girls stayed together enough to render a chaperone unnecessary. He believed that this couple had more than worries over chaperones. They did not want the woman they'd handpicked to rethink her own choices regarding the match, and a three-month voyage allowed plenty of time for rethinking.

Thomas hated how so very few women did any rethinking while on the voyage to Mumbai or Chennai, the two ports he sailed to most frequently. Those women went to India to find husbands, and the few who returned empty-handed acted as though they had failed all of humanity by not making a match. Thomas thought those who returned home were the lucky ones.

Many other captains catered to the demand for proper English wives by hosting dinner parties when they arrived in port so the young ladies could meet the young men, and the not-so-young men, who were available. Thomas did not host any such parties. On occasion, he would be invited to attend balls and dinners, and he was obliged to accept those invitations based on his rank, position, and his personal dealings with trade, but he hated it.

Blast, but he hated it.

He gave a flat-eyed stare to the couple while the woman continued to talk. "My son is a captain himself. Though not of the sea. No, he's a captain in His Majesty's army. You two would probably get on quite well!"

Thomas doubted that and stepped to the side to bypass the couple and continue in his duties, but the woman moved in front of him again.

"And the girl we've found for him! She is ever so lovely. So accomplished. I hear she sings like a songbird."

"But you've not heard her for yourself," Thomas said, trying to point out that perhaps she should have verified this information before putting the woman on a ship bound for her son.

The woman looked perplexed but brightened. "Well, no, I haven't, but those who have said it are ever so trustworthy. And I really do hope that you —"

"If you'll excuse me." He bowed. "You may hand the parcel off to any of my crew as all of them are capable of placing it in the correct cabin. Thank you *ever so* much." He walked away. He hadn't bothered asking the name of the young miss he was supposed to be looking after and was glad the couple hadn't told him the woman's name.

If he knew her identity, he'd be tempted to throw the girl overboard to save her from a future of probable disappointment.

As he walked away, the woman stammered, "But I — well, I — How insolent! So rude. To be treated with ever so much —" She stopped, perhaps realizing that his repeating her turn of phrase meant she said it too often. He should have felt bad for his behavior in spite of her own ill manners, but he had a ship to sail.

But he found that he could not resist turning back to watch the couple make their way to the nearest crewman, Mr. Kilpack, who didn't look happy about being sent off on an errand. Thomas knew the crewman had a long list of duties to tend to before they sailed. The couple was quite insistent, however, and Kilpack eventually relieved the man of his burden.

Odd. They were odd people. After meeting such parents, any sensible woman would do well to steer clear of the son.

But silly people had a way of attracting silly people.

He'd be done soon with the business of entertaining ridiculous people on his ship because he had a plan. He had begun investing in goods from India. He would no longer be simply a captain ferrying goods back and forth for others to buy and sell. He would also be a businessman who would make profits on goods he transported *and* sold. Soon, he would have a fine house and be able to consider settling down and creating a family of his own.

He loved the sea, but it had been his father's dream for him, not his own. Soon enough, he'd have the money to make his own path. But not today. Today, he was nothing but the captain. Which meant he had work to do.

He shook his head and moved to the quarterdeck to verify that the helmsman was in place and the ship was ready to sail. As he did so, something caught his eye. No. Not something — *someone.* A young lady.

A gust of wind snatched her hat from her head, the untied ribbons fluttering free. She reached to save it from being blown overboard but failed. One of his deckhands, Mr. Black, fished the hat from the water and carried it to the woman. She laughed rather than scowling or lamenting as he handed it to her. Then she very graciously shook the water from the bonnet and put it on her head, though it must have been quite damp.

The action was unlike any he had ever seen from a lady before. He wished he had been close enough to hear the conversation between her and Mr. Black. Once the deckhand had returned to his chores, the lady removed the bonnet again, probably to let it, and her hair, dry.

Her white dress was a gauzy fabric — an expensive muslin, he guessed, based on his experience in the textile trade — and fell to the ground in a lovely cascade rather than the stiff, conical shape he'd noticed young ladies wearing during his last trip into town. The lady's long, gauzy sleeves were gathered at intervals, making a series of puffs down the arm. The bright blue ribbon of her dress matched the embroidered wrap hung loosely at her elbows. He considered the ribbon and the color, and smiled. A shipment of indigo waited for him in India. If women's fashion stayed steady, that shipment would be lucrative.

Focusing on the business of fashion helped distract him from his other thoughts. He didn't want to think about why she had caught his attention. He didn't want to think of the curves of her figure. He didn't want to think about how the soft, dark curls framing her face made him wish to see her long hair loosed from the pins and braids that held it up off her neck. He blinked several times, swallowed hard, and looked away.

No woman to ever sail on his ship had gained his notice so quickly, and this one shouldn't have either. The women who boarded were either already married or journeying to become such. And he'd not let a pretty face and soft curls distract him. Not now, when he was so close to securing his own future. He'd worked too hard to gain his position.

Now that his father had passed away, he knew his mother was eager for him to come home and tend to the business of creating a family, but he couldn't see how such a thing would ever be possible until after he'd settled his finances. The sea was his home for now. He didn't want to bring a wife into a situation where she'd be left alone for months at a time. He knew of no woman who would agree to such a situation for herself.

There were some men who brought their families with them on sea voyages. He'd allowed several men of his crew to do just that because he could not bear to be the cause of an unwanted separation, despite the dangers posed by the sea. In Thomas's experience, women liked balls and parties, fashion and gossip. They wanted the constancy that came from a life in one or two places, not the inconstancy of a life where every minute you were on top of a new place in the world.

He looked at the woman as she leaned against the railing with her bonnet now tied to her wrist. The feeling she created in him must have been because, while in port, his mother had forced him into the conversation of settling down.

Yes. That was it.

He frowned and sped away, his bootheels clapping the deck and drowning out that brief stirring he'd felt. Not that there was anything wrong in admiring the lines of the female figure. It was like admiring a sunset. Beauty was what it was, and there was no vice in acknowledging beauty when he saw it.

It was with relief that Thomas heard the bells ringing for all non-passengers to vacate the ship. He watched as people scurried off, and he hoped the pretty young lady was among those leaving. He didn't need distractions of her sort.

Once they were clear of the harbor and out into open sea, Thomas readied himself for dinner. The first dinner of any voyage was either the worst or the best, depending on perspective. He usually liked the first dinner as it proved to be entertaining and interesting. He was able to meet new people, learn new things, and often found himself amused at the way events unfolded as the various guests at his table made discoveries regarding their shipmates. People frequently formed alliances and identified enemies within that first hour. A voyage that lasted more than three months was bound to put a strain on those alliances and an even bigger strain on those who were determined to loathe each other from the start.

Thomas was careful to keep a distance and not get too personally involved with his passengers since a ship — no matter how large — was a small place for those who carried grievances against others.

He joined the dinner party late and startled to find the young woman who had earlier captured his attention in attendance. He tried not to stare, but his gaze kept returning to her. She spoke quietly to another young woman who looked to be of a same age — early twenties. She wore a different dress this evening, the light green as equally lovely as her white day dress. While the other woman talked excitedly regarding the journey, the lady in light green responded with barely visible smiles that certainly never reached her eyes. Questions sped through his mind about why she was on his ship when she clearly felt less than happy about the prospect.

Had she been sent away for some cause or another? He could not see this woman as the sort who would have no prospects and no choices. She was unerringly pretty. Her form perfect, her face fair and open, her hair dark and very likely soft.

He cleared his throat as if such an act could also clear his mind, calling attention to himself, and everyone smiled expectantly at their captain. The dark-haired woman also smiled, a brief flash that was gone far too quickly.

Well, he couldn't just stand there making a study of the woman. There was dinner to be had.

Lieutenant Peterson smoothed back his graying hair before addressing the group. "Allow me to make the introductions, Captain."

Thomas nodded.

Peterson motioned to the dark-haired lady

first. "Miss Caroline Gray of Salisbury."

Thomas bowed to her while she offered an elegant curtsy and a subdued smile. Her steady gaze was one of a poised woman assured of both her standing in society and in her own skin. He would have assumed her to be a woman already taken, already married, except Peterson had called her *Miss* Caroline Gray. Yet, she could not be one of the Fishing Fleet women. When their eyes met, his heart stumbled, and he opened his mouth.

He did not know what he might have said, and luckily he was saved from himself by Lieutenant Peterson's voice.

"This is Miss Jennie Jeffries of Bath."

Miss Jeffries smiled broadly, her freckled face beaming. Her curtsy was essentially an excited bob. He bowed to the woman before moving on to Miss Lynette James, whose eyes were quite large and quite wide; the poor woman seemed to be in a constant state of panic and terror. Miss Monique Bronley seemed too preoccupied by the view of the table of food behind him to really notice him or the introduction. The last of the ladies were Miss Rebecca Cole and Miss Agatha Luke, both of whom had the appearance of high society in every particular — especially the arrogance.

The gentlemen were introduced next: Mr. Alan Liechty, an apothecary for the military, and Mr. Douglas Miller, a barrister traveling under the advisement of the Governor-General. Mr. Miller scowled and sniffed as if the introductions had been an inconvenience.

Six women and two men.

Thomas glanced again at Miss Gray. As if embodying the muted notion of her name, she stayed relatively silent. He pulled his eyes away from her and considered the other ladies, wondering which of them were doomed to be a relation to that garish couple who'd boarded his ship earlier.

The couple's request that he look after their prospective daughter-in-law for their son insulted him. He felt a duty to watch out for *all* the young ladies who journeyed with him and his crew, not that it mattered. Invariably the women all ended up in situations that made him pity them. Many of them were in arranged matches to brutish men they would not have chosen for themselves had the choice been put before them honestly.

His eyes fell on Miss Gray again. He wondered if the stunning beauty was also bound for India on an arranged match. Arranged marriages were a barbaric practice

— a thing of their grandfathers and great-grandfathers. Not a thing that should play a part in these modern times.

She would have to have been outstandingly dull-witted to have agreed to such a thing. Or perhaps there was some scandal from which she needed to flee. Or perhaps she was penniless, though her dress and manners signified she came from wealth and knew how to carry herself comfortably within its confines.

Maybe Miss Gray was not bound to India to find a husband at all. Perhaps she was going to meet a mother and father. He hated how much he hoped that would be the case.

She took the seat to his right, and he settled himself in the chair reserved for him. He glanced at her place card and found there was no mistake; it did indeed have her name on it. She was to be his dining companion for all these months. So, she was of notable class *and* beauty. That left the dull-witted option as the only logical one available. Just his luck to be forced into taking his meals with a woman unable to maintain interesting conversation.

She spoke, but he was so focused on discerning her circumstances that he didn't catch her remark.

"Pardon me?" he said.

She flashed that brief smile again. "I was commenting on the fine quality of dinner. I was encouraged not to expect much, but this is quite lovely. Thank you for your hospitality."

"I am glad you like it," he said. Then, since she'd opened conversation between them, he added, "What takes you to Mumbai?"

Her eyebrows shot up, his question catching her unawares. She smoothed her features quickly. "Business," she said.

"Business? And what business has a woman leaving her home and crossing so great a distance?"

"Business that is my own," she replied.

He almost laughed at that, snippy and cool though she may have been. There was nothing simpering or demure in the comment, which made for a nice change. Maybe having her as a dinner companion wouldn't be so awful after all. For her to be so careful with her own information made her quite a lovely mystery.

Miss James, who sat to Miss Gray's right, spoke up. "I'm heading to India to find a decent husband."

Miss Gray looked embarrassed to hear such a bold admission. Ladies were taught to keep their private matters private. Clearly, Miss Gray had benefited from that education.

Miss James was likely the one the couple asked him to watch over. They'd called her a pretty young woman, but he felt that had been an overestimation on their part.

"And what leads you to believe there are decent men to be found in such a place?" Thomas shook his head and tsked his tongue. "I'm afraid you were wrongly informed, Miss James." He'd had to glance again at her place card. Mercy, but he hated learning new names with every voyage. "I daresay there isn't a single decent Englishman to be found where we're going. I'm afraid you'll have to return home if you want a man of that variety."

Miss James looked alarmed with her wide-set eyes.

"I'm sure the captain is teasing you," Miss Gray said softly, as if apologizing for him.

"Am I, Miss Gray?" he asked, feeling vexed and not at all apologetic to be called out on his own ship. "And do you think you know my character so well after our brief meeting here to assume I trifle with the emotions of the ladies at my table?"

"Not at all, Captain." Her voice was not loud, but neither was it quiet as would be expected from a lady. She spoke boldly and with enough energy to allow most of the table to hear her. "I'm sure such behavior would be abhorrent to you — a gentleman. It is only that you are speaking in absolutes, and absolutes are best avoided in most occasions. Not all occasions, obviously, or the rule itself would be an absolute. But to say there are no decent Englishmen to be found in all of India seems rather impossible, don't you think? It would be like saying that all plants are green. While a great many of them are, all are not. Or it would be like saying there is no cloud in the sky just because one could not see a cloud immediately before them. But that does not mean that all the skies of a country are void of clouds just because one person happens to be blind to them. A world of absolutes would be a colorless, dreary place, would it not?"

Thomas felt as though his eyes would pop out of his head as he stared in surprise at Miss Gray. The other gentlemen went stone silent for a moment, and then the conversation became the affair of the whole table. The two men defended the honor of India's Englishmen, while the women seemed agog at the whole of the conversation. Miss Gray did not demure. She remained an energetic and active participant throughout the whole of it.

So, Miss Gray was not a silly woman lacking in wit or wisdom. Not at all. He took a sip from his glass before finally interjecting. "Do you think yourself a philosopher then, Miss Gray?"

"To love knowledge is neither above nor below a lady's station, Captain Scott." Her cool response came quickly, but pink splotches colored her neck, which meant he had struck a nerve. One of the ladies at the other end of the table laughed at Miss Gray's remark. He felt sorry and not sorry all at once.

He took another drink from his glass and allowed the conversation to flow around him, only answering when summoned by one of the gentlemen who, thankfully, were far enough down the table to make such summoning difficult and therefore infrequent.

His lieutenant at the foot of the table smirked at him. Thomas frowned in return.

One of the ladies at the end of the table smiled at him a great deal more often than he cared for, and she tried to speak to him any time he turned to speak to Miss Gray. He sighed. It was not unusual for one of the female passengers to decide he was a fish who could be baited to her hook. But he hated it.

Blast, but he hated it.

Miss Gray also fell quiet, her eyes fixed on her plate and her mouth closed. He was sorry about her silence, and even more sorry that he had been the one to silence her.

With the vivacity of Miss Gray's discussion at an end, everyone else remembered themselves and their places. Such open discourse at the dining table was highly irregular. Perhaps it was the excitement of an adventure that allowed all present to behave in a manner ill-fitting to their stations, but whatever it had been, they all sent curious looks in Miss Gray's direction, as if to attribute their own free behavior to her impropriety.

As expected, alliances and enemies were already forming. Wide-eyed Miss James was on the outskirts of those alliances and not enough of a threat to anyone to make herself an enemy, but Miss Gray proved she could be a threat. A woman of position, mind, and beauty.

Miss Cole and Miss Luke seemed already thick as thieves with their heads bent close together — Miss Cole being the one who had laughed at Miss Gray and then smiled at him far too often. Miss Jeffries stayed to the side of the alliance forming between those two ladies, purposely keeping herself aloof. And Miss Bronley ate her meal as if the dinner conversation had been a bothersome distraction from the loveliness of such food.

Miss Cole and Miss Luke laughed and cast a meaningful glance in Miss Gray's direction.

And with that glance, Thomas felt he understood what Miss Gray was doing on his ship — she, like the others, was on a journey to find a husband. She had not found one in London; clearly the *beau monde* had not approved of such a mind. He ground his teeth. Being that she was husband hunting, he'd best be careful he did not approve of her either.

CHAPTER FOUR

Caroline's embarrassment turned to anger that brewed and simmered until she felt as though she quite loathed the captain. How dare he call her out when he'd been the one to make poor Miss James so ill at ease. How dare he insinuate that a respectively sized population of young men had not a single man of merit. How dare he assume anything at all about her.

And why had she allowed herself to be tempted into such a conversation? Miss Cole had actually thrown back her head so that her dull blonde curls bounced and laughed aloud when Caroline had said that the love of knowledge was neither above nor below a woman's station. How many women like her had Caroline met in her life?

Too many.

Which made Miss Cole a woman to be avoided, especially when it seemed every word Caroline uttered above a whisper was

53

contested by her jury at the end of the table.

After the meal had been cleared away and dessert served, Caroline watched Miss Cole and came to the conclusion that the woman had raised her sights to the *captain* of all people. The man was pleasant to look at with his well-cut form, dark hair, and dark eyes set in a smooth and chiseled face; a handsome man was a rare enough find, and Caroline was not one to waste the opportunity to stare every now and again.

And being so close to him at the table, she realized he smelled of sandalwood and leather, which made it hard for her not to inch closer to him just so she could breathe him in. But the moment he opened his mouth and dashed the hopes of poor Miss James, Caroline decided that no one on the ship could be less desirable than the captain.

The ladies exited the dining room together, leaving the men to themselves. As they walked down the corridor, Miss Cole mock-whispered to Miss Luke as she kept her eyes fixed on Caroline, "And there is a lady who would surely never be approved by Almack's."

Miss Jeffries stiffened at the insult, the skin beneath her freckles turning pale.

Miss James hurried to take Caroline by the hand. "Don't let that bother you. A lot of women are not accepted by Almack's. I was never approved."

Miss Cole heard Miss James's attempt at solidarity and laughed with scorn hot enough to burn a hole through the floor where she stood.

Caroline turned to Miss James as they stood at the entrance of the saloon. She made certain to speak as loudly as Miss Cole had done to be sure everyone knew who she addressed. "Being approved by Almack's and approving of them in turn is not the same thing, Miss James. I *was* approved at Almack's, but I found the music lacking for a ball of such repute. And worse than the music was the company. The gentlemen and ladies I met there were very dull indeed. There are far better ways to spend a Wednesday evening during the season than with people who work so hard to be fashionable that they will never truly be in fashion." She turned to Miss Cole directly. "And honestly, I don't recall ever seeing you there. It makes one wonder regarding their approval of *you.*"

Miss Cole's face reddened, but she did not confirm or deny Caroline's assessment, making Caroline believe she'd hit the mark.

She shouldn't have allowed herself to snip back. She should have let Miss Cole's comment roll off her shoulders, especially when the truth of the matter was that she'd only been approved to attend Almack's balls during her first and second season.

Once in the saloon, Miss Cole and Miss Luke decided to play cards to pass the evening hours and invited her to play. Miss Cole even pretended that the snub given only moments before had never happened — an action that made Caroline all the more cautious. Women of that sort were to be avoided whenever possible. Miss James had accepted the invitation to cards and gave Caroline a pleading look to stay.

She felt bad leaving Miss James to fend for herself when such terrible cats were ready to pounce with no provocation, but she could take no more of it. She retreated to her cabin as soon as was socially acceptable.

She allowed herself to breathe deeply, to calm herself once she was alone, before she realized there were two cards on the small desk. Two — which meant there would be another person with her. She would not be alone for the voyage. One card had her name. The other was addressed to Miss Gaunt.

Caroline was relieved the name was not Miss Cole or Miss Luke. An entire journey sharing a cabin with either of them would have proved unbearable. Then she frowned. She'd not been introduced to a Miss Gaunt. No one by that name had dined with her and the others at the captain's table. It seemed odd that the woman hadn't shown herself yet. Caroline took the card and exited her room, hoping to find someone who could tell her if she should expect another person to show up in her cabin or not.

The hall outside her cabin was empty in both directions.

Caroline went to the left since it was better lit and therefore more likely to have others working in that direction. She turned a corner and ran straight into Captain Scott.

She stumbled, and he caught her arm to keep her from falling. She hurried to right herself and step away from his touch.

"Miss Gray!" He seemed as startled to be encountering her as she felt to be encountering him.

She had found him attractive while looking at him during dinner, but now, with the two of them so close, she could see the wave in his dark hair and the gold flecks in his hazel eyes set aglow by the low light from the wall sconce. He was more than handsome. Painfully handsome.

Or so she would have thought had she not already spoken to him and found him to be otherwise.

Caroline remembered the note in her hand. She was not supposed to be inspecting the captain's features. She was supposed to be locating a missing woman. Perhaps she had fallen ill before leaving.

"Did you need assistance, Miss Gray?" the captain asked before she could gather her own thoughts.

"Yes. I'm looking for someone."

"Anyone in particular? Perhaps I can point you in the correct direction."

"No. Not anyone in particular, so I suppose you'll do."

His eyebrows shot up at that, and a muscle in his clean-shaven jaw flexed.

How foolish of her to have assumed all sea captains wore full beards simply because the one captain she'd met in her life had worn one. Hadn't she been the one to argue against absolutes? Determined not to think of how his skin looked both smooth and coarse, and how part of her longed to run a finger over his jaw to see which of the two won out, she managed to say, "I believe there was supposed to be another woman sharing my room. Miss Gaunt. Is she on the ship? Perhaps she fell ill and is in a

58

sickroom?"

"More likely she fell intelligent," he mumbled before clearing his throat. "She had a change of mind at the docks and chose to stay in England. She might sail with the next ship. She might not. People are consistent in their inconsistency. Enjoy your privacy, Miss Gray. It is a thing to be envied aboard a ship, not a thing to be fretted over."

"I'm not fretting. I'm merely curious," Caroline said, not liking that the captain seemed to be continually annoyed by her. Had she done something to earn his censure? Surely not. How could she? She'd only been aboard his vessel for a day. Of course, he'd managed to earn *her* censure, but that was another matter entirely. "I am pleased to know I am free to claim the space as my own."

"Claim away, Miss Gray. It is yours for the duration of our journey." He looked like he might say more, but she had no desire to hear anything more from him. The day had been difficult enough. She did not need him to try to goad her into further humiliation.

She dropped a quick curtsy. "Thank you, sir. Please forgive my trespass on your time." She turned and hurried back to her room where she could be certain no one would disturb her for the rest of the evening.

In her cabin, she allowed herself to feel all of what she had lost that day. Her mother had held her so tightly, and there had been tears at the end, but not any from her. She did not want her mother to feel worse regarding the situation than she already did. She did not want her mother to know how truly heartbroken Caroline was over her new circumstances.

Caroline didn't blame her mother. She could not blame anyone besides herself. Hadn't she been the one to throw around facts and figures instead of flirtations and compliments to the young men who would have courted her? Hadn't she been the one to want to prove herself equal of mind? Hadn't she been the one to look down her nose at those other girls who batted their lashes to make themselves look mysterious and pursed their lips to make themselves look kissable?

Now that her cousin had found a wife and she had not found herself a husband, what had she thought would happen? There was quite literally nowhere for her to go except for where she was going.

She would make the best of it. But not tonight. Tonight, she would allow herself to feel all of it. She would allow herself to mourn the nieces and nephews she would likely never see once her sister started having children. She would allow herself to mourn the England she loved, the countryside of Salisbury which she called home, the mother and sister who had been like breath to her in their importance in her life. She allowed herself to feel the ache in every way. The tears were a hot, acidic deluge on her cheeks. The sobs in her throat threatened to choke the breath out of her. She crawled onto the bottom bunk and curled into herself without bothering to remove her dinner dress. She had no maid to help her, and she had no mind to help herself.

Hours passed with crying while the boat rocked her like her mother had done for all those years of her childhood. The soothing motion offered comfort. She had expected to feel ill for the first few days of sailing as many people said they often did. But she only felt consolation being cradled as she was in the ocean's arms. She finally rolled onto her back and looked up at the bottom of the bunk above her.

Someone had carved a little nighttime sky into the wood. Even with the low lamplight from the sconce above the small desk, she could see the clouds and stars and a moon. The carver exhibited great skill in this small piece of near-hidden art. That gave her comfort, too.

She thought of her father throwing a blanket down over the lawn by the river near their home. It had been warm for the beginning of winter, but not warm enough. They'd needed several layers of cloaks and a blanket to cover the top of them as they lay on their backs while her father pointed to the night sky.

"There. Do you see that, Caroline? Do you see that, Josephine?" he'd asked. "Those three stars in a row? Slanted like this?" He used his arm to show the angle and then pointed again.

She followed his fingertip to the three stars angled in the sky.

"That's a belt. It's Orion's belt," he'd said.

She'd laughed and said that Orion's mother would be quite cross with him when she discovered how crooked he'd put his belt on that morning.

Her father had laughed and then helped her see the rest of Orion the hunter in the sky. She'd argued that the shoulders looked more like hands — like the ends of things rather than the extension of more to come. But he finally helped her trace the whole figure.

"And that star, the bright one that makes

up his right shoulder, is called Betelgeuse."

She looked at it for a long time, squinting her eyes to see if what she thought she saw changed at all. "Is it red, Papa?"

He'd laughed. "Yes. Like the ruddy nose of an old man with a terrible cold."

She'd fallen asleep staring at Orion and his crooked belt and red-jeweled shoulder. Her father had moved her into the house at some point.

She could almost feel him carrying her still, feel the rock of his gait as he walked toward the house.

Caroline opened her eyes. It was the rocking of the boat. She'd fallen asleep staring at the carved Orion constellation on the bottom of the bunk above her. She rubbed the crust of tears and sleep from her eyes. The room was dark; her lamp must have run out of oil.

Without windows in her room, she could not guess at the time, but it felt like the middle of the night. She tried to return to sleep, but sleep would not come.

After what might have been an hour, or only minutes, she moved to her feet, put on a wrap over her dinner dress, and left her cabin. She reached the upper deck without stumbling into anyone or over anything in the dark.

The breeze hit her immediately as she stepped onto the deck, and the cool air relieved the ache in her head, a result from all her crying.

She moved to the side and looked down over the black water.

"Seasickness has two stages."

Caroline whirled to see Captain Scott looking at her. He walked her direction in a leisurely fashion, his jacket flapping in the breeze, his broad shoulders seeming to loom larger in the pale starlight. "The first is when you fear you'll die. The second is when you're afraid you'll live."

"I'm not seasick," she said.

"Then why are you hanging over the edge as though in the fits of illness?"

"I was looking at the water."

Their gazes connected as he drew near her. He hurried to look down. "You realize there is nothing but black to see out there when there is no moon? Far better to look up where there is at least a view to be had."

She looked up. "Ursa Major," she whispered, and felt the ache of her loss wash over her again. She traced the familiar pattern of stars with her eyes and then over to Cassiopeia, remembering her father and her mother pointing up and tracing the lines with their fingers while she and Josephine nestled between them.

Papa was dead. Mama and Josephine were out of her reach.

Would it have been so bad to have stayed and been the family spinster? She would have still had Mama and Josephine if she'd stayed.

But no. Not really.

Caroline had been right to choose this path that offered the hope that she might form new attachments to hold and love, that she might have children for whom she could trace lines in the stars.

"You know all your constellations? Or just Ursa Major?" Captain Scott asked.

Caroline dragged her gaze from the stars back to him, noticing how much more relaxed he was on his deck than he had been at dinner.

"It is impossible for me to know them all, beyond academics, since I live in the northern hemisphere, and there are some that I've never seen in the sky." Even as she spoke, she'd heard how much her words sounded like a lecture. Couldn't she simply say, "My, but how lovely the stars are tonight!" Was it so difficult to speak in breathy exclamations?

Intent on recovering herself, she asked him a question. If she could keep him talking, then she could direct his attention away from her. "What brings you from your wheelhouse, Captain Scott?"

He murmured something unintelligible before saying, "I am the captain. It is my job to see to the needs of the whole of my ship, not just the wheelhouse. Besides, I find it healthful to stretch my legs every now and again. And I've found that viewing the stars academically, as you say, through a sextant and charts, makes it easy to forget the majesty of their movement and light. I like to look up and remember beauty."

She looked from the stars to him, startled to find such sentiment from someone who'd been so chilly at their earlier meeting. She was even more startled to find him not looking at the stars but at *her.*

He quickly looked away as though he'd been caught doing something wrong. "Are you apprehensive at all to travel to India?" he asked, bringing the conversation directly back to her.

She sighed inwardly. She knew from experience that men — no, not just men, but *people* — liked to talk about themselves. So why could she never manage to keep a conversation on the other person? Did she not ask complex enough questions?

"No, sir, I'm not apprehensive. I think a

new situation might be vastly interesting, and travel has always suited me. As a young girl, I often accompanied my parents while they traveled to visit friends and family. The journey always seemed so splendid and arrivals always seemed to come too soon. What of you? Has life on the sea been adventurous, or were you ever apprehensive about your choice?"

He looked away again, and she wished she could see his eyes clearly to determine how he felt. "It was not my choice, Miss Gray. Sailing is the family business and has been for several generations. If I'd chosen another occupation, my father would have had me keelhauled until I changed my mind."

His candor surprised her and emboldened her to continue. "That doesn't answer my question entirely. Does the adventure suit you, or does it make you apprehensive?"

He studied her in a way that brought a flush to her cheeks that she hoped he could not see in the veil of darkness. It was likely because of the darkness that he studied her so intently; she was likely as much a silhouette to him as he was to her.

"Apprehensive at first. And apprehensive each time I had to take a new route. Now, my schedules are fairly steady, my course varying but little."

His long pause made her think he'd ended the conversation. She assumed he would take his leave, but then he spoke again.

"Now my apprehension is reserved for the journeys of others, for the choices they think they must make without understanding the realities that await them."

She frowned, unsure what to make of him or his somber declaration. "Surely you feel no such apprehension for me, Captain Scott."

His grip tightened on the railing before he released it. He gave a quick bow. "I fear I've intruded far too long on your late-night ocean views. Good night, Miss Gray."

She hurried to return a curtsy. "Good night, Captain Scott."

Had she offended him in some way to cause him to leave so abruptly? Had he felt her question to be impertinent? Caroline didn't know and had no way of discovering without asking further impertinent questions.

This new adventure in her life *was* giving her a new chance. She had to look at things from that point of view. She had to see this opportunity for what it was. It was a chance to reinvent herself.

She need no longer be the know-all woman.

She frowned.

The problem stemmed not from knowing all, but from earnestly striving to learn more. How did one learn more or improve their understanding without embarking on a frank and lively discussion on all manner of topics?

Caroline did not want to stop learning.

But neither had she wished to be the woman left matchless despite attending several seasons. Yet she had become that woman.

She looked up to the sky. "I have to change," she said to the stars. "I have to be decidedly *not me.*"

The trouble came from not knowing how to become someone other than the woman who had been walking in her own skin for the last twenty-three years.

Her frown deepened as she made her way back to her room.

CHAPTER FIVE

Blast that woman and the mind behind that pretty face. The entire woman was a walking quandary — a puzzle that made no sense since most of the Fishing Fleet women had no prospects. Why else would they be fishing for husbands in other lands? Yet, how could Miss Gray possibly fit into the category of a woman who could not make a match?

He knew the answer. The same reason he felt intrigued by her was why other men had passed her over. Most men preferred their women docile, controllable, though that word would never be spoken out loud since such a thing would hardly be polite. And the gentleman of the *ton* were nothing if not polite — at least on the surface. And the gentlemen who made their fortunes in India were the worst of their kind.

He'd seen their atrocities, the mistresses they took, the morals they shed at the docks because they felt they were beyond the reach of proper governing principles. He had even been invited to partake in their folly, though, of course, he never had. And it galled him to lead these women, no matter their station, to a future with men who were cads at best and monsters at worst.

He tightened his fist as he entered the wheelhouse. *Do not speak in absolutes, Captain Scott,* Miss Gray's voice reminded him. And she wasn't wrong. He did know a handful of honorable British men in India who gave credit to the very concept of gentleman. But the majority tainted that handful.

"Are you all right, sir?" Lieutenant Peterson asked.

"Perfectly. Why do you ask?"

The lieutenant shrugged. "You look vexed, sir."

He wanted to snap that he did not look vexed but doing so would only prove the point. Blast that woman!

He remained quiet as to the condition of his well-being. But before long, the lieutenant started chatting to the other men in the wheelhouse about how the company on this voyage promised to be more pleasant than on voyages past. "That one woman, Miss . . . Oh, what was her name?"

"If you gave a better description than 'Miss,' I could probably help you find the woman's name," Thomas growled.

All right, so maybe he was vexed.

Thomas pushed down his frustration. Peterson didn't deserve such a sharp response. The man was respectful and competent and never seemed bothered by serving under a captain eleven years his junior. Thomas knew he'd found a rare one among men and counted himself lucky to have such a loyal crew member. In truth, he had very little trouble with any of his crew, but he'd found a genuine friend in Peterson.

Peterson continued, ignoring the captain's tone. "Oh, you know the one. The one who didn't beat us over the head with a display of her good breeding or speak breathlessly as though she were about to faint."

"Miss Gray." How easily he remembered her name. How quickly she had called attention to herself.

"Right. That one. Nice to have such an interesting lady on board. Did you see the way the other ladies looked at her? Especially Miss Cole. Open war shall break out between those two, mark my words. Should prove to be entertaining, to say the least."

"Come now, Peterson. You think brawling ladies to be entertainment?" Thomas asked.

His lieutenant shrugged. "Better than the kind who pretend politeness but are later found clawing at each other's eyes. Open battle can at least be understood."

"Ah, but the fine subtleties of subterfuge and warfare are more interesting, are they not?" asked Lyon, the helmsman.

"Not when you don't understand them," Peterson said. "And I must confess to seldom understanding war between ladies. Their rules of engagement are known only among themselves. And Miss Gray doesn't seem the sort of lady to give way to subtle warfare. Her candor makes her likable. I found that refreshing."

Thomas refused to agree, though neither could he disagree.

Lieutenant Peterson accepted the silence as agreement, and the conversation moved toward topics that did not make Thomas want to shift his shoulders in irritation. The officers discussed a few of the other guests, the condition of the cannons that were aboard in case they ran into trouble, and the new ship's boy who'd been brought on to help the cook but who couldn't seem to be kept from the ratlines. Peterson had taken a liking to the boy and made excuses for the child to keep him out of trouble. After a look from Thomas, Peterson promised to talk to him about staying where he was supposed to be and staying *out* of where he wasn't.

Thomas much preferred the conversation regarding the running of his ship. Conversation regarding the ladies, and of one lady in particular, made his mind feel muddy and well . . . vexed. Why did she have to be out of her room and looking out over the sea like she belonged on a ship's deck? Why did she have to have an interest in constellations and give a pert response to his question regarding her knowledge of them? Why did he feel as if he'd taken a dangerous siren aboard his vessel?

"Sir?" Peterson narrowed his eyes, his graying brow wrinkling over the bridge of his nose.

Thomas startled, realizing the man had been speaking to him. "Yes?"

"Are you sure you're —"

"I'm quite well, Lieutenant."

Again, his words came out sharper than they should have, sharp enough that Lieutenant Peterson smoothed his expression and said, "Of course, sir." His raised eyebrows, though, spoke volumes.

Thomas turned to his maps and ignored his lieutenant. Sometimes, the man was too observant.

He determined to put thoughts of the woman out of his mind.

He maintained his concentration up until he saw her again the next day when he'd gathered the passengers to inform them of proper protocol on the ship. As his gaze swept over her, he suddenly felt hot under the too-bright sun.

"Storms at sea are common enough," he said after adjusting the cuff of his sleeve. Blast, but he did that a lot when she was near. "But a squall is just that — nothing more than a squalling child throwing a tantrum. Please remember you are in safe hands with this crew." He indicated his officers and the other crewmen.

He informed the passengers of the rules, restating the importance of staying below deck during a storm to avoid being swept overboard. Restating the importance of staying in their cabins. He felt quite sure Miss Cole wasn't listening despite how her eyes stayed trained on him during his entire lecture. He sighed inwardly and was grateful when he was done so the passengers could go about their business. He gave instructions to the crew and then surreptitiously looked to see if Miss Gray had lingered on deck.

She faced away from him but had a leather

journal or some such thing in her hands. She was in animated conversation with Mr. Black, the deckhand who had rescued her bonnet from being washed away.

Miss Gray was not giving Black a scolding of any kind, rather the conversation had the lively appearance of discovery. Indeed, Miss Gray was asking questions and smiling. She opened up her book and pointed to a page. Mr. Black peeked at the page and nodded.

As rare as it was to see a lady talking to his crewmen, it was even more rare for Black to talk to any woman aboard. Black still held that women on the ship were bad luck, even though such a notion was ridiculous and even though the man's own wife traveled with them.

Thomas edged closer to hear what the discussion entailed, and he managed to catch a glimpse of the page Miss Gray had pointed to. It was a rather intricate sketch of the sails. He would have thought she had brought along a book from a master artist except he recognized the details of his own ship, and her fingertips were smudged with gray graphite.

"The sails are so lovely when they billow as they do. What do you do when there is no wind?" she asked.

Black nodded. "It happens on occasion.

We usually wait it out. There was one time when the ship was becalmed for so long, we ran low on food and water rations. Had to sail by ash breeze."

"Ash breeze?"

"Oars are made of ash. There come times when we've got to pull out the rowboats and ropes and tow the ship a ways."

"The crew physically drags the ship through the water? I can hardly imagine . . . Are the sea and wind such fickle creatures? Are ships *becalmed* very often?" Miss Gray said the word with obvious pleasure at having learned something new.

"Not often." Thomas interrupted the conversation before Black started into tall tales regarding the sea and the wind. There were many traditions on the sea, and many beliefs in what changed the moods of the weather and water. He felt that Miss Gray was a woman who expected facts not folly. He did not want her scoffing an honest, hardworking sailor — especially not where that sailor could hear her.

Miss Gray turned to him, and Thomas felt as though his brain took a stumble at the sight of her in full daylight with the sun kissing her hair and the breeze sweeping several stands free from a decidedly loose bun.

He forced himself to stop considering how

much he approved of this less elaborate and restricted hairstyle of hers, and how much it stirred in him something akin to joy to see her looking so comfortable out on his deck, enjoying the day.

Miss Gray studied him a moment and then asked, "Is the infrequency due to understanding weather patterns at this time of year and sailing around them? Or is it just luck?"

Of course, she had to discuss luck in front of Black, who believed in all the many superstitions that came with it, including the very bad luck that came with anyone onboard saying the word aloud.

Before Black could respond, Thomas hurried to interject. "Mostly understanding, of course. Knowing the seasons and currents makes it much easier to navigate the seas. However, in the last year, it has more to do with the new steam engine that the shipping company installed. With wind and steam working together as equally yoked partners, we make good time and worry less about wind in our sails."

Black's expression soured at the mention of the steam engine, so Thomas quickly redirected the conversation. He indicated the book in Miss Gray's hand. "I see you've taken to sketching for the day."

"She said she'd sketch my likeness, sir," Black said, looking pleased by the notion.

"I'm sure she will at some point, but for now, you've work to do, Black." Thomas gave the man a meaningful look and a nod to the rigging.

"Aye, Captain." He hurried away.

"I don't think Mr. Black much cares for your steam power." Miss Gray's eyes followed the man as he went about his duties.

"Some of the men don't — more than I would have imagined since it eases their workload, but I've been grateful for it on more than one occasion. When the wind dies and our sails are slack, I send my silent gratitude to Mr. Watt for easing my worries."

"So you credit steam power to James Watt then?"

He hated how she could do that to him. He had thought himself to be making an obscure reference far above her notice or care. Yet every time the lady opened her mouth, she proved herself to be something Thomas never imagined. His own mother and sisters would not have understood the reference.

"You know of James Watt?" he asked.

"They say the labors of London's factories are greatly improved by Mr. Watt's work,

79

but it seems misplaced to put all the credit on that man's name when he merely stood on the shoulders of those who had come before him."

"And whose shoulders was Mr. Watt standing upon?" He noted the way the wind twisted and played with the stray strands of her hair and felt a strange jealousy that the wind was allowed such familiarity.

"There were several who began the research into the matter and then worked to further the initial research, but I believe it was Thomas Newcomen who created the first steam-powered machine with moving parts that actually did useful work."

He'd heard the name of Newcomen, but would have never remembered who he was or the significance of his work if she had not just spouted it from her lips with an ease that made it seem she was speaking of something as basic as a spoon.

Thomas leaned into her slighter frame — close enough to smell the floral scent from either her soap or her perfume. It was a nice change from the smell of the ship. He hurried to straighten as he realized his movement could be misinterpreted by someone with a mischievous mind.

Heaven knew, his own mind was scrambling to interpret what his leaning into her might mean.

Miss Gray's shoulders slumped, and for a moment, he worried she had taken offense when he moved away from her. "I never learn," she muttered. She shook her head and her brows knit together, created a crease above the bridge of her nose.

"Never learn what, Miss Gray?"

She glanced at him as if startled to remember he stood with her. "Oh. Nothing. Never mind. I apologize for troubling you, Captain Scott. And I apologize for distracting your man from his duties. I was only curious about . . . well, I was curious." She dropped a curtsy, smiled in a way that made him think she was not smiling at all, and hurried off.

He hated that he watched her until she'd turned the corner and descended the stairs that led to the dining area. He hated even more that she'd left when he'd been enjoying their conversation, enjoying that she knew about steam power, enjoying the way the wind played with her hair.

Putting her out of his mind this time took a good deal longer than it had the night before. The frequency with which his thoughts turned toward her alarmed him. It was clear he would need to take lengths to guarantee he did not run into Miss Gray again.

For the next several evenings, he sent Lieutenant Peterson in his stead for meal-times and asked his second lieutenant, Abramson, to go in the place of Peterson. His passengers would still enjoy the company of two officers, even if one of them wasn't the captain. He took his own meals in the wheelhouse.

Lieutenant Peterson brought back news of Miss Gray each night Thomas stayed away. He spoke of all the ladies and gentlemen, but he seemed to enjoy Miss Gray's conversation in particular — at least enough to discuss it when he returned to the wheelhouse.

"She's quite intelligent; do you not agree?" Peterson asked. The two of them were alone on the forecastle, checking their course in the stars. They were two weeks into their journey with the weather holding strong with wind and, thankfully, no storms.

"Yes. Intelligent. So intelligent that she's gone fishing for a husband in a land where she will likely die of disease." Thomas hated how surly he sounded.

"Oh, don't start on the topic of husband hunters being the ruin of a perfectly good shipping business."

"You only refuse to entertain such topics because you know it to be true. A woman who has to resort to such measures is no woman I would want."

"So no to that lady. Pity."

Thomas knew why he, personally, thought it was a pity. He liked her against all reason and sense, and to find himself attracted to such a woman went against everything he wanted.

"Why is it a pity?" he asked, curious as to why his lieutenant felt any sort of despondence in the matter.

Peterson gave a sheepish look. "I'd rather thought the woman would make a good match for a friend of mine."

"I appreciate the sentiment, but I'm not looking for a wife."

Peterson laughed outright. "Are you so arrogant you think the friend I meant was you?"

"You don't have any other friends. You're too old, and the crew is too terrified of you to think of you as a friend. I'm the best option you've got."

Peterson gave a snort, turned his face toward the sea, and breathed deeply of the evening air. "I hope you don't think you've complimented me and are now waiting for some show of gratitude."

"What's the point of being friends if we have to compliment each other all the time?" Thomas checked his pocket watch but slid a sideways glance and a half smile toward Peterson, who was also smiling.

"So no to Miss Gray for you. But we should marry you off soon before you become old and impossible like me."

"Being like you would not be so bad. You're a well-informed man who refuses to make time for nonsense."

"That's why I'd set my sights on Miss Gray for you. She's nothing like the others."

Truer words had never been said. And it was the reason he felt so especially vexed in the matter.

Peterson continued. "Tonight, she began the most lively discussion regarding Volta's battery. I confess to having been quite ignorant of the matter, but not any longer. She told me this man, Volta, could create energy from salt water and . . . maybe it was gold? Copper? Some shiny metal or another." He laughed at himself. "All right, so maybe I am still ignorant on the matter, but she was most engaging. The man who marries her will never find himself bored."

"No. I expect not," Thomas mumbled. He caught sight of Ursa Major and wished she'd told him what other constellations she knew.

Back in bed that night, he read through some letters from home and wondered what his mother would think of Miss Gray. Peterson reported that the other women acted quite nervous and scornful when Miss Gray spoke, proving them to be rather uninteresting. His mother liked interesting women, and Miss Gray was the only woman he'd met who fit the bill in a good way. Mercy, but how many had he met who were interesting in a less-than-favorable light?

Not that it mattered what his mother would think as she would have no opportunity to meet the lady. For all the women who flirted with him each voyage, he refused to budge. It was his policy to never enter into any kind of flirtations with the lady passengers. His reputation as one who made certain the young ladies arrived safely to their destination made his ship the first choice of many mothers of society. It was good for his business even if it wasn't good for his nerves.

Still, he believed his mother would like Miss Gray quite a lot. Though Thomas's mother had not taken her education to the lengths Miss Gray obviously had, he knew his mother to be a woman of great intellect.

The two women would have been friends. But the lady had her own path, which meant she was none of his concern. But she made him think that perhaps he was wrong to not spend more time in port. He should take the time to meet eligible young ladies. If he had taken the time while he'd been in Bristol, perhaps he would have met Miss Gray when she wasn't a passenger — when she wasn't a violation of policy or principle.

He shook his head and put his mother's letters away as if that would help him put his thoughts of Miss Gray away as well.

After almost a week of strategic avoidance, he felt up to the challenge of facing the lady again. He even believed he welcomed the opportunity, if only to prove to himself that he had overcome the little stumble of weakness she had managed to discover in him. He purposely went out on deck after the breakfast hour when he knew the majority of his fashionable passengers preferred to take their exercise. And yet, the day he decided he welcomed her presence, she never showed up on deck — at least not where he could see.

But he'd been busy with keeping his ship on course and running smoothly. It's not like he'd actively sought her out as he looked over the ship. That's what he told himself every time he lifted his eyes to scan the working crew and the wandering passengers. He was determined to not feel disappointment when she failed to appear.

You will see her at dinnertime, he told himself.

He had to prove that he could be in her company without gawking like a schoolboy, that he was quite in control of himself.

But he couldn't help remembering the last day he had seen her — the day she'd been talking to Black — when she smiled up at the sails and the wind and sun tangled together in her dark hair.

Maybe Black had been accurate and it was bad luck to bring women aboard. He scanned the deck again. She wasn't there. He snapped the box closed on the chronometer and received a curious glance from his watchkeeper for having invaded the space of the chronometer in the first place.

Bad luck indeed.

CHAPTER SIX

Caroline stretched her spine from the bent position she'd endured in an effort to stay relatively isolated while on deck. She preferred to be hidden where she could draw things that interested her rather than draw the other ladies — a favor she'd already done for each woman so they would have no reason to complain. It didn't hurt that Clara, Mr. Black's wife, who lived aboard the ship and acted as chaperone and maid to the young ladies, had taken a liking to Caroline and decided she did not need such a close eye kept on her. Clara had apparently not made the same decision regarding Miss Cole and Miss Luke as she followed them diligently.

Caroline appreciated the freedom. She'd found a spot between some rather large coils of rope and a crate of folded canvas.

She'd noticed it while searching for a good vantage point from which to draw the likeness of the little boy she often saw scurrying up the rigging for the sails. Since first drawing the child, she found herself drawing him again and again. Not only when he was on the lines but also when he was down in the galley preparing food.

She scouted the ship continually and drew everything she saw, but for reasons she could not explain, the boy had quite captured her.

She frowned at her current sketch. Did the child have a bruise on his cheek or was that simply dirt from his work? Had he fallen while climbing the ropes?

She closed her sketchbook, cinched its leather cords tight, and glanced around her before she dared to stand and scurry from her hiding place. She skirted around the mast and ran straight into Lieutenant Peterson.

He looked both startled by the collision and baffled that she was in such a location at all. She didn't apologize for being where she was likely not welcome. She had learned that if she acted like she belonged, then she *would* belong.

After his initial shock wore off, Peterson smiled warmly, his gray eyebrows rising along with his cheeks. "Sketching again?"

She smiled and nodded.

"You'll run out of graphite long before we reach Mumbai if you continue as you are."

"If I told you I have an entire trunk dedicated to this particular diversion, would you believe me?" she asked.

"Of course. And I would think it a good use of space. Has Mr. Black pestered you yet to make good on your promise to draw his likeness?"

She laughed, untied the leather cords, and opened her sketchbook to the page where she had a few rudimentary sketches in process. She had liked drawing him because the lines in his weathered face were deep and interesting.

The lieutenant fairly beamed at the image. "Why, look at that! I don't think I've ever seen an image look so true to life."

"I will take these few quick sketches and make him a gift of a much nicer portrait."

"Quick sketches? I would not be capable of creating such a likeness if I were given eternity to complete it. It is not mere flattery when I say you are truly talented and possess a great skill. It would be a delight to have you draw the officers as well. I am sure the captain would like that."

Caroline did not consider herself a great talent and felt herself flush with warmth from the compliment. "*Would* the captain like such a thing?"

His lip twitched with something almost like humor. "From your hand? I daresay he would."

"I have been meaning to ask. Is the captain well? He has not been at dinner for several evenings." She fidgeted with the leather cord, feeling silly for voicing her worry aloud.

The twitch in the lieutenant's mouth returned as he murmured, "It's probably just the fine company." At her questioning look, the lieutenant smiled fully. "It is likely he is in turbulent waters when faced with a lady so unlike any other he's met before."

Nothing was said specifically, but she felt certain the captain had wanted to avoid *her*.

Had her carrying on about steam power and constellations truly been so awful?

Had the captain been so mortified?

The lieutenant turned to leave, but Caroline stopped him. "Lieutenant? This boy . . ." She turned to the page of the most recent image she'd made of the child. "Who takes care of him?"

"Ah." Lieutenant Peterson grinned outright. "Young Tom! He's the cook's boy."

"I fear the child may have fallen. Perhaps the cook should be alerted to a possible injury." She pointed to the smudge she'd recorded on the child's face. "I think I saw a bruise, but I could be mistaken."

The lieutenant's smile faded. "I will assuredly talk to the cook regarding the matter." He nodded and bid her farewell.

Caroline considered the conversation several times in her mind as she explored below deck. She was looking for a diversion, but only found a crate filled with rope that put her in mind of a coiled snake, a box of various tools, and three dusty buttons that must have fallen off a uniform long ago.

Caroline sighed, realizing she'd put off preparing herself for dinner for far too long. She returned to her cabin, slowly dressed, and then trailed the other ladies to the dining hall. She steeled herself before entering, hoping the captain to be absent again.

Stop, she thought. *It makes no difference if he is inside or not.*

She could not let the captain's opinion of her make her feel anything at all — good or ill. The captain would not be part of her future society. He would deliver them all to Mumbai, and then go back to London, and she would never see him again. His opinion of her was the least important on the ship.

That was what she told herself before entering. So why, on this night after his many absences, this night when she'd decided she could not care one whit regarding him and when she hadn't expected to see him at all, did she feel a jolt shiver up her spine when her gaze locked with his?

His smile faltered.

That small gesture pierced her and burrowed deep into her heart, whispering of her insecurities and failings. She felt her own smile drop, but unlike the captain, it took her a great deal longer to find it again.

Perhaps she had made herself a fool in his eyes, but who was he to pass judgment on her?

She lifted her chin, made her way to her seat, and forced herself to act normally. Well, not *normally* as that would have meant engaging in a conversation with others at the table about the recent discovery of the connection between electricity and magnetism.

In that moment, she missed her mother and sister acutely. Her father, too. They would have enjoyed speculating on what such discoveries might lead to in the future. She would never have such conversations again. The realization that she had not merely lost her family, she had also lost that melding of minds that took place when she was with her family broke her heart again.

Once seated, she swallowed her pain with her glass of water, then smiled at Miss James next to her and wished her a good evening. She would make an effort to create friendships on this ship because, while the captain would not be part of her future society, these people likely would. She couldn't keep avoiding them by hiding on rope coils and sketching everyone from afar. Besides, she couldn't very well speak with the captain after he'd frowned at her so deeply.

It did not bode well for her decision to create friendships that Miss James's eyes widened and she made a small squeak at having Caroline address her. The poor woman had the continual look of hunted prey, and it didn't help that the several times she'd tried to engage Miss Cole and Miss Luke in conversation, they had pounced and turned her into the joke of the hour.

Caroline smiled and started over. "The meals are much better than expected," she said conversationally.

She'd said as much to the captain at a previous dinner, but she honestly did not know how else to start a conversation with ladies other than to remark on the fine quality of food, music, or weather. Since there was no music and they were indoors, the food was all she had.

She widened her smile at Miss James. "People spoke of salted meat, hard biscuits, and sauerkraut and laughed about the savagery of life on the seas." She looked down at her plate of buttered green beans, roasted carrots, and tender beef. "But the food service is quite remarkable."

"Just you wait," Miss James said. "My brother has made the voyage twice. He told me the food starts out well enough, but the appeal dwindles as the days stretch on."

Caroline bit back a sigh. Miss James had an almost vulgar sense of despair to her. It was why Miss Cole and Miss Luke enjoyed baiting her into conversation. Everything for her was simply a "wait and see" for some impending disaster. That, and the woman felt no sense of restraint in speaking of her desire to catch herself a husband.

Oddly, her dinner companions seemed less bothered by Miss James's outspoken plans to make a match than they were with Caroline and her desire to discuss the science of the weather rather than keeping the conversation *on* the weather.

Though Caroline had kept her remark about the food quiet, Miss James had not. From across the table, Miss Jeffries, who was also going to India to fetch a husband, nodded vigorously. "My cousin said much the same when he returned from Kolkata. He said by the end of the voyage, he wished to go hungry rather than eat the fare they called food on his plate."

Mr. Miller looked up from his beef with concern on his face. And Miss Cole's hand went to her heart as if the very idea assaulted her every sense.

"Is this true, Captain Scott?" Mr. Liechty asked.

"I have no idea," Captain Scott said. "I've never met Miss Jeffries's cousin."

Caroline almost laughed aloud at the wordplay, but since no one else seemed to understand the joke, she instead turned her head toward the captain.

Captain Scott surveyed the group with his left brow raised. Caroline had to scold her face into behaving. She'd spent a good part of her childhood practicing the art of brow-raising yet had never perfected it. She found herself wanting to try it again, but it was certainly not good manners to mimic the captain's movements.

"While the food will not be what it is at this moment, it will be adequate to get us to our destination." Captain Scott tugged the cuff of his sleeve, moving the conversation past the awkward silence.

Mr. Miller scowled. Miss Cole noted his

reaction and rushed to console him. She scrunched her nose and squinted as if trying to see the silver lining in the captain's words. "Fish is lovely. And we are on the sea, so I assume we will probably be eating fresh fish toward the end of the voyage, isn't that right, Captain Scott?"

Caroline opened her mouth but stifled the desire to explain. Doing so would upset Miss Cole, and Caroline knew better than to work against her fellow passenger. Besides, the lady was only trying to put Mr. Miller at ease. Inserting herself into Miss Cole's conversation — especially to contradict her — would make her seem like she was a know-all. Caroline promptly closed her mouth.

Which is why it surprised her to see Captain Scott's mouth twitch at the corner. It could only have meant he kept himself in check as well. His eyes met Caroline's, a brief moment of understanding passing between them.

"I am sorry, Miss Cole," he said. "But the fish we will serve while traveling will be of the salted variety. To fish properly, it is best to be closer to the coastline where fish are plentiful. And when the wind is good, we need to keep our sails full that we might cover the distance swiftly and get you all to your destinations safely."

That sobered most everyone as they pondered a future of salted meat and hard biscuits. Caroline found she didn't really mind. Nice food was nice, but there was much to recommend the sea to her. No one held formal balls that required her attendance. The wind felt freeing. The sea slapping against the ship had strength and power, and she felt like it transferred some of that strength and power to her.

The conversation turned back to speculation of what it would be like on land once they reached their destination. The ladies wondered about the food and the weather. The men wondered about the trade and housing.

Captain Scott answered the questions as they came, talking about the unexpected heat of the curry and the unexpected heat of the weather. He spoke in great detail about the rice cakes and bananas and the joy of listening to the hawkers calling out their wares in the market.

He started to explain something called betel quid, but stopped and then gave a warning to perhaps stay away from it to avoid the strange effects it had on one's mind. He talked about the flowers and the riot of color that took his breath each time he saw it anew.

Caroline could almost see the lovely scenes he painted as he spoke.

It made her soften toward the captain. It settled the confusion she felt about him into something friendlier. She smiled at him. He returned that smile.

Maybe we will be on friendly terms after all, Caroline thought.

Such pleasant musings lasted until after dinner when Miss James took Caroline's hand and followed the captain instead of joining the others for cards.

"I so loved hearing about the place that will be our home," she said after she'd called his attention to them, her voice an almost dreamy whisper, as if she were picturing it all. Then she straightened abruptly. "But, sir, you did leave off some information."

"Did I, Miss James? What information would you like to know that I failed to provide?" He smiled at her indulgently.

"What about the gentlemen?" Miss James said.

Captain Scott's easy manner stuttered to a halt. "What about them?"

"I was wondering about the ratio of men to women. Are there many single women in comparison to the men?"

Captain Scott narrowed his eyes and let

out a puff of air that seemed to barely cling to the safe side of thunderous. "Are we talking about your chances of making a match, Miss James?"

She blushed but did not lower her gaze. Caroline had to give the lady credit for the fortitude to remain in a contest of wills with the captain, especially when forcing him into such an indelicate topic of conversation.

"Well, yes," she said. "That *is* why I'm going. That is the concern of chief importance to me."

"Dear lady," the captain began, with civility in words though not in tone, "there are a significant number of single men compared to the number of single young ladies."

Miss James looked relieved to have this rumor confirmed, but her smile fell as soon as the captain continued.

"But I am hard-pressed to call them gentlemen. And I must confess that if I had a daughter, I would never allow her to make this trip in search of a match. I would rather see her thrown to the sorrow and pains of spinsterhood than see her in a situation that is beneath morality."

Miss James blinked, and her lip trembled at the harshness in his tone and message.

Caroline glanced around to see if anyone

else could hear and was glad to find no one in the corridor eavesdropping on the mortifying moment.

"Captain Scott, please." Caroline spared a moment to glare at him before turning to Miss James. "Dear, do not let him worry you. Remember when I spoke before of absolutes? There will be cads aplenty I am sure, but so there are in London as well. I am certain you will find a lovely gentleman who will be exactly what you are looking for."

"So sure, are you?" Captain Scott asked pointedly.

In truth, Caroline wasn't at all confident in her statements, but she certainly hoped. "I am sure that absolutes are not made up of sound science, Captain."

"We're not dealing with science, Miss Gray. We're dealing with the frailties and weaknesses of men. I stand by my opinion."

"Then it is a good thing we will all be able to form our own opinions."

Captain Scott snapped his mouth closed with a click of teeth. He clearly had gone further in this conversation than he had intended.

Fine, if he had more to say, Caroline asked him a question that demanded an answer. "Tell me honestly, Captain. Do you really

101

not know of any gentlemen in India whom you hold in high esteem?"

His jaw flexed, and he finally gave a curt nod. "I confess I do know of a few. But only a few, Miss Gray."

"There are six ladies on this ship, thus, by my accounting, we will need only six."

"What of those of you who have pre-determined arrangements? Those of you living under the black cloud of being unable to choose for yourselves may not have the chance to seek one of only six good men. You may be saddled with a viper of a man instead. Be careful, Miss Gray. There are a great many things that hide in the shadows of India. And if I've discovered anything, it is that things hidden in shadow are usually dangerous."

Caroline narrowed her eyes, feeling as though he no longer spoke in generalities. He was talking to *her*. But how could he? He knew nothing of her situation. And certainly, she had made a pre-arrangement of sorts, but it wasn't an obligation. No contract bound her to marry a man. No offer had been made. No offer had been accepted. She only had to give the man in question a chance to court her.

Yet she felt the weight of the captain's words. What if the gentlemen in India were not true gentlemen? What if they were as the captain had said? Who was this Nicholas Barritt, who had his mother pulling the strings on which she danced across an ocean?

She felt her anger cool to something else. Fear? "You may not like the gentlemen of this colony, Captain, but you do have an obligation to *be* a gentleman on your ship. Frightening the passengers and bringing them to tears is hardly appropriate behavior."

They stared at each other for several long, rather tense seconds. The captain's jaw worked before he looked down.

"No. Quite right. I apologize, Miss Gray." He nodded to her and then turned to Miss James. "I apologize to you as well, Miss James. I truly hope you find happiness in your new lives. But I do not believe my behavior to be ungentlemanly. By opening your eyes to the possible failures of the men who will seek your hands, I do the most honorable thing a gentleman can do. I ask you to be wise and trust that by giving you the full spectrum of information in my possession you will rise to my expectations and actually *be* wise." He gave a stiff bow. "Good evening, ladies."

Caroline glared at his retreating back. She

was half a mind to remove her slipper and throw it at him. How dare he treat Miss James with such callousness?

Miss James had become a puddle of tears while Caroline fumed. She finally realized she was ignoring the problem at hand and placed an arm over Miss James's shoulders. "There, there, dear. How can we expect a man to be a decent judge of another man? I do believe you will find happiness."

"B— but what if I don't?" Miss James sniffled into her lace handkerchief.

Poor Miss James. She was the sort of woman no one would call pretty, and her voice had a grating resonance to it. The embroidery stitches around her handker- chief were done so poorly Caroline's mother would have made Caroline pull them out and do them again. No wonder she prob- ably felt quite desperate.

Caroline understood her own confidence to be a rare thing among women, and, if she felt a little of that desperation herself, how was a woman like Miss James to survive the voyage with the captain carrying on the way he did at every given opportunity?

"All will be well." She hoped she sounded comforting. "You will find a nice man who shares your same enjoyments and who will treat you kindly. That's most important of all. Do not worry so much over his status or means. Pay attention to whether or not he is kind to others and to you. I trust you will find yourself happily paired with someone deserving of you in no time at all."

Miss James leaned her head on Caroline's shoulder.

Caroline realized she'd done as she'd intended that night. She had made her first real friend.

By the end of the next day, Caroline was not so sure having a friend was all that desirable. Miss James trailed after her relentlessly, offering to help Caroline put up her hair or asking Caroline to return the favor. She even offered to help Caroline tie her stays as if the woman was a lady's maid. Caroline assured her that all of her stays tied in the front and that she was quite capable of dressing herself. Heat crawled straight to her hairline over such free discussion regarding her clothing. And people said that Caroline showed an astonishing lack of propriety!

Captain Scott did not show up to dinner for the next several evenings. Uncertain if he stayed away because of her outspokenness, she decided to stop Lieutenant Peterson on his way out of the saloon after cards. Miss James attempted to join her, and Caroline waved her hand to show that she wished to have a private word with the lieutenant.

Miss James frowned, likely worrying over Caroline being alone with the lieutenant, but she did leave after a second.

"Yes, Miss Gray?"

"I do hate to trouble you, and I do hate to reveal my ignorance in these matters, especially since we've already discussed this once, but is it usual for the captain to skip so many dinners with the passengers?"

Lieutenant Peterson's mouth turned up into a full grin. "Ah. That. Well, it is not unusual. A captain has many duties that must take precedence over society. He must make certain our course is clear and unhindered. He must inspect the ship regularly to be certain everything is in working order, and he has to quell any issues that might arise with the crew. His responsibilities are what keep our passengers safe and allow them to reach their destination without trouble."

Relief filled Caroline so quickly, she almost felt faint. So, he did not stay away because of her sharp tongue dressing him down for his brutish behavior. Not that she should have cared — but she did.

"Is there anything else you needed, Miss Gray?"

"No. Thank you, Lieutenant."

He bowed and moved to leave, but Caroline called him back. She had to know. She needed to understand why the captain so unwaveringly spoke out against the gentlemen of Mumbai.

"I wondered, Lieutenant, if you could tell me . . . can you think of any reason the women on board this vessel should feel any apprehension regarding our current course regarding the gentlemen we will meet when we arrive?"

Lieutenant Peterson's posture softened into something sympathetic. "I see. He's admonished you for choosing to follow the allure of India and make you own fortunes there, has he?"

"Yes. No. Well not me, exactly. One of the other ladies asked him a less-than-discreet question, and she received a far-less-discreet answer. It seemed prudent to ask for a second opinion, and as we've shared several meals together and you seem like a well-informed man, your opinion has weight in this matter. Do you agree with the captain?"

"Miss Gray, one thing I can say is that few men are always strictly gentlemen. We do try, but we do not always succeed. But I can promise you that Captain Scott is one of those few who is *always* a gentleman.

His words may have been harsh in nature, but he does worry for the India-bound women. He worries they are misinformed and that misery awaits them.

"But most of the women I see later at some dinner or occasion or another seem genuinely happy in the lives they have discovered. Certainly, their lives are far different than they would have been in London, but their lives are not so changed that they despair of joy."

He bowed and took his leave.

It was an elegant answer.

One that answered very little.

He defended his captain, and he made overtures of appeasing her fears by reassuring her that a pleasant future awaited her. But he had not remarked on the quality of men.

Lieutenant Peterson was a very smart man indeed.

And Caroline's fears were not appeased at all.

CHAPTER SEVEN

Caroline awoke to the sound of something violently crashing against the wall of her cabin. Her eyes popped open to the darkness around her. As she swung her legs free of her bunk, she felt as though she were a child on the swing her father had installed under the sycamore tree. As he pushed her and she sailed up into the sky, there was a pressing against her middle as if she had a string tied around her stomach and the ground was pulling her back. She felt that same disorienting tugging now as she tumbled, rather ungracefully, to the floor.

Her entire sense of direction felt off. She knew she was sitting at an angle; she had become used to the motions of her life on the sea, but this was something else. She started to slide, then bumped up against the leg of the desk in the room. And then she slid the other direction until she hit the corner of her bunk.

109

And then it felt like the ground had dropped out from underneath her, and she plummeted down with it. The next moment found her rising again.

Another great boom thundered around her as if the wood of the ship itself was shattering apart.

"I should never have left my bed," she said aloud, realizing she would be much safer if she tied herself into her bunk. At least then she wouldn't be rolling around the floor.

She wondered how the others fared in their bunks when a pounding on her door broke through the cacophony of noise. She could barely hear the knocking above the storm raging around their ship, amplified by the ventilation slats that seemed to let every slight noise filter into her cabin.

"Miss Gray! Miss Gray! Please help!" More pounding.

Caroline managed to get her feet underneath her and stood, though she required the bunk to balance her. She felt for her robe and quickly swept it over her arms and shoulders, then fumbled her way to the door.

She had recognized the cries for help as Miss James and assumed the woman required comfort in the storm. Though the storm unsettled her as well, she was not about to show anyone that she felt any rising panic. No reason for both of them to be at sixes and sevens.

She opened the door and could barely make out the face of her friend in the darkness of the corridor, but the panic in Miss James's voice told her something was quite wrong.

"What is it? Are you all right?"

The ship took another plunge down that made her feel as though she'd fallen off a mountain. Both women clung to the doorframe to keep themselves from tumbling into the hall.

"It's Miss Jeffries. She's gone!"

"What?" Caroline had to have heard wrong.

"I awoke when the ship took that terrible pitch. I called out to her, but she didn't answer. I became worried."

The ship seemed to roll onto its side. The hull creaked alarmingly, and cries came from other rooms.

"I checked her bunk. She wasn't in it," Miss James continued. "I found her in the saloon. She was in such a state, crying about how we'll all be drowned in the ocean. I couldn't calm her. I'm afraid she went out on deck."

"No!" Caroline cried out.

"I tried to stop her!" Miss James wailed.

The ship recovered from its downward dive, and now seemed to be climbing. Caroline shifted her balance to keep from falling back into her room. She wanted to demand to know exactly what Miss James believed she could do about Miss Jeffries's disappearance. Indeed, the woman looked as if she expected Caroline to calm the seas herself. It terrified her to think that anyone could depend on her so much, because really, what could she do?

"She'll be swept from the deck and into the sea!" Miss James pleaded.

Miss James was right. If Miss Jeffries had gone out onto the deck, she *would* be swept off. There would be no way to recover her.

"Are you sure? Absolutely sure she went up? She wouldn't have gone to one of the other ladies' rooms or to one of the men's rooms?"

"She went toward the stairs! And there's no crew anywhere. I looked. I don't know what to do!"

"I know where to find rope," she said, not wasting time on deliberating plans. "I'll go up and see if I can get her. But I need you to stay here."

"But I want to help!"

"I doubt there's enough rope for us both."

She wasn't sure if there was enough for her. "I can't help her and worry about where you might be at the same time."

Instead of arguing further, Miss James agreed to stay.

With her stomach in her throat, Caroline hurried as fast as the pitching ship would allow. The wall sconces were dark, whether because it was late or because they were purposely doused to keep a fire from starting, she didn't know. She'd heard fire was the greatest enemy to any ship on the water.

She took a step and nearly tripped when the ground rose up to meet her foot faster than she'd expected. Her next step felt like the ground had fallen out from under her. She stumbled in her hurry to return to where she'd seen the rope while exploring a few days earlier, hoping it was still there. She didn't dare go on deck without being properly lashed to the ship.

She called out again and again, hoping she would run into a crewman, but she encountered no one.

The rope was where she remembered it. She nearly wept with joy at the feel of its coils. She also nearly wept with the horror at the task before her. There would be no going back now.

At least she had the rope. She would not

be going out unprotected. Caroline hefted the bulk into her arms and hurried to the stairs that led to the deck. Usually she could see light there, even if only from the stars, but it was totally dark. Frowning, she tied one end of the rope around her waist as she moved, tightening and double-checking her knot to make certain it would not fail her. She added a second and a third knot, her fingers trembling in her panic.

Well, she thought, *if I die, what a jolly adventurous story I'll have to tell Papa on the other side.*

At the top of the stairs, she found a sturdy piece of canvas lashed in front of the door to hold the storm at bay. A stream of water flowed down the stairs from under the door; perhaps whoever had done the lashing had been in a hurry, or perhaps the storm was worse than she feared.

"I'll just look," she told herself. "I'll see if she's out there, and I won't have to go out myself at all."

She pushed aside the canvas, opened the door, and was hit immediately by the cold.

Caroline slid forward, her back to the wall for balance, and exited the stairwell to meet the torrential storm outside. She looked through the rainstorm but couldn't see well enough to know if Miss Jeffries or anyone else was out there or not.

She stepped farther onto the deck, regretting her choice as soon as the blast of wind pelted stinging rain into her skin. Her nightdress and robe offered no protection from the icy needles of water. Her slippers were soaked through with the first step. She tied the other end of her rope to the railing outside the door and tugged hard to make sure the knot would hold.

"Miss Jeffries!" she shouted, but the sound was snatched away in the swirl of storm. Lightning flashed, and a violent clap of thunder followed that made her cry out.

Not willing to allow the rope to be the only thing tethering her to the ship, she groped her way along the railing toward the wheelhouse. She wanted to grip the railing tightly in her own hands. The security that beam of wood provided her was false, she knew, but she wanted it all the same.

She shouted for Miss Jeffries again and again as she stumbled forward and tried to peer into the stormy dark for any sign of the woman. Her soaked hair stuck to her face and blocked her vision.

I'm going to drown, she thought, *even without falling into the ocean. The rain will drown me.*

The ocean seemed determined to come to

her if she did not go to it. The ship climbed each swell and crashed down again, waves washing across the deck.

She took a step back, wanting to return belowdecks where she could tie herself into her bunk and . . . what? Go back to sleep? When there was a woman missing?

She took a few more steps forward, sliding her feet along the deck. She could not go back when Miss Jeffries might need her help. But what if Miss Jeffries had already arrived at the wheelhouse, and Caroline was taking an unnecessary risk? But what if she was only a few feet away and unable to return on her own?

Caroline felt confident Miss Jeffries would have taken her same path. It was the most direct route to the captain's wheelhouse. But as the ship tilted sharply to the side, Caroline thought of Miss James's fear that Miss Jeffries would be swept out to sea. It was possible that such a thing had already happened. The rope around her waist suddenly felt as insufficient as gossamer.

A wave cracked against the side of the ship, startling her enough to make her cry out again. Another wave pounded into the deck as if it meant to drive itself through to the hull.

And then she heard it. Another cry that

was not her own: a cry that hit a pitch higher than that of the storm, a cry that sounded like it came from a woman. Caroline squinted against the rain in the direction of the noise but could see nothing.

Lightning forked across the sky, and in that flash, she saw a pile of sodden, brightly colored cloth against the darkness of the sky and ship.

"Miss Jeffries!" she cried, the sound half-strangled from the water that splashed into her open mouth. The brightly colored lump moved, and Caroline saw the woman's eyes in that flash before all went dark again.

Miss Jeffries hadn't stayed against the railing, but that didn't mean she'd moved to her current position on purpose. It was possible that the lady had fallen and slid toward one of the masts near the center of the deck.

"Come to me!" Caroline shouted, not wanting to leave the edge, not wanting to be vulnerable in the open space of the middle.

But Miss Jeffries didn't move.

Caroline couldn't be sure she'd been heard. *I have the rope,* she thought. And she knew how to tie a knot that would hold. It stood to reason she would be safe to venture toward the middle regardless if the ship tipped or if a wave washed over her. So why could she not convince her hands to release the railing? Because a rope wouldn't stop the weight of a wave from crashing into the deck and bludgeoning her to death. But then, there was nothing to stop the weight of a wave crashing into Miss Jeffries either.

Another lightning flash; another roaring boom of thunder.

She screamed and forced herself to let go of the railing and forge her way toward Miss Jeffries.

The distance wasn't far. Sixty feet? Seventy? Yet it felt like miles as she groped her way along the deck. Lightning flashed again and again while thunder rolled around her and water poured over her, whether from wave or rain she couldn't tell.

Her body felt numb, but she couldn't tell if it was from the extreme cold or extreme fear. Her legs felt like dead weight. She only hoped that weight would hold her fast to the deck of the ship. She desperately prayed that no more waves would crest the railing.

And then she was there, next to Miss Jeffries who had found refuge against a box bolted securely to the deck.

"Come on!" she shouted. "We must go inside!"

Miss Jeffries's eyes were wide with fear, and she shook her head to indicate she could not move. Or maybe she was injured and was physically unable to make the distance back to the door. Regardless, Caroline had no intention of staying out in the open with so much danger swirling around them. If she had to drag the woman, then she would.

"We're going to die!" Miss Jeffries said, barely audible above the noise.

"Not today!" Caroline grabbed Miss Jeffries around the waist and shouted, "Get up! Save yourself!"

Miss Jeffries stood on wobbly legs, but it was enough for Caroline to undo the tie around her own waist and lash the two of them together. She made quick work of it, and she hoped and prayed that the knots would hold until they got back to the stairwell.

Both women cried out as another explosion of thunder crashed over them.

CHAPTER EIGHT

Thomas had felt the storm coming in his bones. As a child, he had believed his father had been magic when he'd insisted he could predict a storm. Now, Thomas knew better. Long hours of experience, not magic, taught him to feel the charge and power of the storm straight to his marrow.

His crew made quick work preparing for the storm. It would likely be nothing significant, but he liked being prepared for the worst. Cannons were secured, and his crew had extinguished all lamps as well as the galley fires, and they had battened down the hatches after informing all below deck to stay put. There were already several men at the helm trying to hold the ship steady. He had some men working on the pumps to make sure the *Persistence* didn't take on more water than she could handle, and the rest of his crew were in the process of reducing sails to bare poles when the storm arrived.

It hit with the violent intensity of a hammer. The seas frothed and bucked the ship as though she were a horse determined to throw the rider. The rain fell in torrents. Visual acuity dropped to almost nothing. He could barely see anything through the torrents. The wind howled around them before ripping one of the sails free from its line before it could be taken down from the foremast. He didn't have to see to recognize that sound. The cracking noise of the sail being whipped to-and-fro was deafening even above the sound of the rain and the waves.

"Secure the sail before it brings the foremast down right through the ship!" Thomas shouted.

Dressed in his foul-weather gear, Midshipman Allen jumped to action and rushed to the mast. He pulled out his rigger's knife and sawed through the heavy ropes, freeing the sail.

Thomas felt a momentary relief until another crack thundered above them.

A yardarm on the sails of the foremast splintered and snapped. The yard came down and struck Allen across the chest, nearly knocking the man off the forecastle deck to the main deck. Part of the railing gave way, but Allen was pinned where he was.

Thomas did not hesitate. With everyone else intent on reducing the sails and monitoring water levels, there was no one to help Allen. As Thomas rushed to the midshipman's aid, the lightning flashed, and he saw something else. Thomas's heart and stomach and lungs all lodged solidly in his throat as he caught sight of two ghostly figures moving down below, across the main deck, illuminated by the lightning that raced over the sky.

Two women.

Miss Jeffries and Miss Gray.

He would never forgive himself if he lost any of his passengers to a storm, yet he knew it was different thinking of losing Miss Gray. Losing her would be like losing a piece of his own soul. Did no one else see them?

How could they with the storm and the duties before each and every man?

He raced to Allen's side. If he could move quickly enough, he would not have to choose. He could save them all.

Lightning flashed, and he looked back to the women. He halted in his attempts to lift the yard as the brief illumination showed the two women rapidly closing the distance

122

to the stairwell leading to the cabins.

His relief was short-lived as a wave reached out and swept over the whole of the deck.

"No!" he cried out. Water slapped up against his own legs and torso. He blinked in an attempt to clear his vision, as if he could will Miss Gray to safety just by laying eyes on her. For several terrible seconds, he saw nothing, and the impossible decision of what to do felt like a chasm stretching open in his soul.

What if he could not save everyone?

What if he had to choose?

The lightning stilled, keeping him in suspense of Miss Gray's safety. But then a flash revealed her and Miss Jeffries near the alcove that led to the passenger stairs. Another wave crashed, but they were protected by that alcove and then they disappeared behind the canvas that should have prevented them from venturing out in the first place.

His worry gave way to anger. He used the strength of his fury and lifted the yard from Allen. He then dragged the man to safety.

"Get this man to the surgeon," he snapped to Black, "and return to duty immediately." He then turned to Mr. Kilpack, who was completing lashing one of the yards to the railings. He jabbed a finger at the alcove leading to the passenger stairs. "Batten down that hatch! And make sure it's done right this time! Go!"

He considered going to those stairs and shouting himself hoarse at those women. But he didn't. He had a ship to keep afloat. He verified that the poles were bare and all hands were occupied accordingly. He ordered a sea anchor to be dropped to keep the ship perpendicular to the waves and then made his way back to the wheelhouse.

CHAPTER NINE

Lightning webbed the sky around them, and Caroline thanked Providence for it. The flashes of light allowed her to see where she needed to go and which route would get them back safely, as well as the wave before it crashed over the deck. She had just enough time to shove Miss Jeffries out of the alcove and toward the door of the stairwell.

Caroline stuffed Miss Jeffries and herself through the door and past the canvas just as another wave broke over the top of them. They tumbled down the stairs as the ship plunged downward again.

They staggered into the saloon where Miss James was waiting with blankets that she immediately wrapped around both women.

"Come!" she said. "If we don't get you out of those wet things and dried off immediately, you'll both die of hypothermia."

She led them back to Caroline's room, which Caroline was grateful for since she was exhausted and disoriented.

The storm had tested her, and she wasn't certain if she had passed that test or not. She only knew the boat still rocked and dropped and climbed.

She knew her body trembled, yet she felt no cold. Her skin had gone numb. She half-wondered if she'd gone deaf in the experience. It seemed Miss James was talking, but her voice sounded far away. Miss Jeffries didn't respond either; perhaps she had also gone deaf.

Thunder still rapped against the ship like an unwanted visitor demanding entrance, but it didn't hold the same menace as it had out on the open deck.

"I trust the captain knows his business. We'll be safe," Miss James said as she stripped the dress from Miss Jeffries's body. Her attempt to comfort them was kindly meant even if she didn't understand what they'd seen. No one could know the raw chaos she'd witnessed. And no one could guarantee safe passage through such a mess, no matter how experienced the captain.

The storm eventually tapered off. Miss James dried Miss Jeffries and then redressed her with one of her own spare nightgowns and robes. Miss James then wrapped a fresh blanket around Miss Jeffries's shoulders before turning to Caroline.

Caroline gratefully allowed Miss James to help her out of her wet things and into dry clothing. Her own fingers refused to obey her commands and fumbled and flailed at her every attempt to use them.

Miss James continued talking, discussing her favorite dessert — a baked apple pudding that her grandmother's cook made to perfection. She discussed horses and puppies and how much she wished she had a better mind for needlework.

Eventually Caroline's body began to warm, and as it did, so did her temper.

"What were you thinking?" she demanded from Miss Jeffries. "To go out in the open in such a storm! We've been told and told again that in such situations we are to remain in our cabins. You could have been killed! You could have been the death of both of us!"

A roll of thunder cracked, making the wood shudder around them.

"I'm sorry," Miss Jeffries replied. "I was so afraid — I was mad with fear — and I thought if I talked to the captain, I might be able to . . . Oh, I don't know. I don't know what I was thinking."

The ship took another plunge, but none of them cried out this time. It was like their nerves had frayed entirely and were completely undone.

"I didn't know," Miss Jeffries continued. "I didn't know how horrible it would be. And I know they came through and told us to stay below, but I hadn't realized . . ."

Caroline hadn't heard the warnings of the storm. She must have been in a deep sleep to have not heard.

Miss Jeffries began sobbing. "If you hadn't come for me, I'm sure I would have died. I owe you a great debt."

Caroline's anger softened. "It was Miss James," she said as she patted Miss Jeffries on the back and tried to soothe her sobs. "If she had not immediately come for me, I don't know that I would have had time to help. But you're fine. We're fine. I'm glad everything has worked out."

Caroline could not help it. She didn't have the energy to be cross with Miss Jeffries, not with the woman crying. Besides, she was crying as well. She'd never felt so grateful and overwhelmed all at once. She had lived. So she would not be telling Papa any grand stories, but she would write of them to Mama and Josephine. She would tell them about how she'd fought a great battle with the storm and the sea — about how she'd won.

Assuming she actually survived the night. Because the weather picked up again, and the storm returned to rage around them. Thunder boomed over them like a promise it would break the ship apart and cast it to the sea for driftwood.

Caroline squeezed her eyes shut and wrapped her arms around the two women huddled in the bottom bunk as the ship rocked wildly between the sky and the sea.

CHAPTER TEN

"How did they get out there?" Thomas demanded from the crew inside the wheelhouse. He stripped off his foul-weather coat and studied the sky; the next strike of lightning would allow him to verify all deckhands were cleared and belowdeck.

"Who, Captain?" Lieutenant Peterson asked.

"Miss Gray and Miss Jeffries. They were out on deck."

Everyone in the wheelhouse shared his horror with the tale he relayed, not only for the two women but for Midshipman Allen as well. Thomas wondered how many others had been hurt in the storm besides Allen. There was no way to know, not until they were under clear skies again.

He noted that where once there had been several men hanging on the helm to hold the ship steady, there were now only two — a good sign that the storm was clearing.

"The doors should have been fortified," Thomas continued to rant. "Those in the cabins and in the steerage should have been warned to stay below deck until the storm passed, and only then would they be given permission to come back up. What could those fool women possibly have been thinking?"

He clawed at his collar, feeling as though his throat had been blocked, preventing oxygen to flow to his lungs. The women had been a crashing wave away from becoming a casualty of the sea.

The storm wasn't the worst they'd seen as a crew. Thomas knew they'd pull out of it right enough, but it still packed a powerful enough punch to make it deadly for anyone out in it. Now that Miss Gray was safe, he allowed himself to stoke his fury. What would induce such a muddleheaded decision? What fool decided to take a stroll on the deck in such conditions?

"Don't be too hard on them," Lieutenant Peterson said. "They likely have an explanation."

One of the two helmsmen shot Peterson a look that showed he doubted it.

"Watch your helm!" Thomas barked in reprimand. No explanation could excuse such a lack in judgment. But for as furious

as he felt, relief was there, too. Miss Gray
had made it to safety.

He would not have to figure out how to
fill the hole losing her would leave in him.

I'm being silly, he thought. *How can she
leave any mark on me when I barely know the
woman?*

Surely his concern for her was because
she was a passenger aboard his ship. Surely
that was it. Regardless of his relief and his
reasons for that belief, both she and Miss
Jeffries would hear his thoughts about their
little escapade. He would make it clear in
no uncertain terms they were in quite a lot
of trouble. He would scold them well
enough to ensure that they would never do
such a thing again.

He would scold them well enough that his
reprimand would ring in the ears of their
great-great-grandchildren.

But not tonight.

The night had been long for the entire
crew, and at the end of it, Thomas fell into
his cot and into sleep in the same instant.

The seas were calm the next day. Thomas
woke and lumbered to his feet. No water
remained in his washbasin, but the wash-
cloth was plenty wet from the water slop-
ping out over it the night before. He dragged

the cloth over his face and caught a glance at himself in the mirror. His eyes were red rimmed, and he looked as though he had aged a decade overnight.

"More likely it was that woman who has aged me," he muttered.

He dressed quickly, made his way to the wheelhouse, where he received the first reports of the crew's well-being. Allen had broken several ribs. Several men had suffered cuts from the splinters flying from the broken yard. But everyone was alive. Exhausted, but alive.

With the reports being good news, he issued the order to call the passengers to gather on deck where he could have a word with them.

He stood on the quarterdeck above them and watched as the passengers from steerage joined the ladies and gentlemen. He eyed them all, and noted every one of them needed a good washing after the experience they'd endured. They all appeared to be in need of sleep as much as the crew did.

"Thank you all for joining me this glorious morning," he said.

He wasn't sure if they agreed with his assessment of the morning being glorious, but they all looked grateful to be alive. He would not make light of their gratitude.

"I would like to publicly thank my crew for their great attention to their posts during last night's adventures, and to assure you all that you are in safe, capable, and experienced hands. They worked hard to ensure your safety. I will be allowing them to rest today so they might recover from the difficult night. Meals will be kept simple."

His eyes flicked to where Miss Gray stood with Miss Jeffries. All the passengers looked to have passed an incredibly difficult night, and few looked as though they would be able to stomach even the simplest of meals, but Miss Gray and Miss Jeffries looked especially haggard and exhausted. Though what would one expect considering their nocturnal adventures?

His anger rose again at the thought of them putting themselves in such mortal peril.

All passengers had been warned of the danger of storms and the proper protocol when dealing with such things, and Miss Gray and Miss Jeffries had not obeyed his orders. They knew to stay belowdeck. They knew to stay inside their cabins.

"If you will trust us to do our jobs, we will see you securely delivered to your destination." Though he was speaking to Miss Gray and Miss Jeffries, it was important for all to hear it. Panic on a ship proved to be a contagious disease.

Maybe he'd been wrong about Miss Gray. Maybe she wasn't as intelligent as he thought because only a daft fool put herself in such danger. A daft, reckless fool.

As soon as he'd ended his rallying speech to the passengers, he asked Peterson to bring Miss Gray and Miss Jefferies to him. When the women arrived in the small sitting room just outside his cabin, he found they looked far worse up close with hair barely brushed and stiff, clothing disheveled.

He stared at them for several long moments hoping to intimidate them the way his father always did when he stared for long stretches of time without saying anything.

Miss Jeffries seemed very intimidated.

Miss Gray seemed irritated — and becoming more irritated the longer she stood in silence.

He had not anticipated her defiance. As foolish as he felt her to be after such a night, surely she had intelligence enough to remember the rules. She had to know she was in trouble for breaking them, yet she showed no signs of remorse.

He cleared his throat and began. "I know

you were both out during the storm last night."

He let that sink in for a moment, hoping it would reduce some of Miss Gray's belligerence and remind her that humility would be her best option. If anything, she now looked hostile as well. Hostile toward *him,* of all things.

Miss Gray said nothing.

Miss Jeffries, however, dissolved into a puddle of tears. "It was all just so frightening!" the woman sobbed. "It felt as though the ship was about to be swallowed whole by the sea! I didn't know what to do! I was frightened out of my mind, and I thought that if I could just get to you and explain how afraid I was that perhaps you would be able to steer us out of the storm and . . . Oh, I don't know. I realize how silly it all sounds now, but during the storm, I was mad with fear."

Had the woman really suggested that he could just steer out of the storm at will? If he had such miraculous powers, wouldn't he have already made that choice?

He stood to his full height, knowing he posed an intimidating form when he wanted to. " 'Mad with fear'?" he repeated. "Your *madness* nearly endangered members of my own crew. When I saw you out there, I was confronted with the awful choice of caring for one of my own who'd been struck down or retrieving you and bringing you to safety. Your being on deck posed a distraction that none of us needed during a time when so much was required of us. What kind of madness could be worth the lives of my men?"

"I know!" Miss Jeffries lamented, wringing the gloves in her hands. "I understand now that my actions were foolish, and I assure you it will never happen again!" She tightened her grip on her gloves.

Miss Gray, on the other hand, showed no such distress. She offered neither explanation nor apology. The way she just stood there, silently looking like she planned on calling up a new storm, unnerved him.

"Do you have anything to say for yourself, Miss Gray?"

"No, Captain," she said.

"No?" He was certain his incredulity at her insolence hung heavy on that one word.

"I have nothing at all to say, Captain Scott."

"And how is it you have nothing to say, not even an apology, when you knew the rules and appropriate behavior aboard my ship, yet still felt compelled to throw all good sense to the side so you and Miss Jeffries could ask me kindly to steer my ship out of the weather? How is it that you have nothing to say to that? You, a woman who always has something to say."

If she seemed unrepentant before, her stiffening at his last comment made her even more so.

She lifted her chin. "You've already deemed me incompetent and accused me of violating your rules when you have yet to ask me why I was out there last night. You do not want reasoning. You want groveling. And I will not grovel when I have done nothing wrong."

That took him off guard. Beyond being unremorseful, she seemed to be accusing *him* of wrongdoing. "Then, please, enlighten me as to your purpose out on deck."

"No."

He blinked. Miss Jeffries gasped and actually took a step to the side as if not wanting to be associated with one so willfully disobedient to authority.

"No?"

"You aren't asking for my side of the story out of a genuine desire to hear, but out of a need to mock and abuse me. So, no. I will not tell you what happened because you do not truly wish to know."

Silence descended and pressed down on all of them. Miss Jeffries looked from

Thomas to Miss Gray and then back again before she sputtered, "It was all my fault, Captain Scott! I am the reason Miss Gray went outside. I went even though Miss James begged me not to, and then Miss James ran to Miss Gray for help. Miss Gray tied herself to the boat and came after me. She is the reason I am alive and able to stand before you." As if to make up for not showing solidarity with her shipmate mere moments before, Miss Jeffries took two steps closer to Miss Gray and linked their arms.

Miss Gray looked as surprised by the physical contact as Thomas was by Miss Jeffries's confession.

"You tied yourself to the ship?" he asked Miss Gray.

"The point of a rescue is not to make yourself a liability to others but an asset to the one in need. Of course I tied myself to the ship. Now, is this interview at an end? As you so thoughtfully pointed out, I had a difficult night, and I'm quite tired." She dipped a quick curtsy and turned and left without waiting for permission or dismissal.

Since Miss Jeffries was linked to her by the arm, she was compelled to leave as well, though she turned back to call out, "It truly was all my fault, sir, and I am truly sorry. I promise to never be so foolish in the future." Miss Jeffries stumbled and had to quicken her pace to catch up to the woman who had been, apparently, out on deck for the same reason he had been — to save a life.

She had mounted a very elegant and successful rescue all on her own. It appeared Captain Thomas Scott owed her an apology.

CHAPTER ELEVEN

"He's an ogre," Caroline insisted as she sat in the dining room with the others and focused on practicing her tambour work. She imagined she was sticking the long hook through Captain Scott's head each time she pushed it through the fabric in her hoop.

It didn't matter where she went on the ship, the odor of illness was everywhere. She took shallow breaths to refrain from inhaling the acrid stench more than necessary. She had been reduced to tambour work because she didn't dare take out her sketchbooks with the ship being so decidedly soaked. The dining room seemed the driest place, so the men and the women were spending the day together.

"He was only worried about us." Miss Jeffries had been making excuses for the man all day.

From the moment Caroline had risen

from her nap, she'd been trailed by Miss Jeffries and Miss James as if they had nothing else to do than whatever it was she happened to be doing. As if the ship wasn't small enough already, she now had the additional benefit of being continually crowded out by company.

"Worried?" With extra energy, she stabbed her hook through the fabric again and lost the stitch due to her hastiness in wrapping the thread. She'd always had trouble casting on and off the hook, and her mood did not improve her work. "If he had been so worried, he would have seen you out there and would have mounted a rescue well before I ever stepped a foot on those stairs."

She frowned when she considered the stairs. All the water that had been running down them the night previous had become quite a mess for the crew to clean out.

With everyone together, and since Miss James felt the night had carried a tale worthy to be told, she had no qualms about telling it. She recounted all the details, including the scolding Miss Jeffries and Caroline had received — details which Caroline would have preferred to have been kept private.

Miss Cole sat on the edge of her seat and clung to every word like the grasping gossiper she was.

"Well, you can hardly blame him," she said. "To so casually set aside the rules put in place for our safety would be a great insult."

Miss Jeffries looked at the floor and said nothing. Miss James also said nothing, as if just realizing that Miss Cole was not a sympathetic listener.

Caroline could not stay quiet, not when people she had grown to care for were being treated poorly. "I *can* blame him. If his crew had been checking on the passengers, they would have been able to aid Miss Jeffries in her panic."

"So you accept no blame for any of the trouble you caused?" Miss Cole seemed incredulous.

"Blame? For helping a friend? Do you think that putting someone else's needs before my own is grounds for blame? And Miss Jeffries was not in her right mind due to fear, so I do not fault her either."

Though such fear had never happened to Caroline, her words were true. She'd seen such panic when her father went out shooting. Birds, who would've stayed safe if they had only stayed put, scattered to the skies and made themselves vulnerable.

"But to blame the captain?" Miss Cole

143

repeated.

Caroline bit back her bitterness. Unkindness and gossip were not parts of her personality she wanted to embrace. She knew they lurked under the surface and worked to keep them there.

"You're right. I do not blame him either, not exactly. I simply refuse to excuse his part in last night's drama. It was not all Miss Jeffries. It was not all me. It was not all the crewmen who were in charge of 'battening down the hatches,' as they say. It was not even all the captain. It was a mixture of all these things that formed a singular outcome. Since he will not excuse me for my part, I am finding difficulty in excusing him for his."

She took a steadying breath. Why did she always feel so cross when working with needles? She never felt such fury when sketching. By way of apology, she added, "I recognize that such feelings do not make me the better person. I am working to overcome my emotions."

"Overcome your emotions?" Miss Cole scoffed. "Do you ever venture to do any such thing? It's a wonder the captain shows any kind of preference for your opinions at dinner when everything about you is so incredibly wild."

Caroline felt her face grow hot and cold all at the same time. She glanced at Clara, who worked quietly in the corner on her own mending. She did not know why it shamed her for the ship's maid and chaperone to hear such words. Would Clara think she needed to better chaperone Caroline?

"The captain never shows any sort of preference for anything I do."

Miss Cole's dark eyes flashed with a malignancy that made Caroline apprehensive. "Oh, but he does. He is always seeking out your thoughts or commentary on any subject brought up at the table. It's appalling. But now that I consider it, he probably only does so to gain the amusement of the great many oddities that exit your mouth, would you not agree, Mr. Miller?"

Mr. Miller made a noise that might have been agreement or might not. Caroline did not intend to remain in their company long enough to discover which of the two it might be.

"If you'll pardon me. I think I need to rest a bit longer."

"Or a *great while* longer if her moodiness is any indicator," Miss Cole said as soon as Caroline stood. The words were whispered to Mr. Miller but were said loudly enough to be heard by all.

Caroline inhaled sharply, gathered up her needlework, and exited the room as quickly as possible. Not quickly enough, however, because, from behind her, Miss Cole tittered a laugh — the laugh of all cruel society women.

"Mr. Miller, I do believe you are correct! She is exactly that sort of woman."

Caroline hated herself for wondering what sort of woman the two of them had agreed her to be, but she did wonder.

And she wondered how she could despise such people and yet want to fit in among them at the same time.

Caroline returned to her cabin, still feeling restless. She was surprised to find that the saloon and her cabin had been mopped up and cleaned as if the water splashing up the sides of her walls as the boat rocked the night before had been nothing but a dream. She placed her embroidery in a basket in her trunk and retrieved her Conte crayon box and sketchbook, wanting to occupy her time until the odious task of dinner and facing down the table and the captain became her immediate burden.

But what to draw?

The crew was likely still busy setting the ship to rights. Then she thought of the steerage passengers she had seen during Captain

Scott's lecture. Perhaps she would find something new to draw among them.

The sea was calm, as if it, too, was tired and needed to rest. Even so, Caroline hesitated at the steps leading to the deck. She would have to cross the deck to reach the other stairs that would take her to the steerage passengers. Her hesitation came from fear on two fronts. First, she could not stop seeing last night's waves crash over the wooden planks again and again. And second, she did not want to see the captain or have him see her if he happened to be in his wheelhouse.

Stop being absurd, she scolded herself. If the captain felt like baiting her into conversation for his own diversion, she would not give him the satisfaction. She would not allow him to make her a fool in front of the others.

And the storm had ended. She had nothing to fear.

She squared her shoulders and forced herself up the stairs. She could not help herself from glancing to the wheelhouse to see if the captain was there with his morose and judging expression. He was not there, nor anywhere else on deck. She relaxed and made her way to the other stairwell without interruption.

Down in steerage, she noticed the water in this part of the ship had yet to be fully cleaned out. The water wasn't very deep, which made her think somebody had tried to mop it up, but the job had not been done quite so fastidiously as everything remained decidedly damp.

Still, she was able to step carefully and keep her slippers dry.

The dank smell of wood left wet for too long mixed with the smell of unwashed bodies, but it wasn't necessarily a bad scent. It reminded her of when her father had been out hunting all day and came home to wrap her up in his enormous embrace. He'd smelled of work and wild.

The stairs were wide, probably to account for the necessity of moving cargo. From the top of the stairs, Caroline heard men laughing and talking over each other excitedly. She even heard the bang of a hand slapping a table. She followed the noise to find several men playing cards on a keg. She recognized one of them as Mr. Black, the crewman who'd rescued her bonnet and explained to her the sails and the rigging, and who was married to Clara.

"Mr. Black!" she said, feeling happy for the first time that day. "How good it is to see you!"

He smiled and opened his mouth as if to greet her but then closed it again and frowned. He nodded at her without speaking.

"Is something the matter?" she asked.

"Sorry, miss. Cap'n told me I wasn't to be fraternizing with the passengers." He stumbled a little over *fraternizing* as if the word had been hard for him but he was determined to make it part of his vocabulary.

"But you're playing cards with these passengers . . ." she said, feeling as though the captain had, once again, cast a dark cloud over her day.

"But that's different, isn't it?" He shrugged and cast a meaningful look at the men who were in vastly different dress from the gentlemen she had left on the other side of the ship.

Different in demeanor as well. Before she had drawn their attention by addressing them, they were boisterous, laughing, and teasing one another in a way she rarely saw gentlemen of the *ton* behave, though she suspected they did behave in such a way when ladies were not present. Why would society men be so different at their core from men of the everyday world?

Her father had often given in to boisterous laughter, but never when ladies other than Mama, her sister, and she were around. When society ladies were present, he was calm and gentlemanly. The girls had also been allowed to play but taught to behave when members of society were around. It made Caroline wonder how many other families were like that in their unguarded moments.

She hoped she found a husband who could strike that balance. One who wasn't all society bred, all good manners all the time. She wanted someone who understood propriety *and* play.

She realized she'd been silent for too long, and she smiled at Mr. Black. "I wondered if there was anything any of you needed. Some help I could offer? After such a storm, I hoped all of you are all right." She might not be able to fraternize with the crew, but surely no one could complain if she visited with other passengers, especially when she was on a charitable errand.

The men looked at her as if they had no idea what she might be and were unsure what to do with what they saw.

"Naw, miss . . . ." said a man with dark, shaggy hair and teeth that looked like yellowed, crooked, broken fence posts. He shook his head, flipping his shaggy hair back and forth. "We got things well in hand 'ere. As it is, yer shoes are already wet being on our side. You should prob'ly go back to yer own side."

She stared at them for a moment, feeling things she scarcely understood. "I apologize for intruding." She walked away, surprised by how hurt she felt by their dismissal.

She had no place among her own society, and was outright denied access to any other. The ship seemed to grow smaller every moment. Was there no one with whom she could confide or have a halfway intelligent conversation? Miss James and Miss Jeffries were good women, and she really quite liked both of them, but they wanted too much the approval of Miss Cole and Miss Luke, which meant they could not be trusted for confidences.

As it was, to have the whole of Captain Scott's scolding told to everyone in her party, and then to have Miss Cole mock her for the particular attention she perceived Captain Scott paid to her, was simply unbearable.

Was there nowhere for her to go? Somewhere she could act as though nothing had happened? No. There was not. Even her own cabin reminded her of how lonely she felt.

So instead of returning to her room or to the saloon or to the dining room, she decided to explore parts of the ship she felt quite certain were restricted.

And she didn't care. Not one bit.

She skirted around the stairs and down a much narrower hall, which led her to another set of stairs. She peered into the darkness and then descended. She stepped carefully to avoid the water and to avoid making any noise that would alert her presence to anyone. Several times, when various crewman walked to-and-fro, she had to duck into the shadows of little alcoves. When a larger group of crewmen sounded as though they were coming her direction, she slipped inside a small room. It turned out to be a carpentry shop, filled with tools and the smell of freshly shaved wood.

A lantern hung from an elaborately carved peg as if the occupant of the room wanted to make his mark on every inch of it.

With her sketchbook in hand, Caroline settled on a bench and opened to a clean page. She began sketching the tools and the curls of wood and piles of dust. The saw was particularly interesting with its handle carved to look like ocean waves and an image of a whale; she focused on the nick in the tip where the teeth were missing.

"You're not supposed to be here."

Caroline jumped to her feet, startled by the gruff voice. She'd been so engrossed in what she was doing, she hadn't heard anyone approaching. "I'm sorry, I was only sketching your workshop. I didn't touch anything."

He scowled and squinted, revealing a map of lines on his face that led to his eyes. His dark skin was even darker in the low light. "Sketching? What could be of interest enough for a lady to sketch?" An accent she couldn't place forced her to repeat his words in her mind several times before she understood them. He reached for her book, and she allowed him to take it from her.

His scowl lifted into something soft. "The saw."

"It is beautifully carved. I assume you are the master of such craftsmanship?"

He nodded and stared at the page in his hand. "Very few call me a master for my work. I thank you."

"Would you like me to sketch you while you work?" she asked, not sure why she dared intrude on him further when good manners dictated she leave and not bother him in his work.

"Why would I wish for such a thing?"

"You could send the picture home to your

family. They would be able to see what beauty you create."

He scratched at the whiskers on his chin. "I do not think my father would care to be reminded of me."

"Oh."

She felt quite crestfallen and was about to bid him farewell when he said, "But my mother might find comfort in such a gift."

And they had an agreement. While he worked and she sketched, she learned his name was Arnav.

"Which is lucky, I guess, because it means *ocean,* and I live on the ocean," he said with a smile.

And though she recognized the impropriety of being alone with a man, she could not bring herself to care. Arnav did not really desire conversation while he worked, which allowed her to sit in a comfortable silence that she hadn't realized she'd craved until that moment.

She did a quick sketch for herself to fill in later with details and then did a more thorough sketch for him, making sure to add the softness and kindness she found in him; she felt sure his mother would cherish those qualities in her son.

She tore out the page and handed it to him. Arnav smiled. "Such art deserves a repayment." He turned and opened a small chest. She began to protest but stopped when he handed her a small, hand-carved wooden elephant.

"It's beautiful," she whispered.

"You keep it. My thanks to you for giving me a way to bring a smile to my mother's face."

She could not refuse the gift, nor did she want to. She felt all the honor of receiving something so beautiful.

She left Arnav to his work as she did not want to distract him from his duties and get him into trouble, but she wished she could have stayed longer. Dinner was still hours away.

She pressed onward, deeper into the ship, until she came across an area with hammocks hanging from the timbers. Caroline glanced around and found she was alone.

Mama and Josephine would love to see this, she thought. Not wanting to be caught unawares again, she tucked herself into a corner and began to recreate the lines of the hammocks on her page. She wished she could capture the motion as the boat lightly rocked while the hammocks seemed to stay still.

She froze when a figure who looked to be more a boy than man entered the area. The boy unhooked one of the hammocks and began to roll it so it looked like a large, white sausage. Without really thinking, she recreated what she saw on her page.

She stopped when the boy finished, tied up his bundle, and slung it over his shoulder. She assumed he would go out the way he came in, but instead he moved in her direction. He jumped when he saw her and gave a small shout.

"You're not supposed to be here," he said when he'd collected himself.

She moved out into the open, realizing it did her no good to hide when he had seen her. "I am sorry," she said. "I was merely sketching your work."

"My work?"

She showed him her sketchbook.

"That's me own self!" he said, obviously pleased.

"You can have it if you'd like." She'd run out of paper before the voyage was through if she kept giving it all away, but she was rewarded with the boy's smile. He took her gift quickly as if she might change her mind.

"Is this where you sleep?" she asked.

He nodded as he scratched behind his ear.

"Is it comfortable?" She thought of her bunk and how much her body ached each morning.

"Good 'nuf," he said.

The idea formed and was out her mouth before she could think it through. "I wonder if you might help me."

He turned out to be a very agreeable boy, and before she knew it, she was back in her own cabin with all the tools necessary to re-imagine her space. She had promised to leave the tools where the boy, Theodore, could find them later and return them. She didn't want him to get into trouble.

Once she'd completed her task, she realized it was dinnertime. The explorations and activities of the day had made her hungry. Missing dinner was not an option.

She carefully dressed and put up her hair in the twists and braids her lady's maid, Miss Niles, had done for her a million times. She usually did not reach for extravagance when she was left to her own devices to put herself together. But tonight, she wanted to be armed in the only language the *ton* knew how to speak: beauty.

She briefly allowed herself to wonder what Captain Scott would think of her styled hair and her fine dress. Then she shook her head. Why did she care what that man thought? Miss Cole was unequivocally wrong about Captain Scott if she believed he acted out of admiration. The only attention he paid her was when he wanted to berate her or disagree with her over something or other. Perhaps Miss Cole was right about him enjoying his time spent mocking her.

Caroline could not understand why the thought of Captain Scott's censure knotted her stomach and made her feel ill. So ill she considered missing dinner after all. But she was already dressed and her hair was already pinned.

She would go.

She would likely hate it, but she would go.

She exited her cabin only a moment before Miss Jeffries and Miss James. She'd purposely taken time enough to ensure that everyone else would have already gone up. Caroline had not anticipated other ladies being tardy as well.

Not that she minded. They were good women and the closest things to friends she'd ever had. She greeted them and suggested they walk to the dining room together.

Miss Jeffries studied her for a moment, making Caroline feel self-conscious. Had she overdone her attempt at making herself fashionable? Had she managed to make herself look ridiculous instead?

"Is something the matter, Miss Jeffries?"

"No, Miss Gray. It's just, well, you look

beautiful enough to be presented at court."

Miss James gave a single nod of approval and agreement. "If you don't silence Miss Cole tonight with your beauty, then we have no hope of her ever being silent. And I am sorry, Miss Gray. I never should have told her about the storm or the captain's reaction afterward. I was wrong, and I do hope you forgive me."

"Of course I forgive you. Though there really isn't much to forgive."

"But there is! She took the information I handed her and abused both you and Miss Jeffries with it. I have already begged for Miss Jeffries's forgiveness, and now I must have yours if I am ever to rest easy."

"You may rest easy then, for it is yours. How were you to know Miss Cole would use such information with ill intent?"

Miss James looked at the floor while she smoothed her hands over her skirts. "I wanted to be her friend. I only told her about your adventures because I knew the story was interesting. I knew she would want to hear. And I suppose I should have known she would use up the information like a flame eats up paper. I've known women like her my whole life." Her voice cracked. "Her sort are the reason I'm on this ship."

Tears began to fall freely over Miss James's cheeks.

"Oh, dearest," Miss Jeffries said, placing an arm over Miss James's shoulders. "You mustn't cry over that any longer."

Caroline badly wanted to ask, "Cry over what?" but did not feel it was her place to intrude, especially when Miss James seemed so heartbroken. But she did cast a questioning glance toward Miss Jeffries.

"You can tell her," Miss James said, having caught the look between the two women.

Miss Jeffries frowned. "Only if you're sure."

"Quite sure."

"If you insist." Miss Jeffries frowned but began the story. "Miss James was engaged before. To an old family friend who had wealth but was neither handsome nor charming in the way most young ladies prefer. But Miss James preferred him. From how she tells it, they were quite well suited to one another.

"But while she was in London during her season, she met a young lady who was as unremarkable as she was — those are Miss James's words, not mine! Only her new friend was not as friendly as she had first thought. This lady spent a considerable amount of time examining the faults of oth-

160

ers for her own amusement. When she heard of Miss James's engagement, she made a point to visit her while they were both still in town. As was her usual practice, the woman asked if there was anything about the man that set Miss James's teeth on edge."

"There really wasn't anything," Miss James interrupted. "He and I had known each other for years. For every one of his flaws, there were at least ten of mine to overlook. I didn't know what to say. She asked the question as if I should have some great secret. I didn't know how to answer, but I shared a few small things in the hopes it would appease her. She was quite insistent. It never occurred to me to stay silent — but, oh, how I *should* have. I am a fool.

"She wrote a letter to his mother, relaying the whole of it — except for her part, of course. She warned his mother against inviting me into their family."

Miss James collected herself and said, "So, of course, they retracted the invitation, and the engagement was broken off. As it turns out my *friend*" — her lips twisted around the word — "found ample opportunities to spend time with him, and now *she* is his wife."

Anger rose up in Caroline. Injustice

always fueled her temper. She felt it quite a lucky break that the woman in question was not currently present.

"I'm so sorry," she said, though she felt more sorry than she could ever admit to the two ladies. Hadn't she found fault with both of them in one way or another? How less guilty was she for doing in her private thoughts what the woman in question had done aloud? But she would never purposely hurt another. She would never sabotage the hopes and dreams of another.

"Did you try to explain to him? At the very least, did you warn him of the woman to whom he chose to unite himself?" Caroline asked.

"How would I even start? And what did she repeat to him that I had not first said? Besides, now that they are married, I'm sure he knows. Poor man. He doesn't deserve such a fate."

Caroline handed Miss James her handkerchief. "Here. We're already late, so it's fine for us to be a few moments longer so you can collect yourself."

Miss James took the handkerchief and dabbed at her eyes. "Be careful around Miss Cole. She might be unkind to me or to Miss Jeffries, but it is you she wants to cut to ribbons and cast into the sea."

162

"What have I to do with her? I think you are mistaken. I believe Miss Cole is the sort of woman who will be cruel to whoever happens to be near her. I doubt I am enough to bring her known malevolence to anything extraordinary."

Miss James looked doubtful but said nothing more. And with Miss James's face cleaned up enough to be presentable, the women moved to the dining room.

"Forgive our tardiness," Caroline said as they entered.

When all eyes turned to her and looks of admiration came from the men, she smiled in satisfaction.

Miss Cole's mouth tightened into a puckered scowl before she could school it back into a pleasant smile. The woman did have all the tools necessary to be dangerous. If Caroline hadn't been looking at her directly, she would have never seen that flash of hateful envy. She could easily see how Miss James had been taken in. Didn't she herself wish to make Miss Cole an ally rather than an enemy?

An alliance with such a woman was never possible. Caroline needed to learn that now if she ever wished to survive in the new life she'd chosen for herself. She flashed her own brilliant smile at Miss Cole, and then turned her attention to the captain.

Miss Cole followed her gaze, which meant that she saw how the captain stared, his surprise and admiration as his eyes fell on her.

The gentlemen stood. Caroline glided to her place at the table, smiling at each guest as she passed.

"You look lovely," Captain Scott murmured.

She smiled and said nothing. She had wanted to be striking this evening, her dress an armor against Miss Cole's anger as well as against Captain Scott's mistreatment of her. But now that she was there, in the moment, she could not account for the way time slowed as he spoke to her, for the way everything else in the room faded until nothing else existed except him and her and his lovely words.

The fine cut of his uniform accentuated his muscled shoulders. His freshly shaved jawline inspired her desire to run a finger over the smoothness. His mouth, so often an unreadable slash in his face, bore a subtle smile that seemed to exist for her alone.

She blinked away her foolish thoughts.

She was angry with him. She didn't like him. Not at all.

Except she did. Quite a lot.

But he didn't like her. He thought her foolish. Hadn't Miss Cole said so?

But he was not looking at her as if he thought her foolish. She had wanted him to be struck speechless. She had not anticipated that she would be the same. That she would feel —

"What could have kept you ladies so late this evening?" Miss Cole's grating voice halted Caroline's thoughts.

"Whatever it was, it was worth the wait," Captain Scott said, his words directed toward Caroline specifically.

She nodded at the compliment, willed her cheeks to not heat up, and turned away from the captain in case he could see the effect his words had on her.

But turning allowed her to catch the eye of Miss Cole. Caroline had miscalculated her attempt at setting herself up as an equal against the likes of Miss Cole because it seemed the lady had accepted the challenge.

Anytime the captain spoke, Miss Cole was quick to offer a response, regardless of the fact that she sat near the other end of the table. And if the captain dared speak to Caroline in particular, Miss Cole was quick to interject, to offer her own opinion before Caroline could say anything, and to offer insult to Caroline in the most veiled yet seemingly polite ways possible.

Caroline tried, for her part, to ignore both the captain and Miss Cole. She tried to engage Miss Bronley in conversation regarding her time spent in Scotland. She asked Miss James about the musicians she enjoyed best. But it seemed whatever she did, Miss Cole was there with a retort and the captain was there to ask after her own opinions. With every new sentence, the conversation took a turn into something tense.

Though Caroline was not particularly fond of the coquettish games ladies played, she recognized them when they were at play. Miss Cole fancied the captain. That much was obvious. If her behavior was any indicator, she had decided she would win him even while trying to dangle Mr. Miller from her strings at the same time.

She thinks I'm her competition in winning him, Caroline was startled by the realization. She almost made the mistake of laughing right then and there. *Competition to win the captain?* What an imagination Miss Cole had.

Caroline did not allow herself to entertain the idea. She did not like how it made her hands quiver. She did not like how her cheeks felt like fire when she thought of him. She tried hard not to remember how she had wanted the captain to see her tonight with her hair in elaborate braids and with her wearing her best gown that accentuated her curves to their advantage.

And see her he did! Caroline was sure he had not stopped looking at her through the whole of the meal. Miss Cole noticed the attention as well and by the end of the meal became desperate to turn that attention to anything but admiration.

"Miss Gray, I *do* seem to remember you from my last season," Miss Cole said. "Well, not you particularly. More your reputation. I recall you being mentioned as the strange girl who was fascinated with public lectures. Was that you they spoke of, or was it someone else?"

Caroline lifted her chin and refused to allow this ridiculous woman to make her feel ashamed. "Yes, it was. It's a shame I didn't see you at any of the public lectures. They say understanding is the first cure."

Miss Cole narrowed her eyes slightly. "The first cure for what?"

Caroline did not answer. She merely smiled and turned to Mr. Liechty to discuss advancements in the medical field.

I tried, she thought wearily. *I tried to get along and be like the other ladies.* She had tried and failed.

CHAPTER TWELVE

A few days passed, and Thomas was still haunted by his outburst with Miss Jeffries and Miss Gray. He felt ashamed of his reaction, of not asking what happened before exploding at the two of them. And then to see Miss Gray later that evening for dinner? His throat went dry thinking of her figure in that gown. How many women had he transported from England? How often had he let any of them affect him the way she did?

"Maybe I'm getting old," he said aloud to his darkened room, shifting on his cot. He laughed then. He knew he was one of the youngest captains of his shipping company. Probably one of the youngest captains ever, having been practically raised on the sea. He was too young to complain about being too old.

He sighed. He suspected his behavior was why Miss Gray had taken to deliberately avoiding direct conversation with him. Though she never actually ignored him — her manners were too fine for that sort of petulance — she had managed to make it through several meals without saying a single word to him. If he asked her a question, she made a point of directing her answer to the entire table. She had a right to be angry, and he didn't blame her, but it made him angry that she should be angry. The entire situation made him a fool of the worst sort.

Lieutenant Peterson told him that he'd recently been stopped by Miss Gray and questioned regarding why the tarpaulin had not been properly tightened over the doorway.

He'd been horrified to learn from one of his passengers that his crew had not followed safety measures and was outright mortified that she had felt it necessary to stop one of his officers to relay her information because she felt her captain unreliable. When he asked Peterson what he'd told the lady, Peterson assured him that he had stood by the captain while also quieting the lady's fears.

He should have been the one to quiet her fears. It was the captain's responsibility to assure the passengers that all was well. But how well had he done that even before the storm? Hadn't he been the one to hoist a black flag of concern over the hopes of the young women traveling to India to find a husband?

But he hadn't raised that black flag for all the young women. He'd only done it for two. In truth, he'd only done it for one, no matter that the other lady had been present and listening.

He had done it for Miss Gray.

What would his mother say regarding this unexpected situation of attraction to one of his passengers and his subsequent treatment of that passenger? She'd tell him that his behavior was reprehensible and that she was ashamed of him.

He let his leg flop over the side of his cot and pushed against the floor to make the cot swing. The sea was calm tonight; he shouldn't be so restless.

"I should apologize to the woman and be done with it." He sighed deeply, remembering there were two women involved. "I will apologize to both of them." While Miss Jeffries *had* been disobedient to ship rules, he felt certain Miss Gray would never accept an apology that was not also offered to her friend.

He felt marginally better having made the

decision to apologize and allowed his mind the peace needed to go to sleep.

The next day, he ran through his inspections and found a few places lacking. He was preparing to call for Clara so she could help tend to some of the necessary work when he saw her heading toward the upper deck. She was invaluable when it came to cleanliness, and the men seemed to work harder under her critical eye.

"Clara, I was just about to send for you. I have some detail work for you to get to today. If you'll follow me, I can show you what I need."

"Of course, sir." She hesitated, casting a soulful look back toward the hall.

"Is something the matter, Clara?"

"Nothing, sir. Just . . . I've naught got but one more lady's room to clean before my morning chores are done."

"I'd like you to get to this first. Cleaning a lady's room would take longer than what I need."

Clara's lip twitched and a small, indelicate snort escaped her. "Not this one, sir. It's Miss Gray's room. Hers won't take but a moment, sir."

"Cleaning a cabin takes long enough. Leave it until later. If Miss Gray minds at

171

all, you can have her speak to me." That was one way to get the lady to talk to him.

Clara laughed outright. "Not her cabin, sir. Miss Gray's room is like a birthday present what comes every day. She keeps everything in perfect shape."

"Making up the linens in a bunk is not quick work, Clara." Blast the woman! He was spending as much time arguing with her about the amount of time it took to clean a cabin as it would take for her to do the work in the first place.

He drew a breath to order the woman to do his bidding when she said, "Miss Gray don't sleep in no bunk, sir."

"Miss Gray — What? If she fails to sleep in the bunk provided for her, then where does the lady sleep?" He dreaded the answer, hoping that no scandal was occurring on his ship.

Clara stifled another laugh. "It's the strangest thing, sir. I entered her cabin a few days ago to do my chores and found that her bunk was made up all tidy-like and as good as if I'd done it myself. I looked closer and realized I *had* done it myself. The lady hadn't slept there at all. Then I got to worrying about what might've happened to her in the night to keep her from her bed. I worried she might've fallen overboard or taken ill or was unconscious somewhere or others."

His patience came dangerously close to breaking. "Yes, Clara. I appreciate your concern for the welfare of our passengers, but where does Miss Gray sleep if not in her bunk?"

She lifted a shoulder and the side of her mouth at the same time as if the two things were connected to one another. "In a hammock, sir."

Thomas blinked. "She doesn't!"

"See for yourself, sir." Clara led the way to Miss Gray's cabin and opened the door. "I don't know where she got such a thing, but I found the canvas and bedding rolled up nice and proper on top her trunks. She rolls a hammock better'n any deckhand."

Thomas prided himself on maintaining the highest levels of propriety and had only once before entered a lady's cabin, and that was only because the woman had taken ill and required assistance to move above deck.

So he hesitated at Miss Gray's door, lingering like a criminal who had not quite pledged himself to committing the crime. Then he tugged the bottom of his captain's coat and brushed past Clara into Miss Gray's cabin as though such a thing was no trouble at all.

173

The bunk was as tidy as Clara professed. He crossed the few steps to Miss Gray's trunks and lifted the canvas hammock roll. He then checked the walls and found she'd installed bolts to accommodate her hammock.

"Where did she get all this?" he demanded, working hard to keep his voice calm. People in his employ always deserved his respect.

Clara shrugged. "I don't know, sir. It was here when I came to clean. And like I said, everything else is always put away and tidy-like."

"Where is she?" He shouldn't have asked. He should've waited until he'd calmed down, but that woman! How ironic that only just the night before, he'd had every intention of apologizing to her for being sharp in their previous time together, and now he had every intention of being sharp again.

"In the dining room, sir."

The answer confused him. He checked his pocket watch. "She's where?"

"The dining room."

"But the kitchen isn't open at the moment."

"Oh, she don't go there for food. She walks the deck in the early morning. She

174

waits until everyone has cleared off and then she goes to bring life to her sketches. That's what she says anyways. She also writes letters and such. She likes the peace and quiet of it as well as the extra space."

He grunted. No wonder he did not see her on the decks. He liked to inspect the ship during the night to verify all was well, and then to sleep a little later into the morning so that he might inspect the ship again when a different crew was up and running. If she always took her exercise in the morning hours, he would be asleep.

Without another word, he made his way to the dining room. When he arrived, he found things exactly as Clara described.

A tin box with various colored crayons was open in front of Miss Gray while her fingers deftly ran a line over a page in her open book. He wanted to watch her work, but he reminded himself that admiring her was not his reason for standing where he was.

"Miss Gray," he said, announcing his presence to her.

She looked up, startled. "Captain Scott." She stood and gave a curtsy while he bowed. How he hated the formalities that delayed him from his purpose.

"Would you follow me, please?"

"Follow you, Captain? This very moment?

May I have time to gather my things?"

He glanced at her tin box, sketchbook, papers, pen, and inkpot, as well as the several books spread over the table. On the open page of her sketchbook was an image of Mr. Black and his wife, Clara. Thomas glanced behind him to see if Clara had noticed the image, but the woman had remained in the hall. He wondered what other images were in Miss Gray's sketchbook and had to force his attention back to the matter at hand.

"You can leave them. We'll return shortly."

"Is something the matter?"

"A few rules have been broken, Miss Gray. And rules are incredibly important to the safety of my passengers, would you not agree?" He moved toward her cabin, glad that she followed without him asking her again. The entire situation was awkward enough without him needing to coerce a woman to her room.

"Since I am one of those passengers," she said, "I could not agree more regarding the need for safety. Yet, I do not see how I could have any impact on such matters."

Oh, but she had already impacted the safety of one of his passengers. Granted, it was for the good of that passenger, but he knew she knew that and likely felt some triumph over it.

He didn't respond. He suspected anything he would say would have exited his lips in a growl. No. Far better to show her. He couldn't say why he was so angry. Perhaps it was this new situation, coupled with the event of the storm. Perhaps it was her willful refusal to speak to him without him either forcing her or groveling for her response. He was tired of groveling.

"Captain?"

Blast her! She refused to speak to him for days, but now when he wished for her silence, she would not give it.

"Is there some sort of trouble that requires my expertise? I have no nursing skills, so if another passenger has taken ill or has become injured, I am wholly incapable of being much help."

"No one is ill or injured, Miss Gray." *Except me,* he thought. *I'm quite ill with the worst headache known to mankind.*

He stepped aside to allow her first access to the stairs. Even with his emotions running hot, he would remember his manners. As she passed, he glanced at her and felt the ache behind his eyes increase. She was not in a fine evening dress, but her day dress still showed her at an advantage. Her dark hair was not schooled to perfection as it had been the other night, but then he preferred the loose tendrils of hair curling over her neck and shoulders. He blinked and turned his gaze to the ground. The lady would be the death of him.

How he felt drawn to her and irritated with her all at once was a puzzle. At the moment, he needed to remember that he felt irritated.

It bothered him, too, that Clara had followed him to the dining room. It was not as if Miss Gray needed a chaperone. He posed no threat to her, certainly. But perhaps it was better that Clara had followed. A chaperone meant no rumors, and the last thing Thomas wanted on his ship were rumors.

I should have been a farmer, he thought. A farmer dealt with animals and plants and was spared the trouble of dealing with people.

As it was, he had not become a farmer. He was a captain, and he didn't have to agree with the reasons people chose to leave their homeland to venture into new situations. He only had to do his job and get them to their destination safely: no questions asked.

But he had asked questions regarding this woman.

And that was the whole problem.

Chapter Thirteen

Caroline stood next to the captain outside her cabin. This was certainly not the destination she'd anticipated.

"Open the door," he instructed.

When she did, he asked her for permission to enter. She nodded, and he strode in and took hold of the folded canvas on her trunk.

The way he went straight to it meant he'd been in her room without her. She narrowed her eyes at him with the realization.

"Who authorized a hammock be placed in your cabin, and who installed it for you?"

If Caroline looked as startled and mortified as she felt over the captain all but admitting he'd been inside her cabin, she was likely a blotchy red from her hairline to her toes.

"No one, sir," she answered. She dared not identify the nice young man who'd fetched the spare hammock for her. "I saw into the crew's quarters while I was exploring the ship, and I noted the hammocks and how still they seemed despite the ship's movement. Rather than tying myself into my bunk during a storm, this seemed a better alternative." What she didn't say was that she slept better in the hammock than she had in the bunk.

"You saw into the crew's quarters? What makes you think you can go wandering around wherever you like?" he asked.

"That's exactly why I needed the hammock. I realized a better sleeping arrangement would keep me from needing to pace the ship at all hours of the night and early morning." She was treading close to outright falsehoods with her statement. Though she had paced during several nights and many early mornings, it'd been in the middle of the day when she'd found the hammock.

He pinched the bridge of his nose. "That doesn't tell me who authorized its installment."

She squared her shoulders, something she found she did quite a lot when he was near. "No one authorized anything. It's my cabin, so I took counsel with the one person chiefly involved in the matter — myself. I fail to see how the matter concerns anyone else."

180

"Miss Gray. It matters to the captain. That would be me. Who did you persuade to install the bolts?"

She lifted her chin, something else she did quite a lot when he was near. "I installed them myself. Do you not think me capable of such a thing? It's hardly a task worth mentioning."

He pressed his lips together tightly, and his nostrils flared before he opened his mouth. "Your *capability*, Miss Gray, is not in question. It is your *right* to do as you've done."

Caroline frowned, feeling her conscience prick just a little. "The holes aren't very large, sir. I'll remove the bolts and patch the wood before exiting this vessel." In truth, the bolts were quite sturdy and certainly not small. They had to hold the weight of a grown person after all. Trusting anything else would have landed her on the floor.

His mouth worked. She wasn't sure what the man might be thinking, but it certainly couldn't be good. When the edge of his lip lifted, she frowned in surprise. Was he laughing? Did he think this whole dressing down amusing somehow? She thought of Miss Cole saying how the captain found her amusing and ridiculous.

"Miss Gray, do you know what sort of vessel this is?"

"It's a ship, sir."

"And on what surface does this ship sail?"

She narrowed her eyes, not liking his mocking tone. Miss Cole was right. He might have admired her the other night when she wore her gown, but that was only based on her appearance. He found nothing of worth inside her. She was only a diversion from his everyday tasks.

"The sea, sir."

"Yes. Quite right. The sea. The sea is an interesting companion. It shoves its way into the most miniscule cracks. To say that the holes you placed in my ship aren't very large is not the issue. The issue is that we are in a ship, and holes of any size are not permitted."

She nodded, her face so hot, she wished she could jump into the ocean to cool it off. She didn't respond. After all, what could she say?

"And no one helped you?" he asked once her silence had stretched out into awkwardness.

Caroline thought of Theodore, the wiry young man with barely enough scruff on his face to qualify him as a man. She'd swallow her own tongue before letting the captain have him. She'd heard of floggings and other such punishment meted out by angry captains, and she'd not let the boy come to harm by her word.

"As I said, I am quite capable of helping myself." It wasn't a lie. She *was* capable. She was also capable of finding help when she needed it. But the captain didn't need to know that.

They stood a moment, neither of them willing to bend to the other, until she realized she was doing it again. Her stubborn insistence that she prove herself equal to whatever task lay before her made her a lousy match. It was for that very reason the captain disapproved of her, that he baited and mocked her.

Would she ever learn? Would she ever change?

She *would* change. She would start changing right now.

"I'm sorry, Captain," she said.

He startled at words he obviously did not expect, and she felt herself flinch inwardly. She really needed to learn that it was the demure woman who found herself in a secure situation. Isn't that what everyone told her?

"Yes," she continued. "I am sorry. I should have consulted with you regarding the bolts. I will fill the holes immediately if it is truly a safety concern."

She lowered her eyes but, before she did, she caught the expression on the captain's face. Bewilderment and perhaps even more irritation? She sighed. It would definitely take more practice to figure out how to actually *be* demure.

As it was, she felt like she'd said enough. Any further discussion would have to come from him.

He waited for her to speak. She waited longer.

He took a deep breath. "I suppose we're fine for now, but please do not make a habit of poking holes in my ship."

"Of course not, sir."

He stood there another moment before bowing stiffly and then leaving her cabin altogether.

"Sorry, miss," Clara said.

Caroline had nearly forgotten Clara had been present for the captain's scolding.

Caroline waved a hand at the woman. "It's not your fault."

"It is, in a way, miss. I accidentally told him about the hammock. I meant no trouble. I only thought to explain to him how clever I thought it all was for a lady to work such things out on her own. I hadn't thought he'd be cross over it."

Caroline laughed bitterly. "Well, it seems the captain is frequently cross, so this is hardly a misstep in his daily routine."

Though Clara smiled, she also protested. "Not Captain Scott. He's as calm-tempered as a man might ever try to be. When my man was hired on for rigging work, the captain took me on as well so I didn't have to be away from him. Not many captains make such allowances. We take on enough lady passengers, it makes good sense to have a woman aboard for cleaning rooms and minding the ladies and such. That's what he told me. He told me I made sense. He's a good one. Got good sense and a good heart."

"I stand corrected," Caroline said, not feeling corrected at all. Clara clearly had a soft spot when it came to the captain. Gratitude allowed for such things. But that didn't mean the captain wasn't a brute in his own way. He was certainly not above reproach. Caroline would just have to learn to stay out of that man's way.

But staying out of his way was impossible when she had to dine with him.

Later that night, when they were all seated for dinner, she looked longingly down to the end of the table where Lieutenant Peterson sat. He often took the captain's seat next to her when the captain was unable to attend meals with them, and she got along with him quite well. Better than she did with the captain, at least.

Tonight, the lieutenant seemed to be in a conversation with Miss Luke and Miss Cole. From the way he rubbed his left eyebrow and his smile came in brief flashes of teeth, perhaps he was more enduring the conversation than *in* it.

She took a deep breath and turned to the people closest to her. She could not speak to Captain Scott without being terse, so she did the best she could by staying silent and letting Miss James do all the talking for the evening.

"I used to have such frightful allergies," Miss James began. She spoke about her terrible sneezing fits back in London, and how often she had to switch out her handkerchiefs to keep herself from being a sodden mess and how wretchedly inconvenient it all was. "Yet, I haven't sneezed at all since boarding the ship and leaving port, can you imagine?"

During her story, her dinner companions had edged away from her by incremental degrees.

"What will you do when you arrive in India?" Miss Jeffries asked. "I hear the pol-

186

len there is thick enough to see it floating in the air almost all the time."

"I'm sure it'll be fine," Miss James said with a frown that indicated she was sure of no such thing.

"If the pollen doesn't get you, the disease will," Mr. Miller said, nodding his head while he buttered his roll.

No one said anything after that. Everyone feared the diseases rumored to run rampant in the tropical environment. There were stories enough of young men who'd gone seeking fortunes and who'd stopped writing home after a time. Stories where someone else wrote home instead to tell the family the terrible news. There were similar stories of young women as well.

Such rumors were enough to keep any sensible person from wanting to travel so far knowing they might not live to tell the tale of the adventure.

Caroline glanced around the table, surveying each of her dining companions. She smiled to herself. Clearly none of them, herself included, were of the sensible sort.

Here we all are, heading toward disease, deadly snakes, and allergies. The thought brought a smile to her face. She couldn't help it. Ranking allergies and deadly snakes on the same level of danger gave her a perverse sort of amusement.

"Is something funny, Miss Gray?" Captain Scott asked.

Knowing that some allergies actually were deadly meant that she could not admit her private musings lest people think her uncompassionate. "I'm sorry, Captain. I'm afraid I had become carried away in my own thoughts and was not listening to the conversation. What were you all discussing?"

The captain seemed disappointed in her answer, but she focused on her meal, not wanting to give him further sport.

The conversation turned to politics between the two gentlemen passengers. Lieutenant Peterson added commentary, though none of the other ladies joined in. When talk turned to the state of Parliament, Caroline felt her heart race with her unspoken words. But taking a cue from the other ladies, she tightened her teeth together to keep herself from participating.

Miss Cole hung on Mr. Miller's every opinion, nodding her head in complete solidarity. Miss Luke initiated a quiet conversation with Miss Bronley. And though Miss James smiled at the debate between the men at the other end of the table, her smile was one of wonderment. She did not understand the implications of the words the men spoke.

Caroline felt Captain Scott's eyes on her as if he waited for something. Did he expect her to join in the conversation? To make a spectacle of herself? Well, she wouldn't. Not for his entertainment, nor for her growing need to share her own thoughts.

She curled her fingers into fists to remind herself to keep closed off in this environment. This was not a place for her to display her knowledge or share her ideas. She could not open herself to further censure.

Mr. Miller and Mr. Liechty began discussing the boon of wealth that came from the spice and textile trade, and Mr. Liechty was agreeing with Lieutenant Peterson that someone needed to see to the rights of the people in the colonies to make certain that trade remained fair.

"Fair?" Mr. Miller demanded. "Since when is business ever fair? No. I say not ever, sir! The intelligent of those people will rise to prosperity as they should, and *that* is fair. An overseer of the people in the manner that you suggest would get in the way of good business."

It surprised Caroline when the captain intervened. "Mr. Miller, you could not be more wrong. The exploitation of the lands and people of India is not at all what I

189

would call good business. Rather, it is bad humanity and bad business. Establishing honest trade that benefits all sides keeps trade flowing and allows a man to sleep at night. Do you not agree, Miss Gray?"

Caroline startled at having been singled out to voice an opinion she had repeated several times in her head already. If she'd been a man, she would have joined the fray with energy. But as a woman? She met the captain's eye with indignation. How dare he bait her into such a discussion? While she agreed with his views, she felt fire in her belly. She opened her mouth to speak, but Lieutenant Peterson interrupted.

"Perhaps, Captain," he said, "we should not be engaging in such conversations in front of the ladies." Lieutenant Peterson winked at her from the end of the table. He must have known she'd been about to answer and was saving her from herself.

"Sounds like a convenient way to avoid your own culpability in the matter." Mr. Miller wagged a long, pale finger in the captain's direction. "You make such a bold statement and then duck behind the ladies for cover? No. I say you cannot want trade to be caught in such a noose when you're in the business yourself. This is a merchant ship, is it not, Captain? I say your indignation when you're in the business of exploitation makes you a hypocrite."

"Here we go," Lieutenant Peterson muttered loud enough to be heard by anyone paying attention to him. But all eyes were on the captain and Mr. Miller.

"A hypocrite, sir?" the captain challenged. "Nothing could be further from the truth. I pay close attention to the men with whom I choose to do business. I work with those who work *with* the indigenous people, those who are against the despoilment of resources. I do not work with those who pillage the lands and decimate resources, who unfairly compensate the people who work those lands, or who take no thought for the future of those lands. Fair trade benefits everyone and keeps us all in business for generations rather than letting us fizzle out like some brightly burned kindling that's wasted ash in the end. Honesty. Integrity. An eye on the future instead of just today. *That,* sir, is good business."

Mr. Miller tightened his mouth and said no more; the captain had won the argument for the evening.

Caroline felt alternately relieved and frustrated. Relieved, because the captain had stated his opinions so eloquently. Frustrated, because if she had voiced those same opinions, she would have been scorned by the entire dinner party. It galled her that her opinion had such little value as a woman. The captain could say whatever he liked, and his rank and gender made it all so much more meaningful. Beyond that, how could *he,* of all people, possibly feel the same as she regarding trade?

How could *he,* a man who'd managed to anger her, mortify her, and drive her to madness on nearly every occasion where they were in one another's company, be of the same mind as she on any subject?

Part of her wondered if the captain's opinions were his true feelings or if they were made solely to get a rise out of Mr. Miller. That was possible — certainly more possible than his feelings on trade being in line with her own.

Another part of her agreed with Mr. Miller. It seemed difficult to believe that a man whose business depended entirely on trade should have any qualms regarding exploiting the weaknesses with that business. How many men could boast such an altruistic side?

Her father could have.

He always treated the tenants of his land as valuable. He made certain their living conditions were kept up and that they had the tools they needed to be successful in their endeavors. Her throat tightened at the thought of her father, which always brought on thoughts of her mother and sister. Her whole family lost.

But she would not think on that. She'd been away from her home for long enough that the pain of that loss had dulled to a familiar ache. It had settled inside her heart, yet her heart had learned to beat a steady rhythm in spite of the obstacle.

She would certainly not let thoughts of her father bring her to tears in front of everyone. The conversation continued around her, but she could scarcely hear it over the memory of her parents rustling pages of the various books they read and their energetic conversations regarding the latest news. Trade was something they had discussed often.

The captain's eyes were on her again, steady and persistent. She forced herself to meet that gaze.

"I am surprised you did not join the earlier discussion," he said quietly. "Not even after you were invited."

"I'm surprised you thought it appropriate to extend an invitation that would surely lead to my censure."

He straightened, evidently surprised by

her words. "Why should I not invite a well-informed woman to a conversation where her intelligence would be appreciated?"

She felt her face flush, those red splotches that tattled on her emotions. How she hated those splotches! And how this man could make her feel so many different emotions. How could he make her feel both complimented and mortified at the same time? Both appreciated and mocked?

She did not turn away from him again for the duration of the dinner. She had read in Machiavelli's *The Prince* that one must strive to hold close his allies, but more importantly to hold close his enemies. Though she could not say if Captain Scott were foe or friend, he was not the sort of man she could turn her back on.

And she very much suspected he was foe.

CHAPTER FOURTEEN

Thomas had shifted his regular routine. It had been several days since Miss Gray had accused him of having some ulterior motive in inviting her to the discussion at dinner.

She seemed wary of him. Which made him wary of her. Wary, but still intrigued. Intrigued enough to have warranted a shift in his schedule.

He did not admit, not even to himself, why he had chosen to go to bed earlier and to arise much earlier. He told his crew it was so he could get a better view of the stars in the early morning so he might double-check their course, but he suspected his men knew the truth.

It was to watch as Miss Gray walked the deck while everybody else was at breakfast. His officers who usually did the morning work did not complain. She had entranced them all as she moved among them in a way none of his passengers had ever done. She drew their likenesses in her sketchbook and gave them copies to send home to their mothers and wives. She laughed with them and listened intently as they described all the ways a ship worked.

There was a part of him that sighed with relief every morning as he watched Miss Gray slowly make her way up and down the deck, keeping her eyes trained on the horizon.

That particular morning, he smiled to himself as Miss Gray spied dolphins jumping alongside the ship. She clapped her hands in exclamation, and her smile was wide enough to see from the wheelhouse.

"What are you grinning at?" Lieutenant Peterson asked.

"I'm doing no such thing." He cleared his throat gruffly and turned his attention away from the young lady. But it was too late. Lieutenant Peterson peered over his shoulder and saw Miss Gray standing at the railing, waiting for more dolphins to jump.

"Ah, I see. No reason to be denying it. If a man can't smile at a pretty woman enjoying the ocean, then what can he smile at?" He whispered low enough that none of the other men in the wheelhouse could hear.

"Why do you continue to assume that I am admiring Miss Gray?" Thomas also kept his voice low and stepped outside the wheelhouse for privacy. Peterson followed.

"Why do you continue to deny it? She's quite pretty, interesting, intelligent, and doesn't get sick on the sea. I seriously cannot think of a better match for you."

"Perhaps it has escaped your notice that the woman doesn't like me. She scowls almost every time we are in company together."

"Mrs. Black believes it is because she does not think you like her."

"Mrs. Black?"

"Clara."

"I know who Mrs. Black is!" He glanced to the door of the wheelhouse and lowered his voice again. "What I don't know is why you two are gossiping about me."

Peterson waved off the accusation as if it were a speck of dust on his sleeve. "We weren't gossiping about you. But we *were* discussing Miss Gray. She feels that you disapprove of her, and so she has decided against you."

"Did she tell Clara such things?"

Peterson shrugged. "I believe she implied it rather than said it straight out. But you only have yourself to blame."

"Blame?" He almost raised his voice on that one word. "What have I ever done?"

"This is, again, only something I've surmised, but you pay her too much attention, which makes Miss Cole treat her terribly out of spite and jealousy."

"What has Miss Cole to do with this?"

Peterson shrugged. "Women are cruel to their own kind. Miss Cole is jealous of the attention you pay to Miss Gray. But beyond your obvious favoritism of Miss Gray, and the consequences that follow, you're far too open with your opinions in certain areas. I don't think Miss Gray appreciates your view that all gentlemen of India are cads."

"How is their ill behavior my fault? I'm not the one rushing to a new land to find matrimony with men of questionable reputation. She should be looking inward if she feels some desire to judge. Or be looking to those same men she's turned into a schoolgirl fantasy." Thomas could not keep the disdain from his voice. He might have to keep his voice low, but his tone could be whatever he liked.

"You sound as petulant and jealous as Miss Cole."

"Don't you have breakfast to attend?"

Lieutenant Peterson let out a booming laugh. "Ah, distraction! A wonderful tool when one does not wish to engage further in a conversation."

Thomas groaned and pointed to the door. "Go to breakfast, you cur."

Lieutenant Peterson moved toward the dining room. "Happily. I'm starved. And this allows you to watch your lady in peace and quiet."

"Go!" Thomas demanded with such fervor he forgot to be quiet.

Lieutenant Peterson did go, but not without leaving behind the echoes of his laughter.

In spite of his denial to his lieutenant, Thomas *did* watch Miss Gray. He found he could not take his eyes off the woman no matter how much he wished he could, no matter how much effort he put into the task.

So it was that he was watching as a child shot up from the stairwell and propelled himself right into Miss Gray's skirts. Thomas could not hear what was being said, but as Miss Gray stooped down to the child's level and placed her hands on his small shoulders, Thomas recognized the child.

It was the cook's boy that Lieutenant Peterson had taken such a liking to. Thomas suspected the child had been coming to Peterson directly and Miss Gray had merely been a casualty of his path.

He hurried down to the main deck.

The boy panted as though his lungs were desperate to take in air. "You gotta help me, miss!"

"What's going on here?" Thomas asked, drawing closer.

The boy's eyes went wide and wild at his approach.

Miss Gray straightened to her full height, whirled around to face him directly, and tucked the boy behind her. She leveled a frown on him that could have stopped a hurricane.

"I should ask you the same question." Miss Gray's eyes were stormy and her mouth tight with barely checked anger. "What kind of ship do you run where a child is so mistreated? He looks to be barely older than eight years old, and yet he is to bear such horrors? What kind of captain — one who declares himself to be the very definition of propriety and gentlemanly behavior — allows such horrific abuse?"

"No one is mistreated on my ship." How dare she say such a thing to him when —

She stepped to the side, revealing the boy behind her. "What is this, if not mistreatment?"

The left side of the boy's face was covered in blood coming from his ear and from a bruising cut above his eyebrow.

Thomas swallowed hard at the sight of the boy, who had clearly been beaten by someone. On a hunch, he reached out. The child flinched as Thomas took hold of both sides of the lad's shirt before pulling it up and over his head entirely.

The boy's shoulders were crossed with lacerations and bruises. He turned the child around and shuddered when he saw the boy's back. There were the purples of fresh bruises as well as the green and fading yellow of older bruises that were striving to heal.

How could so small a back bear the kind of rage required to create such bruising?

"Who did this to you, Tom?" he asked the child, even though he knew the answer.

The boy shivered and looked down, saying nothing.

At that moment, someone else popped up from the stairs leading to the lower deck. "There you are!"

The ship's cook clambered on deck, red-faced and bloody-knuckled. As he moved toward the boy, young Tom cowered behind Miss Gray's skirts.

Thomas moved to intercept the cook. "What's going on here, Corbeau?"

Mr. Corbeau stopped short. "The boy's a layabout! Never gets 'is work done. Today, 'e left the stopper out of the ale, and it ran all over the floor. He spends more time looking at those ratlines than he does slicing potatoes."

Miss Gray's eyes grew stormier with every word the cook said. "So you beat him? A child who is under your care? What kind of monster are you?"

"Mind your tongue, woman," the cook growled at her. "This has naught to do with you." He squinted his eyes as if he could glare her into silence.

She raised her own hand as if she was going to give the cook a beating far worse than the one he'd given his young apprentice, but Thomas intervened. If Miss Gray was willing to raise her hand to a man three times her size, she was clearly not as afraid as she should be.

"Step back, sir!" Thomas demanded of Corbeau. "Do not dare speak to a lady in such a manner. I will not stand for one of my passengers being treated in such a way. You forget your place."

Corbeau blew out a huff. "I know my place. My place is in charge of that boy."

"To be in control of another's future does not give you the right to abuse that power." Thomas wanted to follow Miss Gray's example and take a swing at the man, but he held himself in check. "And it is not the way of my ship. You know that. You agreed to the proper treatment of any apprentice brought to you when you requested help."

"Discipline *is* proper treatment. It teaches them their place. I've a right to discipline what's under my training."

"And I have the right to discipline any under my command. That would be you, sir. You are relieved of duty."

The cook laughed, a guttural, nasty sound, and flecks of spittle flew from between his cracked lips. "Relieved of duty? Ha! And what? Starve everyone for the rest of the voyage? You got naught but me to fill the bellies of your precious passengers and the rest of your crew and your own self as well. You got no other choice but to let me do what I'm doing and pay me what's rightly mine for that work. Good cap'n like you won't let the people starve o'er a bit of disagreement."

"Quite right. A *good* captain. I'm so glad you noticed. Every man aboard my ship possesses more than one skill. You yourself also have experience with cannons and rigging. I like knowing that should certain needs arise, there are men to fill those needs. Should a man fall ill or become incapable of meeting his obligations, there are others who can take that man's place. Any *good* captain keeps men who are trained in many capacities."

Thomas stepped closer and loomed over the cook, close enough to see the dull fleck of brown in his blue eyes. "You, sir, are a replaceable cog in the operations of my ship. You are relieved of your duties and will spend the rest of the journey locked up. When we arrive, you will be paid the wages due you for the time you worked, but not a day more. You will need to find your own passage back to England as you will never be allowed on my ship again. And do not expect references from me."

By then, several of the other officers and a few of the deckhands had gathered. The officers took hold of Mr. Corbeau, who immediately began trying to fight them off, but he was outnumbered. He was quickly subdued and dragged away.

The captain's duties were not over, however. Thomas knelt so he could look the child in the eye. "Come, young Tom. Let us find the ship's surgeon so he can bandage you up, shall we?"

"Am I in terrible trouble, sir?" he asked, still trembling with fear.

The small boy's eye had nearly swollen shut from where his eyebrow was split, but he did not move from the spot. The child's threadbare clothing was torn in several places.

Thomas's heart swelled with sympathy. He let out a breath of air that was as much pity for the boy as it was frustration with himself. How had he not noticed the child's condition sooner? He should never had hired someone like Corbeau.

"In trouble? For a little ale on the floorboards? No. I suspect I understand why you did what you did. Corbeau is a mean drunk, isn't he?"

Tom hesitated but then nodded. "It wasn't your ale, though, sir," he said earnestly. "It was his own private stash, you see. I would not have been so careless with yours."

"But you would be so careless with the cook's?" Thomas raised an eyebrow.

The boy looked down, clearly ashamed.

Miss Gray looked mortified. "Captain, you can hardly blame him for —"

But the boy interrupted her. "You're right, sir. I done wrong in spilling the cook's ale. I reached my end on what I could handle, but I should've been smart, right? Should've tried to find a different way, right?"

Miss Gray looked from the boy to Thomas with fury. She probably would have interjected again if he hadn't started speaking first.

"I appreciate your willingness to own your actions. It's a strong man who can admit when he has done wrong. This ship runs on respect, Tom. I'm glad to see you understand that. I'm sorry Corbeau did not understand that rule because he should have respected you in turn. Do you understand what I mean?"

"Masters don't have to respect apprentices."

Thomas sighed again. "If they are good masters, then they most certainly must respect their apprentices. Respect is for everyone. Poor, rich. Master, apprentice. Female, male. Adult, child. Respect is for everyone. Only a scoundrel would think differently. But for now, you're bleeding all over my deck. Let's say we get you cleaned up."

He stood, handed the shirt back to the boy, and turned to lead him toward the ship's surgeon. He noticed Miss Gray fidgeting this way and that, shuffling her feet as if unsure what to do with them.

"You may come along, too, Miss Gray."

She immediately moved forward, catching up with them in three strides. He would have laughed had he been in a mood for levity, but he had other things to worry about, the boy for one, and replacing the cook for another.

Plus he had to make sure Corbeau had no friends on board who might stir up trouble. If someone were to take pity on the man and let him loose from his cell, well, the ramifications could be deadly. Small-minded men worked the worst kind of mischief, and mutiny would do no good for anyone — least of all him.

"I'm sorry, sir," the boy said again as they walked. He struggled to put his arms in the right holes of his shirt.

"Sorry?" Thomas shook his head. "It is I who am sorry. I should have realized that your time on the ratlines was a way to hide from such a man. I am truly sorry."

"No one's ever apologized to me before," young Tom said. After a moment he added, "I forgive you, sir." The boy looked up at him. "Is that how it's done? Is that what one says when they accept an apology?"

"To forgive is the most honest way to accept an apology. And I forgive you as well." Thomas knew Miss Gray listened intently to their conversation. He was acutely aware of the swish of her skirts as they walked. He wondered what it meant that she had nothing to say regarding the whole situation now that young Tom was out of direct danger. Her silence needled him more thoroughly than her earlier scolding had.

He was glad the boy spoke up again; it helped distract him from his thoughts of the woman accompanying them.

"Will I be apprenticed to the new cook, sir? Or will I be put off the ship when we port as well?"

Thomas grunted. "I've already said you're not in trouble. So yes, you will be apprenticed to the new cook, and I'd wager he'll require a little help easing into a new routine. Also, I wasn't lying to Corbeau when I said it's important for my crew to be trained in more than one duty. Since you'll be with us for a while, and since you've shown such an interest in the ratlines, if you tend to your duties with the new cook well enough to keep things running smoothly, we'll teach you all you need to know about the rigging."

The boy grinned, showing off his mouthful of crooked teeth. "Yes, sir!"

Once they reached the ship's surgeon, Thomas was loath to leave the child and Miss Gray. He didn't spend time examining his reasons for wanting to stay while the child's eye was stitched up, but he knew it had more to do with the woman than with the boy.

"We have the same name," Tom said, pulling Thomas from his thoughts.

"Yes, we do."

"Mama said it was the name of a good boy who would grow to be a good man. Did your mother ever tell you that?"

Miss Gray smiled, making Thomas wonder if she smiled at the innocence of the question or at the idea of him being a good man.

"No," he said. "My mother did not tell me that, but she told me many other things to help me grow up well."

Young Tom nodded. "She did all right, even without the extra information. You should thank her."

Thomas and Miss Gray both laughed, their eyes meeting over the child's head. The energy that crackled between them quickened his pulse. He looked away but not before seeing a lovely blush in her cheeks and her expression soften.

After the ship's surgeon pronounced that the child would heal, the boy immediately bounded off to help ready the workspace for the new cook.

Miss Gray followed young Tom into the hall while he stayed back a moment to discuss matters with the surgeon.

Thomas watched her go and felt her

absence the moment she was from his view, even though she'd been mostly silent throughout the whole of the ordeal. Even then, she never spoke actual words, only murmured soothing assurances as she held the boy's hand while he was being stitched back together.

So it surprised him that she waited for him in the hall.

"I want to say I'm sorry," she started as soon as they locked eyes.

"Sorry?"

"Yes. For misunderstanding the situation with Tom. I should not have accused you of being responsible for his mistreatment."

"I assure you I take my position of caring for the lives of others seriously. If the situation had been made known to me, I would have stopped it much sooner. I will be more diligent in the future."

She frowned, the little wrinkle above her nose appearing and disappearing as quickly as it came. "I see that now. Watching you with Tom helped me see a side to you I had not thought possible to exist." She smiled faintly. "Compassion and good humor and even some philosophy. You've been hiding all of that." She smiled wider to show she was teasing.

The knot that had formed in his stomach

210

the moment he saw the blood dripping down Tom's face loosened with her smile. "Yes, well, you've also been hiding traits. I'd not thought you capable of prolonged silence before now." He feared she would take offense at his jest, but she laughed, a sound that seemed all the more musical to him because he knew he was the cause.

"I can well believe you thought me incapable of any sort of silence. I would beg you to not share this knowledge of me to the others. It would quite ruin my reputation."

"Your reputation is safe with me, Miss Gray." His words reminded him of Peterson's caution that his attentions to her were creating animosity in some of the other ladies.

He'd often been subjected to the flirtations of ladies who boarded his ship, and he'd always cast those flirtations aside. He had made it clear to all the other ladies of this voyage that he had no intentions of ever having intentions toward them.

Miss Gray had not flirted with him, not at all, so he had not made any such thing clear when it came to her. Indeed, he had welcomed her company. According to Peterson, Thomas's unintentional actions on that front had caused Miss Gray trouble.

He did not wish to cause her more trouble.

If her reputation was truly safe with him, then he needed to take his leave before he became incapable of doing so. He bowed and moved to walk away.

"Captain?" she said before he could even fully turn around.

"Yes?"

"Will you not offer your forgiveness?"

"My forgiveness?"

She smiled fully, and he felt certain he'd never seen such a beautiful sight before. How had he not made it his life's pursuit to see that expression on her face at all times? He lingered, battling all the things he felt but knew he should not say.

"I told you I was sorry for misjudging you. You told young Tom that to forgive is the most honest way to accept an apology."

He turned to face her fully, not realizing how she'd moved toward him, not realizing how close they stood to one another. A fire rose in his veins as their gazes seemed hopelessly tangled in each other.

"Quite right, Miss Gray. And so you have it — my complete and total forgiveness."

She put out her hand. He looked at it, confused.

"Come, then. Shake my hand, and we shall form a truce between us."

His mouth dried up as his hand rose on

its own accord and took hers. His fingers engulfed hers completely. He was aware of his callouses scratching her soft skin, but he could not bring himself to release her. Their hands moved together until his thumb softly rolled over the back of her fingers. He bowed over her hand and pressed his lips to her fingers. He looked up again and met her gaze, the fire between them threatening to scour him entirely.

"A truce then, Miss Gray."

A small gasp left her, breaking the spell enough to allow him to release her hand.

He bowed again and hurried away before she could see how much he meant what he said, before she could see how he meant so much more.

CHAPTER FIFTEEN

Several weeks had passed since Caroline had witnessed the incident with young Tom on the main deck, since the captain had kissed her hand and made her feel a hurricane in her soul. Since then, she'd seen young Tom several times up on the rigging.

By the marked improvement of the meals — both in flavor and variety — she assumed Tom and the new cook were getting on quite well together, which is what earned the boy the right to climb those ropes.

Caroline had a hard time watching him when he climbed, though she continued to draw him. She feared he'd lose his footing and fall, but he never acted nervous or afraid. Every time he started the scramble up, his eyes gleamed brighter than the rising sun reflecting off the water. His pure excitement made it easier to watch as he scurried to the top.

"Our boy seems to be doing quite well,

wouldn't you say, Miss Gray?" Captain Scott said from behind her.

Warmth flooded her chest. She turned and smiled at him, welcoming him to join her as she watched and sketched what she saw. She liked that he called the child "their boy," as if that shared sense of ownership gave them more familiarity with one another. The day the captain had faced down the child's abuser, Caroline had felt something she could not deny, at least not to herself. She had become fond of the captain.

"Yes, Captain. He's a natural — not afraid at all."

"When I was a young lad, my father made sure I knew every inch of a ship and could do every job the ship required. I was terribly afraid of heights, but my fear only made my father more determined that I should spend more time on the ratlines and in the crow's nest."

"I would guess all that time aloft helped you conquer your fear."

"Then you would guess inaccurately. I think I grew more afraid every time I went up. I merely learned to hide my fears so that my father stopped torturing me. I'd put on my most cheerful face and get it over with."

"Ah. So that's what you're doing at dinnertime."

"What do you mean?"

She leaned over as if to speak conspiratorially. "You're not truly cheerful when entertaining your passengers. You're merely 'getting it over with.' You see? I'm on to you."

Captain Scott laughed, and Caroline worked hard to not blush. She loved it when he engaged in cheerful conversation and when she felt like she'd been a welcome addition to that conversation. He certainly never acted cheerful with Miss Cole, which gave Caroline a wicked sense of satisfaction since that woman seemed desperate to pull the captain's attention her own direction. As the captain stood near her, she thought of his lips on her hand, and her eyes briefly fluttered closed. Realizing she'd allowed herself to get lost in the memory, she blushed.

The captain made no notice of her blush but gave a quick bow and moved on to tend to his duties. She no longer felt slighted by his abrupt departures. She had come to accept them as one of his personality quirks.

Since the incident with the cook and the child, the captain and she had reached beyond the simple truce and had formed a friendship of sorts. They had begun examining a great variety of topics together. She liked how intelligent and well-read he was.

Here was someone who knew how to match wits and theorize new ideas. Here was someone who showed a legitimate desire to understand the world in which he lived.

Caroline had come to cherish every conversation with him, even when those conversations occasionally turned sour. They would be discussing something about the ship or his crew or about sail versus steam, and he would give himself a little jolt as if remembering something unpleasant, and then his manner toward her would turn flustered, almost annoyed. He would scurry away like a child having been caught doing something wrong.

At first, she'd spent hours wondering if she was the one doing something wrong, but it didn't seem to matter what the conversation was about or if it had been her speaking or him before he would act in a way totally incompatible with the person she knew him to really be. Thus, whatever was going on with him couldn't be her fault. Perhaps he still feared being caught slacking in his duties as if he were still a little boy under his father's watchful eye.

Young Tom was the string that bound them together. The child frequently called out to her while she was taking her morning walk, which encouraged her to stay on deck far longer than usual. And Mr. Black had showed off the picture she'd done of him and his wife, which meant Tom often brought requests from other crewmen for her to draw their likenesses as well.

Young Tom also sought out the captain for constant confirmation and approval. The boy wanted nothing more than to please them both and, in a way, treated them as if they were his parents.

That was how she found herself imagining that they *were* his parents. She imagined she was the captain's wife and that young Tom was their child. She knew it was silly. The captain had done nothing to indicate he wanted her or even really liked her — at least not in that way. And she'd never been a silly, fanciful girl pulling petals from perfectly good flowers in the hopes of ascertaining a boy's feelings for her.

But she could not help herself from indulging in fantasy now. Her relationship with Captain Scott was something different from her relationships with any other man. She admired him for his many qualities. She could not ignore his legitimate goodness.

Nor could she ignore his eligibility. He was well established in his business, a gentleman of good reputation. It certainly didn't hurt that he was handsome enough to elicit a swoon from those sorts of women who gave in to such things. Even she often had to look away from him just to keep herself from staring like a besotted schoolgirl.

True, she recognized her obligation to at least participate in a few dinners with the unknown Captain Barritt once she arrived in India. But the contract between her and the captain's parents did not place her under obligation for actual marriage, which meant she felt quite free to daydream as she wished.

She did hate that they had to stay daydreams, however. Captain Scott would return to England as soon as he dropped off his cargo and passengers. She had no money for a return passage, which meant she would be left behind in India. And she could not play the part of a flirt with him now, not when she had a prior obligation hanging over her head.

But the captain would come back to India. He made the journey often. Would it be so difficult for her to wait until he returned? How would she live in the interim? She had some money, but not a lot. How long would such a return take him? Six months?

And what if he stayed in England for the next season? What if he felt inclined to find himself a bride at home? It was possible that when he came back, he would no longer be eligible.

The thought made her fret as she stared up into the ratlines, no longer seeing young Tom, no longer seeing anything at all except the many flouncy, bright dresses the young ladies wore at balls. She could almost smell the candle wax melting. She could almost hear the instruments and the tap of the many slippered feet on the ballroom floor.

And the laughter.

The sound of callow young girls laughing as they tossed back their curly, beribboned hair. The sound of their feigned interest and manufactured delight in whatever their partners were saying to them. That laughter grated on her more than any other noise in the entire world.

"What has you fretting?"

Caroline jumped at Miss James, who had appeared at her elbow.

"I'm not fretting," Caroline said in a way that sounded very fretful.

Miss James raised her eyebrows and allowed a smile to drift over her face. The woman leaned forward to look around Caroline. Captain Scott was almost at the end of the deck near the stairs that would take him down into the belly of the ship.

"I see," Miss James murmured.

"What do you see?" Was it possible that Miss James really *did* see?

"I see that you fancy him. Though I do not see why. He's a bit frightening, I think. Certainly the sort of man unlikely to be interested in long carriage rides or long walks. He's all gruff and callous. I guess a man like that would hardly care if he made you cry." Miss James cocked her head and inspected Caroline. "But then you don't seem the sort of woman to give into crying very often. I've not seen you cry once this entire voyage, aside from the night of the storm. And I daresay you've seen me cry just about every day."

Caroline frowned. "All humans cry, starting in our infancy."

"No one could accuse you of being impolitic. You admit nothing, while assuaging my own insecurities. Well done, Miss Gray."

Caroline laughed. "You give me far too much credit, my friend. A great many people accuse me of being impolitic." She was glad to change the conversation to her *failings* rather than her *feelings*.

But Miss James was not the sort of woman to sway from topics of the heart. "He has fine features though. The captain, I mean. I admit to liking him for a while myself, until

221

we entered into a real conversation and I realized I would always be afraid of such a man. Besides, I do believe he thinks me too simple-minded."

Caroline felt her cheeks burning, but she dared not turn away to hide them lest she draw more attention to them. She had thought the same of Miss James in those first weeks, but now?

Now she thought Miss James innocent and openly honest rather than simple-minded. Miss James said what she felt rather than playing the coy games that most other ladies had perfected before ever being introduced to society. Since Miss James seemed to feel quite a lot, the things she said were typically sentimental.

"Regardless of what the captain thinks of me," Miss James continued when Miss Gray did not reply, "he thinks quite a bit of you."

Caroline wanted to protest, but she also wanted to hope. "Why would you say such a thing?"

Miss James looked snubbed at the comment. "Are we not friends?"

"Of course we are!"

"Do friends not share matters of the heart with one another?" The woman's bottom lip trembled slightly. She wasn't merely snubbed; she truly felt genuine hurt.

"I suppose they do. I'm afraid I'm rather new at being friends. I've never had a close friend outside of my own sister. You and Miss Jeffries are the first. So I'm not quite sure how it goes. I do hope you'll be patient with me while I learn how to do it well."

"Never had a friend?" Miss James's look of dismay proved that she had replaced her own pain with the hurt she felt on behalf of Miss Gray.

Caroline couldn't deny that it was nice to have someone care who was not family, and therefore obligated. But she also did not want to explain the details of why her social circles remained limited.

"I am your friend," she started again. "And I did not mean to withhold information from you. It's simply that there is no information to share. The captain and I are careful acquaintances."

"What do you mean by careful?" Miss James leaned against the deck railing and looked down into the sea.

"To begin, we are careful to stay out of one another's way most of the time since we irritate each other as often as we enjoy each other's company."

Miss James went up on her tiptoes as if that would afford her a better view of the endless sea. "So how does that make you only acquaintances? You sound like my own parents, and they're far more than mere acquaintances. They're *married.*"

Such was the problem of having a friend who wanted to share matters of the heart. Did sharing a little always mean sharing a lot? "I have no intentions toward the captain."

Caroline wanted to be clear on that subject. As sweet as Miss James was, she had a tendency to say whatever came to her mind, regardless of who might be listening. If she were to say something in front of one of the captain's men, or, worse, in front of one of those biting ladies, such gossip could cause a lot of trouble for both Caroline and the captain.

"I am actually sailing to India to meet a particular young man. While there is no official arrangement between us, there is the possibility of something for our futures."

Miss James turned away from the ocean and stared openmouthed at Caroline. "Are you serious?"

"As the grave." Truth be told, she almost felt her news was as serious as a grave and as equally unnerving.

"Isn't that just terribly exciting?" Miss James's voice rose in pitch.

"Isn't it though?" Caroline could not think

of anything less exciting. Terrifying? Absolutely.

Before Caroline had left on her journey, she had allowed herself to hope that perhaps she would get along with this man she was destined to meet. Perhaps they would even love each other. She hadn't allowed herself to get too carried away in her fantasies, though. She didn't allow herself to consider that perhaps he was handsome or perhaps incredibly intelligent. But she had hoped she would at least like him.

How much harder would it be for her to like him when her emotions were already tangled up with a very different captain?

Miss James stared out at the horizon and sighed. "I wish I had some arrangement waiting for me. I could not bear returning home unsuccessful; everyone would know of my failure. If I cannot find an arrangement, I hope I get sick and die of disease."

"Miss James!" Caroline's eyes felt like they might pop out of her head.

"You don't know what it would be like to go back. To face him again. To see *her* on his arm. I am not equal to such a task."

"You won't have to be equal to it. I am certain you will find happiness in India."

Miss James grasped Caroline's hand. "I do hope you are right!"

Miss Jeffries and Miss Bronley soon joined them, and the conversation turned away from hopes and husbands, though Caroline believed it was seldom far from the thoughts of the other women. Why else would they all be on such a journey?

Later, when the ladies settled in the dining room to escape the direct burn of the afternoon, the talk turned to the men on the ship. First, it was Mr. Miller and Mr. Liechty, then some of the officers. But when the topic switched to the captain in particular, Caroline felt her heart begin to race.

"My aunt got a look at him as we were saying goodbye," Miss Luke said. "She nudged me and declared me the luckiest girl on the planet to be in such company for three months. She said she only wished she had such luck."

"Scandalous!" Miss Cole laughed delightedly.

Miss Luke smiled, clearly pleased with herself for gaining Miss Cole's approval.

"Tell me," Miss Cole said. "Do you have any preference for the captain?" She smiled as she asked the question, though the bite in her words was obvious.

Miss Luke was no fool. Whether she had preference for the captain or not, she would never have admitted it aloud. "Of course not." She dropped her stitchwork to the couch and dramatically placed her hand to her chest, her mouth falling open in horror at such an idea. "What sane wo—" She stopped, stammered a moment, and then resumed. "I mean to say that *I* would never want a man who spent the majority of his life away from home."

Caroline had to give Miss Luke credit for her quick recovery. Obviously, Miss Cole fancied such a man.

"To me," Miss Cole said, "a man who is gone is far preferable to one who is home and underfoot. And, for the short times he *is* around, it helps if he is pleasing to the eye."

"Are you saying you think the captain handsome?" Miss Jeffries asked as if the idea had never occurred to her in spite of Miss Luke mentioning how handsome her aunt found him.

Miss Cole adjusted her shoulders and smoothed her skirts. "I would daresay there *is* a young lady among us who thinks so. Wouldn't you agree, Miss Gray?"

Caroline should have been expecting the confrontation, but she hadn't been. She fumbled for a response before saying, "Which lady are you thinking?"

"How charming. You play such games and think us ignorant." Miss Cole offered a thin smile.

"I do not believe I am playing any games. Miss Jeffries asked if you thought he was handsome. You are the one not answering a direct question."

Miss Cole blinked, clearly not expecting Caroline to turn the conversation back to her. Her fleeting surprise melted into one of her sugary smiles. "Do they not say beauty is in the eye of the beholder?"

Caroline smiled patiently. "They do. That still doesn't answer what it is that your eye beholds."

Miss Cole laughed. "We'll get nowhere in this conversation, neither of us. We are women of mystery, are we not?"

"Are we?" Caroline looked down and pretended to focus on her drawing. "For my part, I hope there is no mystery. I try to speak plainly and appreciate when others do the same."

Miss Cole's laugh sounded more scandalized than amused. "You are a rather open book, aren't you? Flirting shamelessly with the captain the way you do where anyone with eyes might see your intentions."

Caroline looked up sharply. "I most certainly do *not* flirt with the captain! What would ever bring you to say such a false-hood?" Even as she demanded an explanation, she wondered if it might be true. Did she flirt?

"It's hardly a falsehood. Always pulling attention to yourself with your oddities. Putting yourself into his path by involving yourself in matters of his ship, sketching likenesses of the whole crew as if that would recommend you to his notice. Did no one ever tell you that a man is never won by a woman who shows such wild independence in thought and action? At least no *gentleman* can be won in such a manner." She paused long enough to rearrange her skirts. "There's no mystery to you at all, is there?"

The other ladies had gone still and silent. Even the creak and groan of the ship seemed to quiet itself under the weight of the tension in the dining room.

I did this to myself, Caroline thought. *I pushed back against a woman who isn't used to so much as a nudge let alone a shove. What did I think would happen?*

She had thought the lady would back down and be silent. But Miss Cole wasn't the sort of woman to make such allowances. She would always lash out to save herself.

Knowing the behavioral pattern of the lady and accepting it were not the same thing. Caroline gathered her things.

It seemed she was always cornered with only one response when dealing with Miss Cole — leaving. She hated how feeble she felt in constantly backing down, but the ship was far too small for the two of them to coexist peacefully. Caroline knew she had to be the one to give way to the other, for Miss Cole would not, perhaps *could* not.

"Don't go," Miss James called as Caroline walked toward the stairs. "She didn't mean what she said."

But of all people, Miss James knew that Miss Cole meant every word that ever fell from her lips.

As if to solidify Caroline's thought, Miss Cole said something Caroline was glad to have not heard. Miss Luke laughed, though the uneasiness of her laughter proved that whatever Miss Cole had said, at least no one was in agreement with her.

That would have to be Caroline's consolation — the knowledge that no one was truly against her except Miss Cole herself.

Caroline went to her cabin. It was the only place she could be alone aboard this crowded, yet very lonely ship. She did not want to think about Miss Cole's words, which meant she thought about them quite a lot. Though she hated to admit it, Miss

Cole was not wrong.

She knew a woman full of independent thoughts and actions would be less desirable to a man. Did she really think the captain considered her heroic for rescuing Miss Jeffries? Did she really believe he thought her clever for installing the hammock? Could she be so blind to her own inappropriate behavior when she scolded him again and again regarding matters on his ship and opinions that he held? What gentleman would want such a lady?

Caroline had promised herself that she would change while on this ship. But she hadn't changed. Not at all. Even a woman as shallow and vicious as Miss Cole could see exactly how Caroline was — exactly as she had always been.

She allowed herself a good cry. After all, what good was having a private cabin if one did not use it for private emotions?

I am feminine enough, she thought with a faint laugh. *What could be considered more feminine than indulging in tears?*

Though honestly, Caroline felt certain gentlemen gave into a good cry as well.

She believed both men and women hid important parts of themselves from each other. Obviously, women could think for themselves, but they simply couldn't allow anyone to know their wide and varied thoughts that belonged to them and them alone. And obviously, men felt deeply, but they simply weren't allowed to show they had feelings that rivaled the depths of the ocean.

The way men and women danced around each other without the ballroom and music would have fascinated her if she hadn't become trapped in the middle of those dances.

The knock at the door startled her. She quickly swept her hands over her cheeks to make sure they were dry before answering, "Yes?"

"Miss Gray? It's me."

Caroline closed her eyes. Miss James. She was a woman of heartfelt compassion.

"Yes?"

"Are you well? Do you need anything?"

"No, thank you. I'm fine."

"I'm sorry Miss Cole was so unkind. May I come in?"

The bad thing about being on the ship was that anyone in the nearby cabins would be able to hear any conversation uttered through the door. True privacy was a commodity no one could purchase while on this journey. For the unkindness to be brought up in this manner was to admit that Miss

Cole had landed a blow.

"I'm resting just now. Perhaps later."

The hesitation from behind the door told her that Miss James didn't believe her. "I don't care if your eyes are red. Let me in. Please."

Caroline considered how well Miss James understood situations that dealt with emotion. She got up and allowed the lady access to her cabin.

"Oh!" Miss James said. She looked confused by the canvas stretched out across the room. "You've a hammock. Why do you have a hammock? Does the maid know? I'm sure you can ask her to take it down."

"I put it up myself, thinking I might sleep better during stormy weather." The words sounded ludicrous to her own ears. What proper lady would ever want to scramble in and out of a hammock every day?

Miss James looked away from the canvas as if unsure what should, or could, be said of it. "I worried when you never returned."

"Surely you didn't think I would return." Caroline felt like pulling the hammock from the bolts and folding it up. Having Miss James see it added strength to the truthfulness of everything Miss Cole had said earlier. What gentleman would want a woman such as her?

"Will you at least come to dinner?"

"I truly do not feel well." Caroline wasn't lying. Her head ached from the crying, and her eyes felt like sand had been rubbed in them.

Miss James crossed her arms and actually looked angry. "You cannot let her win. You're the only one of us brave enough to stand up to her. If you keep leaving when she starts up, she'll only get worse."

"You can't be sure of that. For all you know, she'll improve."

Miss James fixed her with an irritated eye. "I *can* be sure. There is no reason for you to go hungry. Especially since we are reaching the end of the fresh food. Tonight's meal will be the best we'll have for the rest of our journey."

The logic and good sense could not be argued. The fresh fruits and vegetables had given way to pickled foods and the biscuits and salted meats Caroline had been told to expect. She didn't mind, not like the others did.

"Come to dinner."

"What did she say when I left?"

Miss James paled underneath her sunburned nose. She had forgotten to take a parasol out on deck one afternoon, which had earned her light teasing from the other

234

ladies and outright scorn from Miss Cole.

Miss James did not answer.

"I will not go until you tell me what she said."

"She's a horrible woman. Why do you care what she has to say?"

"Just tell me. Please."

No face could have looked sorrier than Miss James's at that moment. "She said that no one liked to be in the company of a bluestocking. She called women of your sort a blight on humanity."

Caroline let that sink in. "Is that all? I would have thought she could have come up with something more clever." She leaned her elbows on her hammock and allowed it to rock her back and forth on her feet. "But then if she had come up with something clever, she'd be considered one of those blights on humanity as well."

"She did go on and on about you and the captain, but I didn't let her get away with it. I told her I would not listen to such gossip and informed her how wrong she was to spread it in the first place."

Caroline was touched by the show of solidarity. So this was what it was like to have friends. "Thank you, Miss James."

She smiled, which made Caroline smile as well.

"I will come to dinner. You've helped inspire the return of my appetite."

Caroline looked down at her day dress. "I suppose I should get ready."

"I'll leave you to it then."

After Miss James left, Caroline considered how she could not let Miss Cole get the better of her by goading her into impropriety.

Caroline readied herself for dinner with a renewed determination to not be trapped by those battles. "No more," she whispered. And this time, she meant it.

CHAPTER SIXTEEN

Thomas had been bewildered by Miss Gray's fiery personality guttering out and leaving a shadow over the woman. It had happened almost overnight, and he had spent several weeks trying to work out the mystery of it. She was as beautiful as ever, but there was no light in her eyes.

Even the crew had noted the change in her behavior. She no longer asked them questions or offered them her sketches. And when Mr. Black had tried showing her how the yards were lowered, she thanked him for his efforts but informed him she was taking tea with the ladies in the saloon and didn't have time.

She seldom engaged in dinner conversation, and when she did, she spoke softly. In short, she had become as bland and lifeless as the rest of them.

He felt cruel to even think such thoughts, but she had been so vibrant before. And worse, now she seemed sad. The other ladies, Miss Cole specifically, no longer singled her out for disparagement, but he took no pleasure in her getting along with the other ladies when it meant she seemed so unhappy with herself.

The morning had touched him with melancholy. He hated how much he wished to delay the inevitable arrival at port. He usually felt so relieved to be rid of the lady passengers that he hardly knew what to do with these new feelings of wanting one in particular to stay indefinitely.

"What?" He'd been staring off into the horizon, not realizing he'd let his thoughts run so far adrift of the conversation in the wheelhouse until Lieutenant Abramson pulled him back. Thomas was glad he had managed to surround himself with such good, reliable men. Well, except the one who was under lock and key — the one Lieutenant Abramson was trying to discuss at that very moment.

"Corbeau told Mr. Rallison that he's got a plan for exacting revenge."

"Rallison's been delivering his meals to him, correct?"

"Yes, sir."

"Has Corbeau exhibited signs of jealousy knowing we've replaced him with a far superior cook?" Thomas smiled at his lieutenant's forbearance. "I apologize, Lieutenant. A small-minded man with the cruelty of a tempest is no joking matter. Has Rallison been able to glean what this plan might be? Does it have anything to do with the rest of the crew?"

"As far as we can tell, sir, Corbeau has no ally within the ranks of the crew. We all knew him to be a miserable sort. And he owes most of the men gambling debts." The way Abramson narrowed his eyes at his last comment made it clear that he was one of the men to whom Corbeau owed money.

Thomas allowed gambling on his ship, though he seldom indulged in it himself. As a younger man, he'd lost a month's wages in a game of cards. His father refused to advance his pay to help him, and he'd had very little savings. He barely ate during that time, but he'd learned a great deal.

"If Corbeau has no friend on this ship, how bad could any revenge plot actually be? He's a powerless, pathetic man, which means I have no reason to fear him."

Abramson shifted, visibly uncomfortable.

"Do you have more to report, Lieutenant?"

"He laughs, sir."

Well, that was unexpected. Thomas

239

rubbed at his eyebrow, a habit he thought he'd overcome until Miss Gray boarded his ship. "I am to be fearful of a guffaw, Lieutenant?"

"I told Rallison you'd say that. But he seemed most sincere in his concern. He said the man is unstable, and his laughter is a mirror into his instability. Rallison said it is most disconcerting."

"But is there an immediate threat?"

"No. But we're nearing port, and he'll be put off ship soon. I do believe we should be cautious."

By cautious, Abramson meant he believed they should have the man trailed once they docked. Keeping tabs on the man would help them avoid any surprises.

"You have my permission to have him followed once we are in India. Report back any information the endeavor manages to uncover. In the meantime, I will visit him myself."

"Thank you, sir." Abramson looked relieved.

"Thank you, Lieutenant. I appreciate your help in keeping me informed."

Thomas glanced out of the wheelhouse and saw young Tom waiting for him, a frown on his face.

Thomas stepped outside and gestured for

the boy to join him. "What's this? I thought you were excited to have a tour today." He had promised to show young Tom his personal quarters and the wheelhouse.

The boy had become a favorite of the entire crew, and he was relentless in his curiosity about the ship. Clara spent a fair bit of time keeping him away from the ladies and gentlemen's cabins.

"I was, sir. I *am,* sir." He hurried to correct himself.

"Then why do you look like you've swallowed a pail of slugs?"

"Miss Gray is unhappy."

The boy's words gave Thomas pause. "And why do you think that?"

The boy lifted a bony shoulder. "She never waves at me anymore when I'm climbing the rigging. It's like she can't even see me. But I know she *can* see me. She just doesn't."

Thomas glanced about the deck but saw no sign of Miss Gray. He frowned but quickly cleared his expression so Tom would not see. The boy noticed everything, which meant that if the lad had noticed Miss Gray's sadness, it was probably true.

Her ongoing despondency bothered Thomas a great deal. But he could not allow himself to brood over her situation. He had the boy who required his attention, and he had a would-be traitor locked up on his ship. The feelings of a single passenger could not get in the way of his duties.

While he showed Thomas his quarters, he decided to put the young boy's knowledge to task. "How well did you know Corbeau?"

He hated himself for asking when the boy flinched at hearing his old master's name.

"That's hard to say, sir. He was my master and an adult besides. He's not like you."

Thomas tried to hide his laugh.

"Right." Tom looked up from the spyglass in his hands. "You're an adult, too, but not like most of 'em. Cook never talked to me like I was a regular person like the way you and I talk." Tom squinted one eye and turned so he could look out the window through the spyglass.

"So you didn't talk. But what did you observe about Mr. Corbeau? Does he have friends? Did he ever mention people he knew in Mumbai?"

That was the question he needed answered. Corbeau had served on other ships and was no stranger to Mumbai.

Young Tom lowered the spyglass and looked uncomfortable. "He mentioned a few places I shouldn't mention to you."

"Whyever not?"

"They aren't nice places. He talked about women —"

"You can stop right there. I understand." Tom put the spyglass on the desk. "He does know people in Mumbai, though. He talked about drinking with them." The boy watched as Thomas processed this information. "Does that make trouble for you?"

"It might. Do you know locations? Did he give names of businesses he deals with? Inns where he may stay?"

Tom shook his head. "I don't remember."

He let the subject go. He would have to go down and talk to Corbeau to see what he could glean on his own.

He returned Thomas to the galley after teaching him how to load powder. He did not understand why he felt some great necessity in teaching the child everything about the ship the way his father had taught him. But the child was oddly charming with his mouth full of crooked teeth and his brown eyes that were entirely too big for his head. Somehow the boy had managed to burrow into Thomas's heart — a thing his mother joked he didn't have. A thing Miss Gray likely did not believe he had either, considering the way she had withdrawn from him.

He groaned and pushed thoughts of the

243

lady away. Now was not the time. He needed to know if Corbeau had the power to do him or his ship any real damage.

As he descended the ladder into the depths of his ship, he wondered if visiting the man might only spur him on to greater mischief.

Too late to change his mind now.

When he reached the iron bars separating him from Corbeau, the cook scuttled to his feet. The man sneered, the whiskers from his unshaven face bristling.

"Come to visit? I'm touched." Corbeau stunk of sweat and urine — the smell magnified by the humidity and close quarters of the cell.

Thomas refrained from covering his nose with a handkerchief. He didn't want to show even the smallest weakness to this man.

In the dim light of the lantern he'd brought with him, he saw the filthy space behind Corbeau even though he had been given water and the supplies needed to maintain cleanliness.

The captain felt it was best to open with an olive branch. "I wondered if we might discuss your options for employment when we reach Mumbai. In spite of our earlier discussion, I don't wish to leave you in port with poor references."

"What care you what I do?"

"It troubles me to think you might not have the means of getting back on your feet."

Corbeau wrapped his filthy fingers around the iron bars and pushed his face through the bars as much as possible. "Come to offer me my job back?"

"No. That door has closed. I've come to see if there are other doors in your life."

"Why? So you can bolt those closed too?"

"No. I want to help provide you other opportunities."

The man started laughing. "You don't care what happens to the likes of me. You're worried about what will happen to the likes of you!"

"I'm here for the reasons I stated. I would like to help you find gainful employment in another position."

"No, you don't! You want to keep me from knocking you off your position! I've got you scared like a little rabbit!" His laughter grew frenzied.

Thomas tried to not let the sound disturb him, but he now understood why Mr. Rallison had become so alarmed by the cacophony of insanity.

He stood for as long as he felt capable,

which in truth wasn't long enough. Realizing the man refused to give in, Thomas took his leave. As he climbed the ladder to fresh air and the sound of the sea to calm his nerves, he was chased by that raucous laughter and Corbeau's calls of "Run, little rabbit! Run!"

A shivering chill ran deep through him.

The chill stayed with him throughout the rest of the day, making him clumsy as a captain because he simply could not pay attention to his duties. He dressed hurriedly for dinner, and, with Corbeau's distraction still at the front of his thoughts, headed to meet the others in the dining hall.

Approaching the room, he suddenly stopped. Miss Gray stood alone by the dining room door, having arrived earlier than the others.

The stumble of duties exhibited earlier was nothing compared to the stumble of step he took now.

She had pinned her hair in multiple small braids, but left two long, dark ringlets to frame her face. She quite took his breath away. But more than with her appearance. She stood before him, making him somehow feel steadied, anchored, and capable.

The crazed cackle that had tumbled over and over in his mind throughout the day fled and was replaced by calm.

He opened his mouth to speak, but in that moment, the others arrived.

Mr. Miller passed Thomas and went straight up to Miss Gray. He actually circled the lady and then smiled a grin that showed too many teeth. "You're looking well, Miss Gray."

At hearing those words, Miss Cole, who had also joined the group, whipped her head around to see for herself.

Caroline returned his smile with one of her own. "Thank you, Mr. Miller," she said softly, dipping her head in acceptance of his compliment.

Did she not see how his smile was that of a wolf? It frustrated Thomas enough to make him want to look away, but he did not — could not.

"Quite right," Mr. Liechty agreed. "You've done something with your hair these past nights, haven't you?"

"She does something with her hair every night," Miss Cole said with a huff and a roll of her eyes.

Thomas had taken to not paying as much attention to Miss Gray in the hopes the other ladies would treat her better. It had seemed to be working. But not tonight. For whatever reason, tonight, Miss Cole had poison in her eyes when it came to Miss Gray.

"But the past few nights, it has been different, has it not?" Mr. Liechty pressed.

"Not so different," Thomas interrupted. He wasn't sure if he had huffed in the same manner as Miss Cole had done, but he didn't care. "It has always looked lovely and looks lovely still."

Miss Gray met his eyes and tilted her head in a way that seemed a question. Her cheeks bloomed into a lovely blush that happened when she felt pleased and embarrassed at the same time.

The other men were quick to agree with the captain's compliment. And then a wretched length of silence followed as the other ladies, who had all gathered by this time, stood about awkwardly as if slighted by his compliment to Miss Gray and not to them.

Thomas realized his error and hurried to amend. "As do all the ladies in our company. We are the lucky fellows who are graced each evening."

The lovely pink that had risen in Miss Gray's cheeks gave way to something pale and less appealing. Her eyes dropped from his, and her mouth tightened into a straight line. He'd offended her somehow.

He should have stayed away from dinner tonight. Peterson was far better suited to entertaining this particular party of ladies and gentlemen. Even Abramson handled them better.

"Why, Captain Scott!" Miss Cole's voice clawed over his thoughts. "You're positively scowling!"

"Am I?"

She laughed as if he'd said something amusing and placed a hand on his arm, but her touch only enforced his general irritation. He was sure he *had* been scowling and wasn't entirely sure that he wasn't still. He stretched his mouth into a smile he did not feel and changed the subject.

Blast, but Corbeau had rattled him. He had no sense of himself. And for Miss Gray to stand before him like a lovely broken seabird made his chest swell and collapse again and again. The relief he felt when they entered the dining room and were finally seated was a blessing.

Mr. Miller and Mr. Liechty moved from ladies' hairstyles and asked after the logistics of deep-sea fishing, inquiring if Thomas or any of his men had any experience with the endeavor. Peterson jumped into the conversation with zeal as he had a great love of fishing.

Miss Gray picked at her food, a sign that young Tom and he were right to worry about her despondence. She smiled at something Peterson said regarding fish as big as boats, but the fleeting expression never reached her eyes.

When the gentlemen moved the topic back to Parliament reform and the sad business of a protest at Manchester, Miss Gray opened her mouth, but immediately snapped it closed again. She had done so with nearly every sentence any of the men uttered on the subject. The other ladies listened politely, well . . . some of them listened. Miss James and Miss Jeffries had entered into a quiet conversation of their own, but he noted how none but Miss Gray seemed to become more agitated with every passing moment.

When Mr. Miller declared, "Served those radicals right," Thomas was shocked.

He opened his mouth, prepared to lecture the men at his table to watch themselves, but Miss Gray beat him to it.

"Many innocent people were killed in that protest!" she interjected with horror in her voice.

"Innocent?" Mr. Miller scoffed, looking at Miss Gray. "If they were so innocent, why were they marching and carrying on like an army drilling its recruits? The local magistrates wouldn't have sent for help if the intentions of those protestors were at all peaceful. Henry Hunt and the others who were speaking to those crowds that day knew what they were about."

The other ladies were suddenly very involved in the conversation with one of their own hoisting the colors of her political leanings. Though none of them offered support for or against Parliament, their eyes showed a keen interest as they listened.

Thomas should have been ashamed of himself for delighting in seeing the fire newly stoked in Miss Gray's eyes, for the iron in her convictions. But he was not. Here was the woman he'd admired.

"Yes," she said firmly. "Those men did know what they were about. Only they were not made aware that the government would turn on its own people. I hope those reformers do as Percy Shelley encouraged and rise like lions after slumber."

Mr. Miller gave her a dismissive wave. "Captain Scott, please don't tell me you've allowed a woman whose sympathies align with that radical Hunt aboard your ship."

He had not been prepared to receive a question of such flaming disregard for the delicate nature of ladies and did not have an answer ready. But he hadn't needed one.

"Whether he has or hasn't, no one could say, Mr. Miller," Miss Gray said sweetly while fluttering her long, dark lashes and offering a smile that had bite. "But after listening to you, we are all assured that he has allowed a man to smuggle his absurdity aboard the ship, are we not?"

Lieutenant Peterson and Mr. Liechty laughed, showing their support of those reformers and those harmed at St. Peter's. The ladies were equal parts horror at the topic of conversation and disbelief that Caroline had called Mr. Miller absurd.

Thomas merely smirked and said, "Perhaps we should refrain from such discussions in the future, Mr. Miller. Especially when you're so clearly outmatched at this table."

He cast a meaningful glance to Miss Gray, but she'd gone stiff and silent and her eyes were fully downcast as if her plate had suddenly become terribly important. Her mouth tightened, and the crease above her nose never smoothed.

Miss James offered a painful smile and said, "I do hope the weather doesn't become too much warmer, Captain. The heat has made sleeping almost impossible."

And the conversation returned to those

safe topics of the weather, humidity, and music.

Miss Gray never looked up from her plate. Thomas wished he could do something to make her glance at him, to make her see how much he approved of her answers. He wanted to tell her how much he'd come to care about her smiles — and her.

CHAPTER SEVENTEEN

The night had been a disaster in spite of its promising beginning. Caroline had wanted to leave the table early but knew that would only make things worse. She had to see the evening through to its end — an end made all the more bitter by Miss Cole's lazy half-smile and the captain's unreadable expression. She'd been grateful no one suggested cards. She'd fled the dining room as soon as civility allowed.

Now, she stared out at the black sea. The crescent moon offered little in the way of light, and for that she was glad. It meant she would be unlikely to be seen by any the crew who might also be out.

"I'm a fool," she said to the waves.

"Not at all."

She whipped around, startled by the captain's approach. How could a man in boots walk with the silence of cat paws?

She hurried to apologize. "I am sorry I

brought contention to your table." Except she wasn't sorry. Not at all.

"Are you? I'm not. Why should you be?"

"I was rude to Mr. Miller. I'm afraid I may have damaged his pride." Though, in truth, she wanted to go back and hit Mr. Miller over the head with a sterling silver platter for his boorish attitude toward other humans.

Captain Scott laughed. "My dear, it is true that your trenchant wit is enough to shred any man's pride to ribbons, but I believe the gentleman in question deserved your words. Rest easy, Miss Gray. You have not offended beyond repair. Perhaps the man will think before speaking or behaving thusly. A little thought would do a man like him some good."

He'd called her "my dear." Her pulse raced at the implications of such words, but she stifled her feelings immediately. He surely hadn't meant them to be taken so personally. But his words were kind, soothing, and so needed. She may have made a fool of herself. He may think her a bluestocking who was a blight upon society. But he was still kind to her even if he did not think of her the way she thought of him.

He stood next to her at the railing, as if planning to spend a moment with her.

Whether that moment be short or long didn't matter for Caroline knew to love it for what it was. The exact occasion of joy was so often fleeting, but the memory lasted.

She turned back to the water, grateful to not be facing him directly.

"Are you sad, Miss Gray?" he asked.

The question surprised her, especially since at that precise moment, she felt suddenly happy. "Sad, Captain?"

"Tonight was the first time I've seen you be yourself in a long time. I have missed your spark."

She hardly knew what to make of such a comment — especially since she'd made such a mess of the evening. "I am always me. How could I be anyone else?"

"You've taken to pretending to be like the other women."

Caroline swallowed hard and placed her hands on the railing so she had something to hold. "Who says I am pretending? And why should you believe that behaving like the other ladies would make me sad?"

"Young Tom says you are sad as well. He's quite a clever little chap. I tend to trust his instincts."

Caroline could not be sure if the captain was teasing or not. It bothered her to think that her demeanor fell so easily to interpretation. "I'm not sad. I am behaving exactly as I ought."

" 'As you ought' and 'as you are' are not the same thing, Miss Gray."

The ship hit a larger wave which tilted the boat unexpectedly. They both grasped the railing to keep their balance, and his arm brushed against hers, causing a fluttering in her heart.

Incapable of allowing him to discover just how deeply absurd she'd allowed her feelings to go, she changed the subject. "Should I be worried when the ship feels as though it might roll right over into the sea?"

He sighed but followed her new discourse. "I'm not saying such a thing never happens, mind you, but it is unlikely. At times, she can roll more than sixty degrees. It's then that your heart thumps a little faster, and you know what it means to be alive."

Caroline laughed and allowed herself to look at him. "Life on the edge, is it?"

He looked out toward the horizon, cutting a profile that made Caroline's heart thump a little faster in a way that showed *her* what it meant to be alive.

"Out here, they used to believe there was nothing but the edge, and they were right."

Caroline scoffed and tightened her wrap around her as she tucked her hands under her arms. "Don't tell me you're a seafaring man and yet believe the world is a flat plate and that one day you'll sail over the edge." He laughed. "No. Not that. But there is an edge to the sea, sharper than any blade, more terrifying than if the world were flat." "And yet you love it," she said. "The affectionate tone you use for this terrifying foe is the same one might use for a betrothed." "And so she is that as well. A creature who is at once bold and soft." "It's a pity men do not like their actual women the same way they prefer their ocean." She frowned and wondered at herself for saying such a thing out loud. "Who says they don't?" He was looking at her, though she'd turned away from him. She felt his gaze like the burn of the hottest day in summer.

She should not have said such things, should not have ventured so close to the truth of her ache and despair. But she *had* ventured to the edge. Should she not at least look over and see what was in its depths?

"So says the woman who went through several seasons and, at the end of all of them, could not even keep a female friend let alone a male beau."

He considered this before asking, "The

women too?"

"Yes, well, one does not like to be so near a woman who has been declared unmarriable lest the condition prove contagious."

"I would wish for a contagion of your sort. A bright mind and a curious heart are virtues to be applauded not shunned."

She turned toward him, pulled by the tide of his words, the gentleness in his tone. He spoke of her with the same caress he'd used to speak of the ocean. When she met his eyes, she swallowed hard.

Had a man ever looked at her like that after she'd opened her mouth to speak? Plenty had looked at her with interest, even desire, before she had spoken to them, but after, the heat in their eyes dimmed to a cold and awkward winter from which they skulked away.

Captain Scott had exchanged many conversations with her, not all of them kind, yet here he stood, looking at her, his face barely a breath away. She tilted her head up and wanted to flutter her eyes closed in anticipation of the kiss that must surely be born of such heat, except she did not want her eyes to shut, not when she felt so much more than she ought.

"I have been sad," she admitted in a whisper so quiet, it may have been only a thought.

But he heard her. "Who has you feeling in such a way?"

"Honestly, Captain? You."

"Me?"

He did not pull away in confusion. If anything, he seemed to edge closer as if to prove her words false.

That movement broke her emotionally, forcing a torrent of truth to flee her mouth. "Yes. You speak to me with such energy one moment, then the next, you leave as if you cannot get away fast enough. You compliment me one moment, then you take it back the next. It is quite a painful process. And I know I should not expect anything from you. I know it is not right for me to . . . think of you in any way other than as the captain of this ship, but I do. That is . . . I think of you. I . . ."

"I think of you as well," he said. His hand moved closer to hers on the railing, his fingers lightly touching hers.

"I completely understand if you do not think of me as more than a passenger, and, wait. What did you say?" She'd misheard. She had to have misheard.

"I also think of you, and not as a captain thinks about a passenger but as a man thinks of a woman."

260

She reeled at his words, at his intensity. She peered into his face, searching for a hint of insincerity but found only the same heat in his eyes that she felt stirring her soul.

It wasn't possible. He could not be saying the words she had imagined him saying for the last several weeks of their voyage. "How could you? When I've done so many things wrong?"

He placed his hand fully over hers on the railing, his warmth welcome even in the sweltering heat of the night. "What things have you imagined yourself to have done wrong?"

She stared at their hands, inconceivably together, and felt as though she might never be sad again. "I went out on deck during the storm."

He turned so he faced her, though he did not remove his hand from hers. Instead he slid his thumb alongside her fingers. "Which was very brave of you to put another's safety before your own, and very wise of you to tie yourself to the ship first. I should not have scolded you for that."

Her pulse raced. She felt light-headed. "I installed a hammock in my cabin and put holes in your ship."

"Which was industrious and clever. I should not have scolded you for that either."

His fingers lightly brushed the top of her hand, leaving a fiery trail across her skin. It made it hard for her to think — hard for her to protest his having any affection or good opinion of her.

"I yelled at you for young Tom's bruises and cuts."

"Which shows you have deep compassion and are willing to protect others." His face drew nearer to hers. His body leaned close enough, she feared he would hear her rapidly beating heart. "But *you* should not have scolded *me* for that." A slow smile formed on his lips.

She felt her lips curve upward as well. "I have no control over my thoughts, and they far too often exit my mouth without restraint."

His smile softened as his eyes dropped to her lips. "I love everything about your mouth, including the things that it says. It is the things your mouth says that have drawn me to you."

Tears filled her eyes and blurred her vision. How many seasons? How many dances where the men were charmed at first and horrified at last? How many years had she waited until she felt certain it would never happen for her?

"I don't know how to believe you."

"Then believe this."

He touched her waist and drew her close, his lips settling on hers. One hand tangled itself in her fingers while his other hand reached out to cradle her face. Was this what it felt like to be cherished, to be — dare she think it — loved?

She welcomed the heat of his nearness, the trace of his lips against hers, the way they seemed to fit together with her smaller frame filling the space of his arms, the way the wind swirled around them as if even nature celebrated their embrace.

He pulled away and rested his forehead against hers. Her eyes stayed closed for several beats of her racing heart. The backs of his fingers trailed down her jaw. She opened her eyes to meet the intense stare of his gold-flecked gaze.

"Was that all right?" he whispered. "I just don't think I can keep my distance any longer. I cannot pretend to feel less for you than I do. Not any longer."

"Is that what you were doing?" she asked. "Pretending to feel nothing for me? Is that why you always left me so abruptly?"

"Peterson said my attentions toward you were making the other ladies mistreat you. I thought if I kept my distance . . ."

"Your distance is what made me so sad."

He pulled back and gathered her hands up in his. Relief dawned across his face. "Then it *is* all right that I kissed you?"

She gave him a soft laugh. "It is definitely all right, Captain Scott."

"Please call me Thomas. It's a fine name. My mother would be pleased to see it getting some use."

She felt an elation she had not known possible. "Thomas, then. And I would very much like if you called me Caroline." She wanted to tell him to kiss her again, but she'd already said more than she'd ever dreamed she'd have the courage to utter aloud.

He cared for her. He was not the sort of man to trifle with a woman's feelings. He would not have kissed her if he did not care for her in the same way she cared for him. No. This was real.

"I cannot believe I am here," he said.

"Here?"

"With you. Feeling so much. I had thought love a thing for other people."

Love.

He loved her?

"I had never thought such emotions would be mine either," she said. "You must know how much I have admired you these many weeks, but even I had no idea I would come

264

to love you as I do."

"I am grateful you found worth in me, Caroline."

She thrilled at hearing her name from his lips. "Do you know what I'm grateful for?"

When he tilted his head in question, she couldn't keep the smile from her mouth.

"I'm grateful Clara believes I have no need of a chaperone." A new boldness overtook her, and she fully blamed this exasperating, loving captain for what she did next. She grasped the lapels of his jacket and tugged him down to meet her lips again. She felt his smile against her mouth, and for the first time ever, Caroline had hope that her life would be everything she had dreamed.

CHAPTER EIGHTEEN

Thomas went to bed with a smile on his face, and he awoke the next morning with the very same smile. After daring to kiss Caroline, he had stayed up talking with her late into the night.

He needn't ignore or avoid her anymore. He needn't worry about complimenting her for fear of how the other ladies treated her, because she said she did not care what they thought or didn't think. He would continue to practice discretion when the other passengers were around because he did not want her to feel uncomfortable. He had told her as much the night before, and she had sighed with contentment, stating that she would not mind now that she understood why he held back.

It went against all the things he had said he'd wanted for himself. He'd wanted to wait for love and marriage until he had secured his future on land.

But here he was.

He was in love.

He felt silly and reckless and delightfully so.

Oh, how Peterson would tease when he found out. Thomas wouldn't even mind it. Not when it came with such a wondrous reward. Caroline Gray. She had even given him permission to use her Christian name. That alone sent a thrill through him every time he thought of it. *Caroline.* How good it sounded.

The day never offered a chance to be alone with her again, so he simply thought the name over and over, even going as far as to say it aloud every now and again under his breath.

He continued the practice the next day. And into the next after that, this time sending sly glances in the direction of the lady who owned that name.

The following day, he walked the deck with her out where everyone could see she had taken his arm. That small act might have been inconsequential to most men, but he seldom offered a female passenger his arm. Doing so now felt like a nonverbal declaration of his affections.

After his walk with Miss Gray — *Caroline* — he entered the wheelhouse to gather up

267

Peterson for inspections of the cannons.

During the inspections, he took a deep breath, inhaling the scent of sulfur and saltpeter that hung in the air. He was grateful not to have had to use the cannons in anything more than a drill, especially when Caroline was aboard his ship. The thought of her instantly brought the murmur of her name to his lips again.

Peterson peered up from where he'd been recording their inspection findings. "What are you mumbling over and over? You've taken on the appearance of a lunatic. And your behavior secures a good chance of dragging me to the asylum with you."

For the briefest of moments, Thomas panicked. It was one thing to walk on deck with the lady, and one thing to think about telling Peterson, but it was quite another to commit to the scheme. For days, he had kept those private concerns between him and Caroline. He wasn't sure he was ready to explain himself to anyone, not even to his lieutenant.

But then he thought of her, of her fire and passion, and realized he needed to tell someone his good fortune of locating and securing a woman of both sense and beauty. "I am repeating to myself the Christian name of Miss Gray."

"Miss Gray? I don't know that I even know the lady's forename. And saying her name doesn't save you from the appearance of a lunatic."

"You know how you said I should consider her as an option for courting?"

Peterson snorted. "You mean when you laughed outright at me and told me to shove off?"

Thomas eyed his friend. "Do you see me laughing now?"

As Peterson peered into the captain's face, Thomas smiled indulgently.

"No," Peterson answered, suddenly subdued. "I do not."

"It is because I now see the wisdom in your suggestion. I do believe I shall become a tenant for life."

"You mean to marry her?" Peterson wavered between incredulity and delight. "That's . . . well, that's wonderful! I am assuming the lady knows of your intentions and is in agreement?"

"She does not know of my exact intentions, as I have not made an offer yet. But for agreement? Yes, she is."

Peterson's graying eyebrows shot up. "You mean to tell me you shared actual feelings with a lady? And you didn't explode or melt or grow an extra eye in the process? That is

269

astonishing. When did this all happen?"

"A few nights ago, after the altercation between her and Mr. Miller. She was up on deck berating herself for letting her tongue get the better of her —"

"You mean the better of *him*." Peterson laughed. "You can trust a woman with such strength of convictions. And to have her convictions be so thoroughly on the side of right is a comfort. The massacre at St. Peter's Field was horrible. All those people. For your lady to champion those who were harmed is a sign of her good character. But, my friend, you were on deck, in the dark, unchaperoned?"

"I merely went out to offer her comfort. I had no intention of opening my heart to her. And certainly no intention of anything inappropriate."

"You are a lucky man that Clara is too much in awe of you to suspect you need supervision in order to protect the ladies in her charge. Take a care now that an understanding has been formed between you and Miss Gray. Some of these ladies have the claws and jaws of a wildcat."

Thomas leaned against a cannon. "Did you know that Miss Gray has been wretchedly unhappy due to advice you gave me regarding her and the other ladies? I had been staying away from her on your counsel to do so, and she thought my inattention meant I didn't care for her. So should I now take your counsel?"

"Yes. Because had she not been unhappy, you would not have sought to offer comfort, and no agreement between you would have ever been reached. I do believe you owe your happiness to me." Peterson's teasing smile faded, and his mouth pulled down into a frown. "You are happy, aren't you?"

"I am bliss itself."

Peterson's smile returned even wider than before. "Well, then, may I offer you a most heartfelt congratulations?"

"You may. I believe I am destined to be terribly happy. Such a consequence deserves congratulations."

It wasn't many days before the other passengers realized something had shifted between Caroline and Thomas. The two had agreed to not announce their intentions, knowing that the more people who knew, the less time they might have to speak alone.

He had not formally asked for her hand yet. Every time he thought it a good idea to do so, it seemed they were interrupted. Often, by Caroline herself. If he did not know better, he would worry she was having a change of heart.

They only had two weeks left before they would arrive in port. He felt a great deal of relief in knowing she would not fall prey to the wolves who would greet the young ladies and offer dinner invitations and ball invitations and marriage offers, sweeping those ladies off into potentially untenable situations.

His own loveliest Caroline Gray would not be caught in such a mess.

He was walking from the galley where he'd been checking on young Tom when he heard someone hail him.

"Oh, there you are, Captain!" Miss Cole called out again, stepping quickly to catch up with him. "I heard some rather interesting news."

The heat did not agree with Miss Cole. Her face dripped with sweat. She frequently mopped her face with her handkerchief, but the cloth was already so soaked that it did little good.

Beneath the layer of perspiration was a ruddy face. She had tried masterfully to keep a parasol on her person at all times, but the covering only shaded most of her face, often leaving a portion of her neck and jawline exposed. Now, she was a patchwork of red and white.

He'd heard her make rude remarks to Miss Bronley regarding both her sunburned face and the tan that emerged when the burn faded. He also remembered his own Caroline silencing Miss Cole by commenting on her red jawline in return.

At the thought of Caroline, he smiled, not realizing he was offering Miss Cole a smile as she approached him, a thing he tried never to do lest it encourage her flirtations with him.

"Why, you seem happy to see me. Time together has made us fond of one another, hasn't it?"

Blast. That was definitely not the sort of conversation he wanted to engage in with her. Did he lie and say yes, he was fond of her? Or did he tell her the truth and explain all the ways in which she repelled him?

"A good captain works to take care of his passengers. All of them. Equally."

"Equally?" She ducked her head in a way that allowed her to look up at him through her eyelashes. The move had clearly been practiced many times, and she probably thought it made her look flirtatious, but to him she only appeared to have kinked her neck. "Do you never take a fancy to any of your lady passengers? Do you never indulge in a harmless flirtation?"

"There is no such thing as harmless when it comes to flirtations, Miss Cole. One member of the party involved is usually in earnest. I am not the sort of man to trifle with the feelings of any lady."

"I see."

He very much doubted her ability to see anything.

Miss Cole took his arm. "You must forgive me for relying on you for support," she said. "I find I am not stable on the ocean."

He didn't bother mentioning how the sea was calmer that day than it had been their entire journey.

"As I said before, I come bearing interesting news. It appears Miss Gray has come under the impression that you have been engaging in some mild flirtation with her. I feel I must warn you that the attentions you've given her might have been misinterpreted. Perhaps it would be best if you did not give her so much attention if you truly do not wish to trifle with the young woman's feelings."

He should have walked away right then, right there. But for reasons he could not explain, the woman had gotten under his skin like an infection that would not heal.

Instead, Thomas responded, "I thank you for bringing this to my attention. I certainly do not mean to give the wrong impression to anyone. That being the case, you should know I am not trifling with that particular lady's affections. I am seeking the great happiness that would come from her returning my regard." They had reached the stairs leading up to the wheelhouse, and he pulled his arm free from hers. "If you will excuse me, the ship has needs that require my attention. I would not wish for us to face any mishaps so close to the end of our journey. Good day."

If Miss Cole's face had been red before with the exertion and the patchwork splashes of sunburn, it was now entirely one shade — the red of an angry sunrise that often preceded a storm.

He tried to smile and gave a slight bow, hoping to ease the sting of his brash comment. Caroline would not be pleased with him, considering they had both agreed to not make their situation a thing of public notice.

But he did not know how to play the games that women of society played, and he was of no mind to put up with them.

"Miss Cole looked to be a thunderhead as she watched you walk away," Peterson said as Thomas entered the wheelhouse. "Did you tell her that her frock failed to flatter?"

"I fear I did worse," Thomas whispered to keep the other men from overhearing. "I told her that I held Miss Gray in esteem."

Peterson shook his head and tsked in genuine concern. "That would do it. Let us hope your blunt force will not create problems for Miss Gray."

Thomas hoped as well. But he feared it might be in vain.

He worried over his misstep all day, and when he saw Caroline arriving first to dinner, he took her by the hand and pulled her into an alcove barely big enough for the two of them to stand in.

"I had no idea this little nook was even here!" she said with a laugh. "And I thought I had thoroughly explored the whole of this ship."

Rather than explain that the ship had many such nooks, he kissed her. He'd been wanting to kiss her again for so long and could no longer resist the temptation. She melted against him and wrapped her arms around him.

"We can't stay here forever," she whispered. "Yet how are we to leave? If the others are on time, they will be right outside this door."

"I'll go first. Then you wait a few minutes while I usher everyone into the dining room.

You can exit safely then. But first, I must apologize."

"You need never apologize for a kiss like that!"

Oh, how he loved this woman! "Not for the kiss, dearest Caroline. I spoke to Miss Cole today." He explained all that had transpired there and explained his worry that he might have set Miss Cole against Caroline, but she laughed it off.

"Knowing you are mine means never worrying over what any other person thinks of me. I will be well, Thomas."

Hearing his name from her lips sent a thrill through him. He had never imagined being so happy.

He exited the alcove and tried to set aside his worry regarding Miss Cole. The slim possibility existed that Miss Cole would behave herself at dinner because it was clear that Mr. Miller was another one of her targets for a potential match. Surely, she would not allow things to become ugly in front of him.

At dinner, Miss Cole proved that, while she would not lead the parade into the battlefield of words, she had no hesitation nudging it that direction. If he hadn't been so frustrated with her, he might have admired her incredible skill with manipulation. She wielded it as a master artist would a brush. She brought up the massacre again, praising Mr. Miller for his exemplary show of standing behind Parliament and being a true patriot.

Mr. Miller, his pride fueled by the compliment, immediately took up the topic again.

Caroline, driven by the encouragement Thomas himself had given her, did not bridle her opinions on the matter as much as she might have if she did not feel so free to speak.

The rest of the table remained subdued in their mortification.

Wanting to protect Caroline from the machinations of a scheming woman and a blundering man, he brought the discussion to an abrupt end.

Miss Cole smiled into her glass and made sure to catch his eye over the top so there could be no mistake as to why she'd sought such a discourse.

After dinner, Mr. Miller sought an audience with him. Thomas feared the meeting would aggravate the headache that had come over him during the course of the evening, but he agreed to meet Mr. Miller out on deck.

The cooler air would aid in abating the headache, and, if the man proved too bothersome, there was always the hope that a wave would pluck him off the deck and hurl him into the sea.

Mr. Miller puffed on his pipe and huffed out his words. "I am most disappointed with our dinnertime discussions. The freedom with which some of the ladies speak is intolerable."

"Odd." Thomas frowned at the smoke that ringed Mr. Miller's head. He'd never been taken with the fashion of a pipe. His father had been a pipe smoker, and the graying ends of his mustache and beard were always stained yellow as a result. "I rather thought it was the freedom with which some of the men spoke that made the conversation intolerable."

"You know of whom I speak. That Miss Gray. It is no wonder she finds herself aboard a vessel bound for a land where no one knows her. I cannot think of a single gentleman who, upon learning of her reputation, would be willing to take a woman of such brazen independence."

"I find her brazen independence refreshing."

"And it is regarding that sentiment that I wish to speak to you. Your participation in her behavior is troubling. You encourage her to her disadvantage, Captain. A woman with

279

such ideas sets a bad example for her sex. Her opinion on matters of Parliament are better left to her own private musings. She should not feel so free to speak of them to the gentlemen at the dinner table."

"It is precisely because of those gentlemen that I encourage her to speak her mind. At least, because of one particular gentleman." Thomas gave him a scathing look. "Perhaps you don't realize that you should not feel so free to speak of a massacre at my dinner table. Perhaps you don't realize the incredible impropriety of such a conversation. I am hoping you will take a lesson from this and go forth and act better in the future."

Mr. Miller's face had grown quite red before his eyes narrowed and he poked a thick finger in Thomas's direction. "You only say such things because you've taken a fancy to her. What a scandal for a captain to become involved with one of his passengers. I don't think you properly thought this through."

Thomas laughed. The man had no sense of decorum. England lost nothing when this man had decided to go to Mumbai, though, sadly, England's gain would be India's loss. The man had a cruel streak in him that was ugly to behold.

"You laugh, sir. But you cannot say I did not warn you. You should be checking into that woman. You should understand what she's about before you defend her like some lovesick pup."

"I know of her past, and there is nothing in it that is shocking to me."

Mr. Miller offered a tight smile "Ah, but do you know her future? You should ask her sometime before we make land. Ask her what arrangements have been procured for her future."

Mr. Miller tipped his hat and walked along the deck, leaving in his wake an insecurity Thomas had not anticipated when it came to his affection for Miss Gray.

CHAPTER NINETEEN

Caroline could not stop thinking of the feel of Thomas's arms around her. She worried at first that she'd imagined his affections. But no. Every day she grew more certain of his affections. This was real. Their love was real.

She didn't know what would come next for them. After all, there was a great deal to overcome to make such a relationship work. He was a man of the sea, so where would they make their home? There was the business she had to finish up in Mumbai. But she could get it over with quickly and get on with her life with the man she loved.

Caroline realized her error in allowing Miss Cole and Mr. Miller to cajole her into that heated debate at dinnertime. She had walked right into it with both eyes wide open. She considered how, as a captain's wife, she would probably have to entertain a great many people who had opinions and beliefs that differed from her own. She would need to understand how to rein in her own tongue to keep herself from embarrassing her beloved captain.

She would apologize to him as soon as she was ready for the day. She dressed with deliberate care, pinning up her hair into perfection. She found she liked putting herself together without the help of anyone else.

If Miss Cole was determined to froth over with jealousy, the least Caroline could do was give her good reason. She might only be wearing a day dress, but it was her best one.

She went to meet Thomas out on deck, as planned, so they might walk together.

But he was not there. She looked up to the wheelhouse but could not discern any of the shadows behind the glass to be the one shadow she was looking for. Happily, Miss James was out taking in the air, so at least she had company.

"May I join you?" she asked as Miss James stopped to look out over the ocean.

"Of course," Miss James replied without looking away from the view.

Caroline joined her at the railing. But when she glanced out to the horizon, she gasped. The water was entirely still. The sea blurred into sky with no discernible break of horizon.

"Have you ever seen anything like it?" Miss James asked.

"No. Not ever." In all of Caroline's experience, the sea was endless waves and movement. As lovely as this particular version of the sea seemed, she wasn't sure she liked it.

"Have you ever felt such peace?" Miss James asked.

"Peace? I don't know that I would call it peace for my part. The sea is a looking glass, flat and unflinching in a way that makes me suspect its treachery, as if a sea monster lurks beneath that perfect surface."

Miss James laughed. "You sound like one of those Gothic novels. What treachery might you worry about? You have a future made secure with a respectable captain."

Caroline jolted, her head snapping toward Miss James. Did she know about the captain? Caroline had asked Thomas to keep their understanding between the two of them. She had used the other ladies as an excuse, but in truth, her reasons had to do with her obligation to accept the company of Captain Nicholas Barritt.

Miss James smiled wistfully. "I wish I had someone waiting for me on land. I wish I had the security that you have of knowing he will take you into his society and give you every opportunity to show him your value."

"Of course!" Miss James meant Captain Barritt, not Captain Scott. "That. You should not consider me to be luckier than you. You have no obligation and are therefore free to like whom you will without any tethers."

Miss James continued to lament her own situation. Caroline only half listened.

She would have to tell her captain about her arrangement with that other captain, and she would have to do it soon. They had less than a fortnight before arrival, and she needed him to understand the situation in full. She'd meant to tell him the night he professed his feelings for her. But how could she tell him when the evening was full of stars and kisses and promises of futures? She could not bring herself to ruin such a perfect moment, not when there was time yet to unveil the unpleasant truth.

But he would understand. He would leave her in India to meet her obligation, leave with his cargo, and when he returned, they would both be free to be together. He would know she waited for him in India, and he would not partake in the offerings of the season in London. Yes. He would understand. He was a forward-thinking man of good sense and discernment. He recognized the plight of women and the limited choices offered to them.

Besides, how angry could he really become when the arrangement with Captain Barritt was her sole reason for being on his ship? Without it, she never would have met Thomas. So, really, they should both be grateful for the circumstances that brought them together, no matter how inconvenient or ridiculous they may be.

She shivered with the chill of a sudden breeze that rippled over the glassy sea to the horizon. A cooler breeze would be welcomed in the relentless heat, but it brought an internal chill to her as well. She needed to clear her mind and figure out how to tell Thomas.

"Oh dear," she said. "I forgot my wrap. If you'll excuse me."

Miss James nodded and went back to looking at the sea.

Caroline returned to her own room, trying to formulate how to explain her situation to Thomas.

He will understand, she thought. But if she really believed that, why did she feel so afraid?

She sought opportunities throughout the

day to find Thomas, but he remained elusive. He was never in the wheelhouse or anywhere else she usually found him.

And he was not at dinner.

"Is the captain unwell this evening?" she quietly asked Lieutenant Peterson.

The lieutenant glanced at her and tightened his mouth, his jaw flexing before he answered, "He had duties that required his attention." The lieutenant then asked Mr. Liechty if he had ever used the stethoscope.

The lieutenant's crisp answer and unusually cool behavior toward her made her worry all the more. Was something wrong? Had she done something wrong?

She tried to smile and listen to the conversation about the modern stethoscope and how Mr. Liechty had heard of its use in Paris but had yet to try it for himself. Normally the subject matter would have been a wonderful diversion, but she barely attended to any of it.

"Do you know where I might find him?" she whispered to the lieutenant as she was gathering up her skirts to leave.

He hesitated, then said, "I am sure if you go out on deck, he will find you."

"Thank you, Lieutenant Peterson."

He shook his head. "Do not thank me, Miss Gray."

"And what is all that whispering between you and the lieutenant?" Miss Cole's voice sent a wave of nausea through her.

When Caroline turned a false smile to the woman, Miss Cole let out a little laugh. "Why, Miss Gray, you look positively panicked. Is something the matter?"

"No," she said. "I'm sure everything is fine."

She hoped she was telling the truth. As she hurried away, she heard Miss Cole call out, "Won't you join us for cards in the saloon?"

Caroline had to pause to give her apologies for declining the invitation. When her eyes met Miss Cole's, she thought she saw something, a glint of triumph.

If she had been worried before, she now felt as panicked as Miss Cole predicted. She fled to the deck.

She paced the wooden planks back and forth for a long time waiting for Thomas to find her.

"When were you going to tell me?" he asked from behind her, surprising her with his sudden appearance.

"Thomas! You frightened me!" She pressed her hand to her heart to calm its racing rhythm. "And tell you what?" When she caught sight of his expression, her fear heightened. Even in the shadows, she could see his brows furrowed and his mouth pulled into a hard line.

"Will you really toy with me? Will you really say that you don't know to what I refer?"

She tried for a small laugh and a smile to lighten the mood, but the tension between them felt heavy enough to sink the ship. "Thomas, you're not making any sense. And you're frightening me."

She stepped closer to him, to take his hands in hers and perhaps smooth out the furrow in his brow, but he stepped back, staying out of her reach.

"What is it that frightens you? That I might learn the truth regarding you and your appointment in Mumbai?"

She could not lie to this man, but she scarcely knew how to explain the situation in the face of his anger.

"You made an arrangement with a man's mother." His voice was a low growl.

She recoiled from his words even as she stood perfectly still. He knew the truth. She had meant to tell him, but she had simply waited too long. Now it was too late to divulge her reasons for being aboard his ship without appearing to have toyed with his affections. "Who told you?"

"So you don't deny it? Your only concern here is who betrayed your secret when your concern should be that you kept such a secret from me in the first place."

That was not at all her only concern. She had to make certain he understood that. "I can explain. This is not as bad as it sounds." She believed they would still be all right, that everything would be fine once she explained.

" 'As bad as it sounds'?" He leaned in to whisper harshly, "How bad does something have to be for you with your modern ideas? You had an arrangement already in place, yet you still felt it fair to pull me into your web and allow me to —" He closed his eyes and shook his head. "I've never felt such disappointment regarding anyone, not even in the silly women who board my ship with no ambition other than to marry a man, no matter his character. I would take dozens of such women over what I am experiencing now. You are no friend to the truth. But do not worry, Miss Gray, I release you to meet your prior obligations. You need not concern yourself with me any further." He turned away from her.

"Thomas!" she cried out, incredulous that he would leave without allowing her a chance to explain, terrified that he would never allow her that chance.

He did not turn back to her, but said, "I feel it best that we do not speak so informally to one another, Miss Gray. Please call me 'Captain' or 'Captain Scott.' " With that, he was gone.

She considered going after him, but his anger was a physical force keeping her feet firmly where they stood. She could not say how long it was before she was able to put one step in front of the other all the way down to her cabin.

Once, when she'd been very small, she had wandered to the river and fallen in. The water swallowed her and dragged her downstream, beating her against rocks and logs as the water kept to its path, her small body bearing the brunt of its determination.

Her mother found her shoved up on the shore and carried her home, though she had no recollection of being found or carried.

What she did remember was the pain when she woke. They called it a miracle that she lived, but the pain in all her limbs, muscles, and bones had been so intense, she wished for death.

That pain was nothing to what she felt as she lowered herself onto the bunk and looked up at the carved constellations. She'd not been capable of attaching the hammock. In fact, she wanted to rip the thing to shreds — to lash out. But instead she stared at the stars in the wood and let silent tears drip from the corners of her eyes and into her hair. She would not sob. She would not cry or lash out. She would not allow anyone to hear her heart shatter over and over again with each tear that slid from her eyes.

CHAPTER TWENTY

It had been a week since Miss James had answered his questions regarding Miss Gray's arrangements once she arrived in Mumbai. A week since his altercation with Miss Gray. And less than that until he would be able to put her off his ship and be free of her spell over him.

He had not allowed her to explain because he already knew what he needed. She had a prior arrangement. An agreement. She had no right to represent herself as free to love whomever she might desire. He remembered the first day of the voyage when that wretched couple had stumbled aboard his ship and asked him to pay close attention to the woman they'd handpicked for their son. If only they knew how closely he *had* watched her. He had hardly been able to do anything else.

Fool.

How had he not seen the signs earlier?

Why had he believed Miss James, Miss Jeffries, or Miss Bronley could be the woman in question? Why had he so quickly cast off the notion that it was his Miss Gray?

No.

Not *his* Miss Gray.

His heart felt like it had been drowned. Every beat felt like it expelled its last breath, and yet it kept beating still further. When she was no longer on his ship, he would recover himself and drag himself from the depths of his own despair.

He had divulged his sorrows only to Lieutenant Peterson when they were inspecting cargo together.

"Engaged?" Peterson had said, his face a mixture of horror and incredulity.

"Yes. I had the misfortune of meeting her intended's mother and father. They were absurd people, which does not bode well for Miss Gray if the son is anything like them."

"But *engaged*? Are you certain?"

"Quite certain."

Peterson had shaken his head as he squinted down at the ledgers. "No. I can't believe it. And even if she is, her affections for you are strong enough to overcome that obstacle."

"Don't be such a cad. I would never

involve myself in that sort of stickiness. And what of her betrothed?"

Peterson had shrugged and moved closer to the lamp as he made a notation. "What of him? She's never even met the man. We could tell him she fell overboard during the voyage and that we're terribly sorry to have lost his bride, but we have all these lovely secondary options for him to choose from."

Thomas had laughed out loud at the thought, glad no one else was with them to overhear. "Do you not think Miss Gray would have something to say if we told her intended that she fell into the sea?" Of course she would. The woman had opinions enough to distribute through a small country and still be in surplus.

"We'll simply lock her up in her cabin. If she felt any obligation to him, surely she would not have . . ."

Thomas's grin had fallen. "But she did, didn't she? And how can a man trust a woman who cannot keep her word? As a captain, I am often away for months at a time. If I am to tangle myself in the web of a woman, I need to know I can count on her word to be worth something."

At the time, Peterson seemed to understand, to commiserate, to be on his side.

Since then, Thomas took his dinners in

the wheelhouse, sending Peterson or Abramson to represent him.

But tonight, Peterson refused to go. "You need to speak with her. I will not be your surrogate any longer."

"I have nothing to say to her." They were in his private quarters — a place where he seemed to spend more time than he had ever done in the past.

"Then go and say nothing. It would be a far braver and more honest thing than what you're doing currently, which is hiding out like a scolded schoolboy."

"I gave her up. How much more honest can I be? If I'd known she was spoken for, I never would have allowed myself to look in her direction."

Peterson stood at the windows and stared out through the leaded panes. "She's not engaged, you know."

That startled him. "What do you mean she is not engaged? She has an arrangement with this Barritt fellow — may he never have a day's good luck."

Peterson tsked and turned back to Thomas. "Goodness, you are slipping if you dare mention luck during a voyage."

"I'm in my own quarters. I can mention whatever I like here."

"As you choose." Peterson turned back to

the windows.

It bothered Thomas that his lieutenant could be so calm when he felt anything but calm.

"What is her arrangement, if not for marriage? Heaven knows it wouldn't be the first of that sort."

"True, we have seen many arrangements of that sort, but that is not her obligation."

He shouldn't ask. He knew he shouldn't. He waited for Peterson to speak, but the man remained resolutely silent. He finally gave in. "What exactly are her obligations?"

"Dinner."

"I already said I'm not going."

"You misunderstand. Her *obligation* to Captain Barritt is that of a dinner, which you would know if you were not avoiding Miss Gray as one might a diseased rat."

"Dinner? What sort of obligation is that?" He stood and began to pace. He was going to wear a hole through the rug he'd purchased for himself on his first voyage to India.

"Exactly the point. It's such a trifle as to be barely worth mentioning, which is likely why the lady did not. Besides, she feels foolish over the whole affair." Peterson wandered to the desk and lazily flipped through a few of the charts.

"Though I understand her feeling foolish, as she ought if she has any shred of decency, I don't understand anything else you're babbling on about."

"Nor will you if you refuse to speak to her. She will step off this ship, and you will be left undone. For the rest of your life. You'll end up old and alone."

"You are overstepping yourself, sir."

Peterson snapped up a chart, rolled it closed, and pointed it at Thomas. "I am overstepping myself as a lieutenant, but not as a friend. Old and alone is never a pleasant prospect. Believe me. I know what I'm speaking of in this."

Thomas conceded the point.

"Who told you she was obligated to merely dine with the man?"

"She did."

Thomas was sure he'd heard wrong. "You spoke to her regarding this affair?"

"Someone had to, since the man-child she's taken a fancy to has decided to pretend she does not exist on this vessel."

He stopped mid-pace. "What else did she say?"

"Ask her yourself. At least look at her. She has lost herself in this whole business. I am truly worried for her wellbeing." Peterson dropped the rolled chart back to the desk and bowed. "Your presence will be required at dinner." He quitted the room with as much pomp as any officer of the British navy could muster.

They had only five days left of the voyage. He couldn't continue hiding for the rest of the journey. What would his men think? Blast. What were they *already* thinking? He knew they were besotted with Miss Gray; there would be mutiny if he sent her away under a cloud of imagined disgrace.

He had a ship to run, and while he'd made some wonderful progress regarding inspections and ledgers during his time spent away from the passengers, he had not been fit as a leader.

What had Peterson meant by saying she had lost herself? There was only one way to find out.

When he walked into the dining room, Caroline — no, *Miss Gray* — looked up at him and paled as if she'd seen a ghost.

Miss Cole smiled wider than ever as if she had achieved a personal victory at his appearance. Thomas suddenly realized that Mr. Miller's words to him that had cast initial suspicion onto Miss Gray must have come from Miss Cole. Ladies had a gift for knowing the business of other ladies, and

Mr. Miller was not the sort of man to have intelligence of anything that was not spoon-fed to him by another.

His deduction did not leave him with any sort of warmth toward Miss Cole.

When he did not return Miss Cole's smile, she turned her attentions to Mr. Miller and acted as though she'd never even glanced in his direction.

She was a woman not to be trusted in any capacity. He hoped Mr. Miller *did* saddle himself with her. They would make each other perfectly miserable.

He took his seat at the table.

And he sent up a prayer for help in navigating these unknown waters.

"Captain Scott," Miss Gray said quietly. "How nice of you to join us."

That she spoke first startled him. When he turned to respond, he felt saddened by what he saw. In just over a week, she'd gone from a vibrant blossom to a colorless, wilted reed.

"Miss Gray. Are you unwell?"

The merest shadow of a smile crossed her lips. "I thank you for your polite interest, but do not trouble yourself. I am well enough." She lowered her gaze and pushed the food around with her fork.

The rest of the party at the table discussed

their excitement to be on land again and having more space to walk than the few decks allowed to them. Miss Bronley declared she would walk for hours and hours as therapy for her confinement these last months. And Miss Jeffries declared she would never again take for granted the many luxuries of having one's own personal space.

In his own misery, Thomas had forgotten the renewed energy that invigorated the passengers toward the end of the passage. The first week and the last were always the best for the tempers of the people onboard. At least they were for most.

Miss Gray ate little and spoke less. She did not comment when Mr. Miller referred to the political state of Mumbai. She did not seem to be listening to Mr. Liechty as he discussed the success a British doctor had recently experienced in doing a transfusion of human blood. And she did not look his direction at all.

Which made him angry.

How dare she act like the victim in a situation entirely of her own making? How dare she let guilt settle into *his* soul when he'd been the wronged party? His temper brewed until it nearly bubbled over. No. He would not stand for it.

As soon as the meal was through, he said, "Miss Gray, I require your company to visit young Tom. He has asked for you several times over the last week and has wondered why you have stopped visiting him. You promised to give him the drawing you made of him. If you would be so kind?"

She blinked as if waking up from a long and dreadful sleep. Her slow movements pained him, stirring a compassion he did not want. "Tom?"

"Yes. I'm afraid he feels that you've quite neglected him. Clara is waiting for us in the hall." He made sure to add this small white lie to keep the gossiping tongues from wagging.

She nodded. "I will need to fetch my sketchbook."

Once they were in the hall, she didn't mention the absence of Clara, nor did she seem to expect the woman to be where he'd said. She led the way to her cabin, the swish of her skirts the only sound.

He missed that sound. The sound of her laugh, the blush in her cheeks, the feel of her lips on his. He shook away those thoughts and waited outside her cabin while she retrieved the drawing she had promised to give to young Tom. Then they moved down toward the galley where the boy would be cleaning up after the dinner meal.

While they walked, he began. "I am willing to hear your explanation now."

"How generous," she murmured, the words sullen.

A flash of anger burned through his compassion. "Generous? You act like I've beaten you black-and-blue, when you are the one who allowed a connection to form between us when you knew full well that you were not a free woman. You are the one who has obligations that must be met when we arrive. I am not going to let you make me the villain here."

She stopped in the narrow hall. "You think I'm trying to vilify you? The guilt you feel is yours alone, as I have done nothing but stay out of your way these last days. I am tired, *Captain Scott.* And I do not have time to worry if you feel guilt or giddiness because, as you have been so kind to remind me, I have obligations once we are on land. Obligations I am not free to shirk."

He winced when she called him by his full title. However, he preferred this familiar, energetic version of her. He did not like the broken version at all. It did not suit her.

"So then tell me," he said, hating how the storm in her eyes stirred a storm in him. "What exactly is your obligation?"

"Dinner, sir."

So it was exactly as Peterson had stated, though the answer didn't make any more sense from her than it did from his lieutenant. "What does that even mean?"

"It means that Captain Barritt's mother noticed me at a ball. It turns out, I have some charms to recommend me when they are viewed from a comfortable distance. She asked my mother if I had any prospects, to which my mother divulged that I had none since my dear cousin had decided to marry and collect his inheritance — a decision which would leave me homeless and near enough to penniless as not to make any difference."

She stepped closer to him with every sentence, her fury forcing them closer. "His mother proposed an agreement where she would pay for half of my voyage to India to meet her darling son. For my part, I was to get on this ship and, when it lands, get off it again. Then I am to accept an invitation to dine with her son on three separate occasions. Well, four really. There is no other arrangement. Just that. We are not obliged to like one another. And for his part, if he doesn't like me, he is free to release me after the first meeting."

She related the tale with enough energy to

power the sun, and by the time she was done, seemed as furious as he felt. She stood barely a breath away.

"Why didn't you tell me?"

"I was going to if you'd ever given me the chance. It isn't as if I had accepted the man's offer of marriage before coming aboard your ship."

"But you did act as if you would accept *my* offer, if I made any, while you were yet on your way to meet him." And he had planned on making an offer. He had planned on a happiness that now seemed entirely unattainable.

She sagged with his words. "Yes. You're right."

"That matters, you see. A person's word matters to me. A man who is at sea for months out of the year needs to be sure of the woman waiting for him at home. He needs to be certain she *is* waiting. I could never accept one who has shown such vacillation of mind and feeling. I could never be with someone who seems a stranger to the truth."

She blanched, her former energy fading in a flash.

He stiffened, refusing to feel guilt over the truth. Guilt came from lies, and she had lied. He had told the truth. The guilt belonged to her and her alone.

The breath she took quaked her shoulders. "Of course. Of course a person's word matters. It matters to me as well, in spite of my behavior to the contrary. You may choose not to believe it, but I am a friend to the truth. I had allowed myself to believe I still had freedom of choice, but you have reminded me that I do not and will not until things with Captain Barritt are decided. You have reminded me that women seldom have any choice in anything, even in their own lives. Thank you for that reminder."

She stood close to him in the narrow hallway. If he so much as flinched in her direction, he would touch her. He ached to do just that, which was why he stepped back. He needed some room for his mind to clear. "I am not angry, Miss Gray. I want you to know that. And I wish for your every happiness in India."

She nodded, seeming to understand why he'd distanced himself from her, seeming to understand that he was saying there would never again be anything besides distance between them.

"I wish for your happiness as well," she said. "I know my way to the galley. I do not require an escort. I thank you for reminding me of my neglect of young Tom. For my neglect on all parts."

He nodded. Their gazes locked for several moments before he gave a stiff bow, turned, and went the opposite direction. He made it all the way to the wheelhouse before he allowed himself to consider what had transpired.

He had said goodbye. He felt as though a cannonball had been shot through his heart.

"Are you all right?" Peterson asked.

"Of course. I have obligations as well, you know. The sea is a jealous mistress."

"Yes." Peterson's low, sad tone showed he did not approve of the obvious outcome of the interview with Miss Gray. But then again, he wouldn't. Peterson had the heart of a hopeless romantic.

As for Thomas . . . well, with the hole in his chest, it was apparent he had no heart at all.

Not any longer.

When land was sighted, everyone crowded out on deck, pointing and excitedly talking. Their futures had finally caught up to them.

Thomas had his own preparations to make as land neared. As such, he had legitimate reasons to avoid the passengers aside from mealtimes. Miss Gray had resumed some of her earlier liveliness, but something was off regarding her behavior. He couldn't quite explain the difference in her, but he knew there had been one.

It was during dinner on the last night of their time together when he finally managed to pinpoint the difference. While Miss Gray was lively and engaged in conversation, she was not talking about steam power or politics. She was not asking Mr. Liechty to explain medical procedure. She was not locked in a battle of wits with Mr. Miller.

Instead, she was every part a young woman making her formal debut into society. She was all the things he'd witnessed when he'd found himself in London during the season: charming with smiles and attentions, careful in manners and dress, and most of all, quiet when it came to topics usually engaged upon by the men.

If Miss Cole's burning gaze didn't catch the ship on fire by the end of the evening, he would be surprised.

"What are you doing?" he quietly asked Miss Gray when the rest of the table had turned to their own conversations.

"Adapting."

"To what?"

"To society's expectations. What better place to practice than here and now?"

"So you will falsify yourself to others?"

308

"Why not? According to some, I am no friend to truth."

He opened his mouth to protest but was interrupted by Miss Bronley. He did not get another chance at private conversation.

He saw her again on deck. It was late, and the other guests had retired for the night. But Miss Gray leaned on the railing and tilted her face toward the moon as if trying to soak it all up.

He wanted to go down to her, to take her in his arms, to lock her up in her cabin if she gave him any indication that she was willing to return to England with him.

He stayed still.

And watched.

She finally moved, trailing her hand along the railing as she made her way back to the stairs. She kissed her fingertips and pressed them to the door before she opened it and disappeared into the darkness.

I am making a mistake, he thought. But even if he believed himself, he did not do anything to rectify that mistake.

CHAPTER TWENTY-ONE

"I had hoped November might mean cooler weather." Miss Bronley fanned her face as they all stood on deck and looked toward their futures.

"It wasn't cool yesterday. Or the day before that," Miss Jeffries said. "I do wonder if it will ever be cool again."

"It was cool enough at the Cape of Good Hope," Miss Luke said with a shudder. They had all felt like they might freeze to death for those weeks during the unseasonable weather of storms and cold. "Though I cannot say which is worse, that unbearable cold or this unbearable heat."

They watched the shoreline grow larger, and the heat, it seemed, grew in intensity. After a moment, Caroline slipped away from the railing; it was time to say her goodbyes to the friends she had made with the crew.

First was Mr. Black and his wife, Clara.

She handed Clara the drawing of the couple standing in front of the ship's railing with the ocean in the background.

Mr. Black looked at the image and shed real tears. "It's very nice. Quite a talent, Miss Gray. You weren't unlucky at all — even though yer a woman."

Clara cuffed her husband on the shoulder. "Your superstitions, man!" She smiled at Caroline. "Thank you for the fine gift. You managed to make us look respectable."

Caroline smiled back. "You do that without any help from me."

Next, she went to the carpentry shop, then to the ship's surgeon, until finally she was at the galley.

"You are a fine young man," she told Tom as she hugged him fiercely, hating the thought of letting him go.

"I wish you could stay," Tom said.

She thought of the captain, and wished she could stay as well.

The process of docking took an age, but the bell finally rang, indicating they were allowed to disembark.

On land.

She wasn't sure her legs would know what to do without the rise and fall of waves.

"What have I agreed to?" she murmured

311

to herself. Once she left the ship, she would have no choice but to face her new life in this new land. She thought she could handle the adventure, but her roiling stomach protested. She was not up to exploits of any kind. Not any longer.

How am I now sick when I was healthy the whole of the journey? She took deep breaths, willed herself not to vomit, and followed the others down the gangplank.

She did not look back at the wheelhouse. He had called her a deceiver and told her he could not be with her. What more was there for her to say? After all, hadn't she broken her heart over him enough already? The tightness in her chest indicated her body did not think she had.

"Goodbye, Captain Scott," she whispered as she took the last step onto the dock.

After that, there was a flurry of action and no time to mourn her farewell. People were everywhere. The explosion of color — vibrant, and eye-twisting — made her wonder if she'd caught a fever. The various hues somehow felt *louder* than the myriad conversations in languages she did not understand and the noise of animals stamping, clucking, braying, and mooing.

Women dressed in bright skirts and dresses fluttered about the dock like bright birds. Their necks and ears dripped with gold jewelry. Some of the Indian women wore styles that revealed bare stomachs, which made Caroline blush, and she redirected her gaze to the hills rising beyond the harbor. After collecting herself, she turned her attention back to the people on the dock around her. Perspiration slid down between her shoulders, which she squared in order to gain control of her emotions. Everyone moved with a great sense of purpose, all of them seeming to know what they were about.

She did not know what she was about. She stood on the dock and clutched the letter from Mrs. Barritt that she was to give to a Mrs. Annabelle Williams. Mrs. Barritt had arranged lodging with Mrs. Williams for whichever woman she would be sending to India to meet her son. Mrs. Barritt had been plotting the arrangement of her son's future for many months, it seemed.

But Caroline wondered if those plans had fallen apart during the many months it had taken for her to actually arrive on land. Would Mrs. Williams greet her at the dock? Mrs. Barritt had assured her she would. How hard would the woman be to find? And if she was found, how willing would she be to take Caroline under her wing?

She was grateful her mother had sent her with a small purse that would prevent immediate homelessness. If no one came to collect her, she could arrange lodging at an inn while she figured out how to proceed. She didn't have much, but enough to survive for several weeks.

It turned out she needn't have worried. A rather large contingent of well-dressed English women surrounded the six women who had been passengers on the *Persistence.* They inspected the women as if they were at market and looking to make a purchase.

Introductions were quickly made, and each of the women with whom Caroline had spent the last several months left the dock. Caroline waved to Miss James and Miss Jeffries as they were collected and taken away. She felt a sense of loss without them. But she did not allow herself to give in to the melancholy. Caroline identified Mrs. Williams among those ladies and immediately handed her Mrs. Barritt's letter.

Mrs. Williams's smile encompassed the whole of her narrow face when she saw the flowing script on the envelope. "Dearest Alison Barritt! How I miss her." She tucked the letter into her reticule and pursed her lips. "Well, dear, let us have a look at you."

She wasn't old, but her hair and clothing were out of fashion enough to age her several years. Her sharp gaze made Caroline feel as though she'd been pricked by a needle.

Mrs. Williams circled her, making little murmurs that could be either approval or criticism. When she'd completed her circuit, she looked to Caroline with a wry smile. "Well! However did Alison manage to get someone like you on that ship?"

Caroline did not pretend to misunderstand what the lady meant. She knew her outward appearance to be pleasing enough. But she felt uncomfortable with the way the lady stared and then smiled and then stared and smiled some more.

At length, Caroline's trunks were collected by a small contingent of Indian men in turbans. And suddenly they were surrounded by several small children whose appearance bore enough resemblance to Mrs. Williams that she had to be their mother. The children begged Mrs. Williams to stay until the ship had been emptied of its cargo.

Caroline worried Mrs. Williams would give in to their requests. She did not wish to stay near the *Persistence* and its captain any longer than necessary. But an Indian woman clucked at the children and said something Caroline did not understand. The children fell into line behind the woman and their mother and they were off, weaving their way through the chaos of the dock.

The children and the woman Caroline believed to be their governess took a separate carriage. As Mrs. Williams watched the carriage drive away, she frowned. "Their *ayah* is far too lenient with them. And I do not like that she speaks Hindi to my children rather than English. I'll have to do something about that."

Caroline didn't know what to say to such a statement. She'd never heard anyone outside her own relatives ever complain publicly regarding domestic affairs. She busied herself by straightening her skirts while settling into the carriage. Mrs. Williams said no more.

After an exchange of only a few sentences, Caroline realized this woman would be nothing like the mother she missed.

The carriage took them away from the dock, away from her captain and the ship she'd grown to love. A blasting trumpet sounded, and she clutched the side of the carriage tightly as she hastily looked to her left. An elephant stood just off the road by a grove of trees. She had read about the animals and seen sketches — Arnav had even given her a small carving — but she never thought she would see one with her own eyes. A man in a white turban sat on its back just behind its ears and looked as regal as King George himself.

"Oh!" she exclaimed, consumed by wonder.

"They are noisy, to be sure." Mrs. Williams twisted her mouth in distaste, apparently impervious to the charms of the creature and its master.

In spite of Mrs. Williams's dour expression, Caroline was fast falling in love with the beauty of the land that was destined to be her home for the foreseeable future. Caroline regretting having packed away her sketchbook in her trunk.

At the house, the children and their *ayah* were nowhere to be seen, though Mrs. Williams didn't seem to be troubled by their absence. She showed Caroline to a small room upstairs — a room with no door — where she immediately set about detailing the house rules.

"I do not abide animals in the house, so keep your windows shuttered if you are not directly at them. An open window invites monkeys, snakes, and all varieties of animals. A woman in Kolkata left a window open on the first floor of her home, and she ended up with a leopard in her parlor. She was very lucky to have survived to tell the tale. You'll be sure to follow this rule, won't you?"

Mrs. Williams then gave instructions for mealtimes, and for how the servants were to be addressed, and for the absolute need for dressing appropriately for dinner. She gave instructions on how Caroline was to behave during dinnertime. She made derogatory remarks regarding other ladies who flaunted their personal achievements and other unladylike behaviors and fixed Caroline with a narrowed eye.

"You are not one of those sorts of women, are you? I have not brought such absurdity under my roof, have I?"

Caroline wasn't sure how to respond because she felt certain she was exactly the sort of woman Mrs. Williams would have dismissed as absurd. She merely smiled. It must have been a sufficient answer because the lady continued her instructions.

She spoke for what felt the better part of an hour while they both stood in the heat. Caroline grew tired, and it seemed the world under her feet still moved to the rhythm of the waves.

At length, Mrs. Williams left her alone, telling her that a servant would come fetch her when it was time for tea.

Caroline seized the opportunity and sank heavily to the white coverlet of her bed and closed her eyes. She slept, but her dreams were disturbed by fretful images of the captain drowning in a great storm, of the ship sinking, of her world spinning and spinning and spinning.

She awoke soaked to the skin from her own perspiration. A dark-faced woman peered down at her. Caroline gasped at the surprise of having someone watching her and grabbed at the thin bed curtain as she scrambled to a sitting position.

"Sorry, *memsahib*. It is time for tea," the woman said.

The words were English, but the heavy accent forced Caroline to repeat the words in her head several times before they made sense to her. "Of course. Tea. Thank you."

The woman nodded and left.

Caroline went down after freshening up as best she could, feeling a great degree of concern about Mrs. Williams, who was clearly a marked traditionalist and who appeared to have an unyielding personality. What was she to say to such a woman? Especially considering how much she owed the woman for not abandoning her at the dock.

She joined Mrs. Williams, who was already seated in the parlor.

Mrs. Williams poured the tea and smiled. "So, tell me everything about the other ladies who were passengers with you. I want to know everything."

Caroline had not anticipated her first real conversation to be a discussion of the other ladies who had traveled with her on the *Persistence.* Caroline was careful in the details she related. Gossip revealed far more about the one who shared it than it did about the subject. And though she did not necessarily like all the ladies who had served as her companions during the voyage, she did not wish any of them ill.

Mrs. Williams, however, did not hesitate to share her own gossip regarding those who took in the other ladies from the *Persistence.*

Rather than respond to any of Mrs. Williams's snide or less-favorable remarks, Caroline said, "To take in any of us is generous indeed. The hospitality of the ladies here in Mumbai is quite astonishing."

"You mean the boredom is quite astonishing." Mrs. Williams took a sip from her teacup. "We quite nearly fight for the right to have guests of a certain repute stay with us. New society is rare. We see the same people every day. We have the same conversations every day. We tell the same stories, embroider the same patterns, drink the same tea. It's exhausting.

"The only bright part of our lives is when a ship comes in with new trinkets, new needles, new patterns for dresses, new people. You'll see. Once the thrill of the chase is over and you've been caught and settled into a proper marriage, you will also come to love the day a ship comes." She set down her teacup and leaned forward slightly. "Now. Tell me everything. What is happening at home?"

After a short time discussing England and all the current events that had at least been current at the time Caroline had left, it occurred to Caroline that Mrs. Williams wasn't so much a cruel and unrelenting traditionalist so much as she was terribly lonely and afraid. The longing she felt for England was clear in her eyes as Caroline fed her bits of societal gossip and the latest in face creams and hairstyles. Mrs. Williams yearned for a life she had not seen in many years. She went on and on about missing snow, of all things, and the soft, silent way it fell outside the windows of her home in Ipswich while the fire blazed brightly inside.

Will I be like this someday? Caroline wondered. *Will I someday bend the ear of a poor newcomer to hear any details of the world I've lost?*

She didn't know. Though she found the little she'd seen so far charming, how long would such enchantment last? It hadn't for Mrs. Williams — if it had ever been there at all.

She listened as her hostess spoke of her life in Mumbai as well as her former life in England. Mrs. Williams used to be Mrs. Corbett. Her late husband had died of dengue fever, and Mr. Williams had proposed to her less than a week after her husband's funeral, and they were married less than two weeks after that. She told Caroline all of this matter-of-factly as if there was nothing strange or horrendously inappropriate at all in having no time for mourning.

The whole conversation stirred Caroline's sympathy, and she felt the woman's lot in life to be pitiable. Mrs. Williams did not even seem to take much joy in her children.

Caroline was glad to have tea come to an end so she could mourn what could have been with Thomas. She asked if she might see the gardens and was given permission to do so, but not before being reminded of the several invitations that had already arrived for her to attend this dinner and that ball.

Mrs. Williams was also quick to remind her that her first loyalties were to Captain Barritt. Caroline's first meeting with Captain Barritt would be at dinner the next night. She felt loathing at hearing his name, knowing what that name had brought to her and what it had cost her.

But no. She would not give in to her despair.

Caroline lifted her chin, determined to make the best of her new situation. She also felt determined to never resort to gossip to alleviate any possible boredom with life in India or the melancholy from the life lived before. She would push forward and find happiness.

Her mother had told her to find love, and she had — though she'd had to let it go. Now, she must do what she could to find some other way to love. Even if her marriage became a business arrangement as had happened for Mrs. Williams, there would be children. And if nothing else, she would love them.

The next evening, they attended dinner with a rather large party at Colonel Eden's home.

Miss Jeffries was present, which delighted Caroline. Miss Cole was also present, which did not delight Caroline. She was sorry not to see Miss James among those of the party. She thought of Mrs. Williams saying that the society was small and therefore tedious. She had thought her society would grow once she quit the ship, but here she was, surrounded by faces she already knew.

There were differences, however. The men outnumbered the ladies three to one, which made for a startling difference to how things were back in England.

Captain Barritt was also present.

She was surprised, and also relieved, to find he was pleasant to look upon. His mass of dark curls gave him a boyish sort of charm. He had a straight nose and smiled with teeth that were also fairly straight. He bowed low over her hand when Mrs. Williams introduced them. There was no missing the intent behind her words as she said, "Here is a young lady brought all this way because your mother felt you must have an introduction."

Did Captain Barritt know his mother had handpicked him a prospective bride?

If he minded his mother's tampering, he made no sign of it as he smiled. "Miss Gray, how lovely to meet you."

"I am pleased to meet you as well."

"At this first impression, was I worth the trouble?"

Caroline faltered, searching for the right words. "I'm afraid I don't understand the question."

He laughed, a lilting sound so different from the gruff, throaty laugh of the captain — *her* captain.

Stop it, she scolded herself. *Do not make comparisons. They will only hurt each man. And yourself.*

"You came an awfully long way, did you not? Surely, you've already passed judgment on whether or not the journey was worth it." With his next laugh came a teasing glint in his eyes, which relaxed her.

"To ask for an answer puts me at a disadvantage. If I am pleased, saying so would make your possible desire to spend more time with me far too easy. If I am disappointed, saying so would make my possible desire to spend less time with you far too difficult. So I will say nothing. But I will smile." Which she did.

She continued smiling as Captain Barritt laughed and declared her to be lovely and witty. Perhaps this match could work.

She stopped smiling when Thomas entered the room.

His face, pink from a fresh shave, swirled in her all the emotions she had been determined to forget. His coat looked fresh and new; she had not seen him wear it on the ship. She thought about the time she had tugged the lapels of his coat to bring his face in closer to hers —

"Are you all right?" Captain Barritt asked, reminding her that she'd been staring across the room. "If this gentleman upsets you, I could have Colonel Eden ask him to leave."

"No!" Caroline placed a hand on his arm. "No one has upset me."

Though it pained her to see Captain Scott, she would rather be in pain than to have him leave. Seeing him felt like seeing home in this foreign land. But though she wanted very much to call that man her home, he had declared it would never be.

As for Captain Barritt, once she had her hand on his arm, he seemed to forget anything else. He placed his hand on top of hers and gave a comforting pat. She could not say why his action bothered her. Many a man had done a similar thing over the course of the years she'd spent at balls and at dinner parties. It was one of the few intimacies a chaperoned woman could possibly hope to enjoy.

She could not remove her hand without

looking foolish or without drawing Thomas's attention. Perhaps he was why she was troubled. She did not want it to seem like she was throwing herself at Captain Barritt.

Except . . . Wasn't her moving on *his* fault?

Irritation bubbled and brewed within her belly. Thomas had been the one to say goodbye. So what did she care of his presence? Her goal this evening was to become acquainted with Captain Barritt, continue her friendship with Miss Jeffries, and avoid Miss Cole — if it all possible.

She had seen dozens upon dozens of young ladies flirt so easily that men fell over themselves to win their hands. Tonight, she would do the same. She would not talk about politics or inventions. She would not insert herself into conversations that were considered reserved for men. She would be lovely tonight. She would make certain Nicholas Barritt would want to see her a second time. She would fulfill the obligation for which Captain Scott had abandoned her.

And so she smiled until her cheeks hurt, laughed at jokes she didn't necessarily find amusing, and kept her teeth tightly clenched to keep herself from revealing too much about herself.

While she smiled, Thomas frowned. She

hated how often their gazes met. She hated that he noticed her behavior. She hated how she imagined him hating her.

The only thing that gave Caroline any source of pleasure was watching Miss Jeffries, who was seated across from Mr. Apsley. He was neither young nor old but was, by all appearances, enamored with her. The two of them blushed and smiled their way through three courses.

Caroline could not help but smile as well while watching them.

"Oh, my fair Mona Lisa," Captain Barritt whispered near her ear. "What is it that makes her smile, I wonder."

She drew back slightly, not appreciating his sudden nearness. "Do you compare me to the work of Da Vinci?"

Captain Barritt leaned back in his chair and swirled the amber liquid in his glass. "Is there another in this room who matches her beauty? Or is there another in this room smiling so mysteriously? I daresay there is not. It must be you."

His calling her mysterious made her glance down the table and meet the watchful gaze of Miss Cole.

For Caroline's part, she had never seen the *Mona Lisa*. She very much doubted that Captain Barritt had seen it either, but she did not call attention to his possible misrepresentation since the compliment was all hers.

After dinner, they brought out tables for cards. Captain Scott declined to play, and Caroline was paired with Captain Barritt. She looked to Miss Jeffries, hopeful she and Mr. Apsley would make the other pair, but was saddened to see the couple had already been seated at another table.

Miss Cole, seeing the vacancy at Caroline's table, was quick to join them.

With no other choice, Caroline settled in for the game of whist. Her neck ached from forcing herself to not turn to check to see where Captain Scott stood in the room, to see if he was talking to someone or if he had left altogether. When he did leave, she felt the sensation as a prickling along her skin. She thought she would feel some relief at his absence. She thought it might free her to more fully relax into the role of flirt.

It only made her sad, as though the light in the room had been dimmed by half.

She returned her attention to the table as they started another round.

"You're so different," Miss Cole said, looking at her cards.

"Different, Miss Cole?"

"Yes. You did not say one word to Captain

Scott when he came in. Nor did you say anything to him the whole of the evening. Were you not great friends during the voyage?"

"We were friends, but to no greater or lesser degree than anyone else who made up the passenger list of the *Persistence*."

"But to ignore him entirely? It's all so strange. I wonder what it could mean."

While dying on the inside with Thomas now gone, Caroline forced cheerfulness to reign supreme on the outside. "Perhaps I was merely so preoccupied by my new acquaintance that everything else quite escaped my notice."

Captain Barritt beamed at the suggestion. Miss Cole glowered.

The woman soon gave up trying to bait Caroline into a misstep in favor of trying to work her own charms. As soon as the second game ended, Caroline excused herself from the table. Captain Barritt attempted to follow her, but Miss Cole managed to keep him with her as she regaled him with her experiences of crossing the equator.

Caroline stepped out onto the balcony that overlooked Colonel Eden's gardens and breathed deeply of air unfettered by gentlemen and ladies trying too hard to impress.

She lifted her face to the moonlight and enumerated all she had lost. First her mother, sister, and home, and then Thomas and the *Persistence*. She supposed she would be married by the time Thomas returned, considering that Captain Barritt seemed interested in her, and considering how he seemed amiable and informed enough to be someone she could like. Not that she would make a decision after a single meeting. Still, she was glad to be able to say she liked him.

All while loving another.

Like a ghost conjured from her thoughts, Thomas stepped out of the shadows.

CHAPTER TWENTY-TWO

Thomas had spent the better part of two days trying to discover all he could regarding Corbeau. After Corbeau had been escorted off the ship, Abramson had slipped after him to see where the man slept, ate, gambled, and drank. Abramson had not yet returned to the inn with any intelligence, which worried Thomas. He hoped the man hadn't run into trouble.

The former cook's laughter still rang in Thomas's ears. He was determined to stay alert while remaining in port. He asked Peterson to stay with young Tom. He worried the lad might be a target for his former master.

When he arrived back at the inn after visiting several of the less-reputable establishments near port, he had no messages from Abramson. He did, however, have an invitation to dinner at Colonel Eden's home. He wanted to decline, but Colonel Eden had

helped him make the appropriate trade con-
nections necessary for him to be successful
in shipping and cargo. Not attending was
not an option.

When he'd arrived and seen Caroline,
he'd wished he *had* declined the invitation.
She had barely glanced at him, had refused
to speak to him beyond a slight inclination
of her head, and, worst of all, she had put
her hand on Nicholas Barritt's arm.

Captain Barritt was the single most unde-
serving man in all of India, if reputations
were to be believed — which Thomas did.
He'd checked the man's reputation as soon
as he'd arrived in India, and learned Barritt
was the conceited sort of man who would
want a pretty woman on his arm. A pretty
woman who remained firmly in her place
lower than him.

Thomas had planned on leaving as soon
as would have been socially polite, but he
could not leave without warning Miss Gray
that this young man was not worth the
trouble of her pretense.

He'd planned on waiting until the card
tables were put away; he'd have no chance
of speaking privately to Miss Gray during
such games. He'd gone out to the balcony
for some air, when the lady herself took up
a position by the railing, her face turned

toward the moon.

He stepped forward before he could stop himself. "I never thought to see something that could compete with the stars at night. But then I saw you standing here."

She did not startle at his approach, but neither did she turn to face him directly. She merely glanced at him from the corner of her eyes as if to verify it was really him. "That is a dangerously flirtatious thing for you to say to me."

"To admire beauty is no crime. And it was not a flirtation. It was the truth."

"There are three sides to every story. There is your side. There is my side. And then there is the truth. What you have said is your side. My side would take it as flirting. The truth . . . ."

"And what is the truth?" he asked.

She finally turned to him, her expression unreadable. "I'm surprised you dare ask me such a question since you find my friendship with truth to be so relaxed."

He breathed out his own frustration with the sarcasm she threw at him.

Despite her apparent anger, she answered his original question. "Truth is somewhere in between, I suppose."

Strands of her hair had escaped her pins and clung to her neck in the heat of the night. But unlike the other women, she did not constantly wave a fan at her face and neck. She simply bore the heat without complaint. Much as she bore the distance he had imposed upon her before trespassing back into her life.

"I was surprised to see you this evening," she said. "Are you not heading back to England immediately?"

"No, actually. I will stay for a few weeks while my cargo is acquired and loaded."

"You're staying? In Mumbai?" Her disbelief and displeasure was apparent in her rigid posture and tight lips. It looked like she was planning on forcing him back to his ship and sending him straight back to England.

So. She must have taken a liking to the Barritt fellow, or she would not have been so anxious to see him go.

He shouldn't have cared. He knew that. He should not have given one whit how she felt. Hadn't he been the one to tell her they had no chance together? Hadn't he been the one to say there could never be anything between them because she had not been honest at the front?

Yes. But blast, he still hated it.

"So," he began again. "Nicholas Barritt."

"Yes." The word exited her mouth with an

abruptness that meant she had anticipated his objections. "He is the one whose mother sent me."

He fidgeted, a thing he had stopped doing in childhood after his father glared him into standing still. "I don't think he's a good match for you."

Her eyebrows shot up.

He hurried on, saying, "I mean this as a friend when I say that Nicholas Barritt is a man best left avoided. His reputation is one of a gambler and of a man seen in houses of ill repute. I advise you to dispatch your obligation to him quickly and find a more suitable arrangement elsewhere."

"Tell me. Do you have more suitable suggestions for me? Is there perhaps a list you've drawn up of which I am unaware?"

He rocked back on his heels and stuffed his hands in his pockets. "No. I am not renewing our relationship if that is what you mean by more suitable suggestions. I only —"

"I most certainly did not mean for you to renew anything between *us*. Captain Scott, I am working very hard to make my own way here and to form my own opinions. I would be happy if you respected that."

"Miss Gray, I only meant you would not be happy with a man for whom you must make yourself absurd."

"You're calling me absurd?"

"You're behaving like a girl at her debut ball."

Her mouth thinned to a tight slash across her face. "Well. Perhaps you are right. Perhaps I am behaving as such."

He felt the briefest relief that she'd finally seen sense until she added, "But perhaps if I had behaved as such when at my first ball, we would have both been spared a great deal of inconvenience, for I would have had no need to have been a passenger on your ship."

"The inconvenience did not come from you being a passenger. It came from you not being forthcoming about prior commitments. It came from your estrangement with the truth." He clamped his mouth closed as soon as the words were out. He hadn't meant to say them aloud. He felt them, but he should not have said them. Not again.

"I believe I have offered my apologies for that. I would hope you could offer your forgiveness."

He didn't respond. He wasn't even sure how he could.

"Please, Captain Scott," she said, her tone soft, her eyes dull with something like exhaustion and irritation and hurt. "You are

337

not in a position to make suggestions or recommendations. You've made your opinions clear regarding how you feel about me, which makes me no longer your concern."

He had not expected that. He should have, but he hadn't. He had also not expected his own anger. "Don't be foolish and discard solid information merely because it wounds your vanity. You cannot pretend to appreciate illumination and then insist on sitting in the darkness out of sheer stubborn pride."

The hurt in her eyes melted into fury. He expected to be thrashed about by her response when a voice from the doorway called out. "There you are!"

They both turned to where Nicholas Barritt stood. He leaned against the doorframe and appeared casual, but the captain had heard enough rumors to believe Barritt was incapable of casual behavior toward anything he was set on acquiring. And from the look in the man's eyes as they settled on Miss Gray, he was very much set on acquiring a bride.

She gave him a playful tilt of her head. "Why, I'm flattered you were looking for me."

"I would imagine all of England has been looking for you from the moment you stepped onto the ship that brought you here."

For pity's sake, how could any woman with any degree of sense fall for such a ridiculous line? It wasn't even that clever. Not that his line of comparing her to the stars had been so original, but it was not so ridiculous either. He glanced at Miss Gray to verify she had seen through the man's absurdity, but she'd begun walking toward Barritt.

He wanted to call her back, but she had already told him that she believed herself no longer his concern. She was wrong, of course. Just because he felt he could not marry her did not mean he wished for her to go to the likes of a man like Barritt.

She reached Barritt's side and took his outstretched arm.

As they went inside together, he heard Barritt say with a laugh, "It sounded like you were arguing."

Thomas's fists clenched.

She did not laugh. "No," she said. "We were merely saying goodbye." She looked back at him, her expression one of painful determination.

It bothered him that she did not take his advice. It bothered him that he felt so keen to give advice. He groaned at his own foolishness and followed them into the house. It was time to bid farewell to Colonel Eden and get back to the inn. Perhaps Abramson had returned. Even if he hadn't, Thomas had no desire to stay and watch Miss Gray make herself ridiculous to a man who was not worth the trouble.

Back at the inn, Abramson sat in the common room with a drink in his hand and a rag to his forehead. His split lip seeped blood down his chin, and his purpled eye swelled.

"You look like I feel," Thomas said. "What happened?"

"I was jumped from behind at some squalid little inn not too far from the docks. Actually, I cannot know for certain that it was an inn. More likely it was a brothel that permits long-term guests. I wasn't sure Corbeau was there before, but I'm quite sure now."

"How do you know this isn't the work of street thugs?" Thomas indicated the battered face.

"As they tackled me, one of them called out to a third to tell Corbeau he was being followed."

"Blast!"

Abramson smiled and then winced as his

cut in his lip widened. "Are you really worried that he reached Corbeau to relay the message?"

Warily, Thomas said, "Did he not?"

"I'm offended, sir. Do you not remember that I can kill a man three different ways with my bare hands?"

"Did you?"

Abramson lifted a shoulder as he tossed back his drink. "Of course not. One doesn't have to kill a man to render him inoperable. They are all snug in a cell and unlikely to see the light of day until we are well out to sea."

"And Corbeau? What of him?"

Abramson's grin turned to a grimace. "We know where he is. And we know he is up to mischief or else he wouldn't need to be concerned with being followed. What we don't know is whether that mischief involves you or something else equally nefarious. I will keep a watch on him."

"Are you in any condition to continue your duties?"

"I think the bruises give me a more devil-may-care look. I'm sure to be the favorite of all the balls, which is why I shall stay away from them. I would hate to give the rest of you such fierce competition for the ladies' affections."

341

His comment made Thomas sigh.

Abramson grunted and slid his glass to Thomas. "That bad, is it?"

"Ladies are notoriously bad for a sailor. Remind me of that the next time I allow my gaze to linger too long on one."

"Are we speaking of a particular lady who happened to have been a passenger recently?"

Thomas's small smile faltered. "She's with Nicholas Barritt tonight."

"No! Not really? And he's interested?"

Thomas swirled the golden liquid around in the glass. "I would say more than interested. He was a man at market and ready to buy."

"I daresay Barritt has no idea what he's getting himself into. Of course, I have seen India take the fight out of a woman — maybe it's the heat or the insects — but I've seen it put the fight into a woman, as well. We'll see which sort of woman Miss Gray is next time we're in Mumbai."

Next time they were in Mumbai.

Abramson meant when they returned and Thomas found Miss Gray either married and docile or married and kicking against the pricks. Peterson would not have let her go so easily. Peterson would have told him to go to her, fling her over his shoulder, and cart her back to his ship like a Viking warrior of old.

But how could he? A pretty face and a keen mind were admirable, but they were not enough. Trust. Loyalty. Faithfulness. Those were the things that made a marriage.

No. He'd made the right choice. He even wished her well in whatever life-altering choice she must make in her near future. For it would be her near future — Barritt wouldn't want to wait long before claiming his prize.

Thomas turned the conversation back to Corbeau as he and his lieutenant tried to guess what the man could be up to. With supplies coming from the subcontinent, he worried for the safety of his future cargo and the men bringing it to him. He had cloth, indigo, and a variety of spices that he'd already spent a fair amount of money acquiring because he had a buyer in England who was willing to pay top prices for the goods.

To lose this particular shipment would be to lose everything he had worked so hard to achieve.

He drained the rest of Abramson's glass. He needed to get his ship loaded and leave

the trouble of mutiny and women behind.
The sooner the better.

CHAPTER TWENTY-THREE

Caroline had been to dinner with Captain Barritt twice and had taken several rides with him as well as walks in the city. She would see him again that night for a ball, and she found herself pleased with the prospect.

He was not overly clever, but neither was he overly stupid. Caroline found him to be amusing more often than not, but she had also seen his anger flare at his servants over minor mistakes. She hardly knew what to make of his character.

Her father had always been generous to those in his employ.

She tried to politely inquire after Captain Barritt's character, but the only people she could ask were those within his own circle of friends, so every report was glowing. But still, he could not be so wicked if he had so many friends. She tried to focus on his positive qualities rather than dwell on those

345

things that needled her. Captain Scott had warned her of Captain Barritt's less-desirable qualities, but how could she trust a man with information when she had not been able to trust him with her heart?

Captain Barritt meant security if she chose him. She was certain *he* had chosen her. His decision manifested in his every action toward her: in the flowers he left for her after riding in his curricle and in the attention he paid her when they were together. He listened as she spoke delightedly of the things she saw as they walked through the marketplace — the fruits and vegetables mounded high on carts, the baskets of spices overflowing with the heady fragrance of curry and cinnamon mingled with tube-roses and jasmine.

He was patiently indulgent as she stopped to sketch monkeys and birds. When she watched as a craftsman pounded out brass bowls and goblets and the sort of jewelry that so many of the women wore, he bought her a bracelet and insisted on being the one to latch it around her wrist.

Yes. He had definitely chosen her.

She also felt the shadow of that choice in the way he paraded her on his arm and glared down any other man who ventured too near. And there were many men who did, stalking her like hunters might their prey. It was a wonder to have so many gentlemen expressing such interest. Caroline felt as she had during her first season, before her reputation haunted her every step. But those men during her first season in London had not known her, and these men here did not either. They saw only what she dared show them. Her long voyage over the sea surrounded by other ladies of society had taught her how to behave.

How to pretend.

Thus, she had not revealed everything about herself to Captain Barritt. While she allowed him to see her active interest in the world around her, she did not tread into those topics that were not considered polite for ladies. She did not ask about the solutions the tanners slathered over the hides stretched out in the sun. She did not ask where the brass and other metals were mined. She did not inquire about the many different religions and societal hierarchies she observed.

She ached to know the whole of everything. She wanted to know about the spices and the flowers and the elephants and the people. She wanted to talk to everyone, the Indians who clamored to sell their wares from their carts and tiny shops and those who stood silently tugging the rope of the great fans that were so common in English households.

What would Captain Barritt do if he married her and discovered that the puddle he'd stepped into was actually an ocean? Would he be angry? A man had a right to expect his wife to act in a manner that pleased him. At least that was what all the ladies of her acquaintance said, and that was what all the men believed.

She was grateful that her father had been pleased by his wife's behavior, had even encouraged it. How different Caroline's life would have been if he'd been repelled by his wife's brazen behavior.

The one man who had not been repelled by Caroline's true self was also not willing to have her.

Do not think of him, she scolded herself. But she did. The hurt from his rejection deepened and spread like an infection in her blood. He had said he could not have a woman he could not trust. He had called her such a woman. It proved he did not know her any better than the men of the *ton* had known her.

Do not think of him. She had someone in front of her who had not turned her away. That gentleman needed to be her focus.

348

Ironically, just as Thomas had warned her away from Captain Barritt, Captain Barritt had warned her away from Thomas.

"He treats those in his employ worse than dogs," Captain Barritt had declared.

She had laughed and replied, "I can safely say after months at sea with the man and watching him interact with those in his employ that they are treated quite well."

Captain Barritt had gone on for several minutes, sharing more rumors of Thomas designed to make her think ill of the man. When she easily refuted each rumor, Captain Barritt finally let the matter drop.

She assumed Miss Cole had been the source of his rumors, but since her own reputation as a know-all bluestocking had not yet been spread, it seemed the woman had remained silent.

For now.

The two weeks she'd spent in her suitor's company felt both too long and too short.

The problem with her visits from Captain Barritt were that they were not nearly long enough. When she was with him, it meant she could be away from Mrs. Williams and her unyielding opinions regarding Caroline's desire to venture into the city.

"You'll catch something if you keep insisting on spending time with the natives, even if it's only fleas," the woman had said.

Caroline had recoiled at the sneering cruelty in such words. Did the woman have no Christian feeling?

Mrs. Williams warned Caroline over and over that the Indian people were not to be trusted, and eventually compelled her to take a guard with her when she went past the neat lines that marked the part of town the British people claimed as their own.

The guard's name was Balvan, and he turned out to be a delightful companion as, after she put him at ease regarding her expectations of him, he answered her questions more freely and more fully than she had ever hoped. She liked him immediately and considered him one of the few friends she had in India.

One day, as she prepared to leave on another tour with Balvan, she heard shouting.

She walked downstairs to find the front doors open to the courtyard despite Mrs. Williams's rules.

Caroline moved to get a closer look when Mrs. Williams appeared at her left and shut the door, muffling the sounds from outside.

"Come, Miss Gray." Mrs. Williams took hold of Caroline's arm and forcibly guided her into the parlor.

"What is happening?"

"Miss Gray, these people have their own ways, their own traditions. All you need know is that Balvan can no longer work for my household, which is a terrible inconvenience as now I must find a new guard." Her forehead creased and her lips puckered with irritation.

Her inconvenience?

"Mrs. Williams, what can we do to help Balvan?" Caroline felt quite distressed.

Mrs. Williams cut her hand through the air to end the discussion. "It has nothing to do with us."

She acted as though that was the end of the conversation.

"But certainly it does. If he can no longer work for you, what of his future? His family?"

Mrs. Williams sniffed, her mouth pursing tighter, deepening her wrinkles. "Ladies do not discuss such matters." She gestured for Caroline to sit in the parlor, then she sent for tea.

"You were sent here for Captain Barritt." She settled her hands in her lap and cast her cold, calculating gaze on Caroline. "I wonder how well his mother knew you before she sent you."

Mrs. Barritt had not known Caroline at all, so she remained silent.

She was a guest in this woman's home. And more, she keenly felt the necessity of maintaining this woman's good opinion of her. A single word from Mrs. Williams could send Captain Barritt in a different direction, and, if Captain Barritt and Caroline *did* reach an agreement, she knew Mrs. Williams would certainly be in communication with her mother-in-law and send back reports of her behavior.

"I must remind you, Miss Gray, that in England, a bluestocking with an audacious spirit isn't the most disgraceful thing a woman can be."

Caroline nearly laughed. Mrs. Williams clearly had never been a woman of intelligence and audacious spirit in England, or she would know how wrong she was.

"Here," she continued, "things are not the same. Here, you will be an example to others when you become a wife. New brides will look to you to guide their own actions. We, all of us, know our roles. Do you understand?"

She forced herself to show some semblance of control and nodded, because that was what was expected. Mrs. Williams also nodded as if ending the discussion. Except there was more.

Thus began a lengthy lesson on how British wives were expected to behave. Some of the rules Caroline understood as they were the same in England. Discussion of politics was simply not allowed. But other forbidden topics made no sense. They could not discuss the arts. Conversation regarding literature would make her an outcast of society in India.

Caroline could converse about sports, which she was expected to love, about servants, which she was expected to rule with a tight hand, and about children, which she was expected to have as soon as possible after marriage.

And which she was expected to send away as soon as they were old enough.

"You mean send them to England?"

"Of course. For school."

She had heard of children in such arrangements, but the entire concept bothered her more than she could say. To be so far from one's children . . . Could they not come home at all?

"I don't know how I —"

"Oh, but you will. No child of Captain Nicholas Barritt would ever be allowed to gain an education anywhere else. The Barritts would never allow it."

"But holidays . . ." Caroline persisted.

"They will stay with their grandparents, of course. If it's convenient for Mr. and Mrs. Barritt."

Mrs. Williams never seemed to consider that Caroline had a mother and a sister in England who would want to be involved in the lives of Caroline's children.

The idea that her possible future children would be gone left her wounded.

The tea had gone cold, but the lessons marched on. Mrs. Williams appeared determined to make Caroline into a wife that would make King and Country proud. Caroline felt worse with every passing word.

Caroline only managed to escape because Captain Barritt was coming for her, and she had to ready herself for the ball, which took a great deal longer to prepare for than if it had been a simple ride in a curricle.

With her head full of worry for Balvan, endless lectures of propriety and behavior, and thoughts of a ball made her wonder what she would be like in a year of living in such a society. What would she be like in five years? Would she be the sort of mother who would *want* to send her children away?

She looked at her reflection in her mirror and shuddered as she thought she saw Mrs. Williams staring back at her.

CHAPTER TWENTY-FOUR

Thomas hated that his attendance was required at social gatherings where people fawned and swooned over each other. But he had business ties that required him to play his part.

For the two weeks he'd been in port, he'd only run into Miss Gray once, but he'd heard of her nearly everywhere he went, whispers of the lovely, new lady who had caught Nicholas Barritt's eye. People expected an announcement soon. Many were surprised the pair were not already married as Barritt was a man of decisive action. Such was the way of things in India among the English. Speedy marriages and speedier gossip.

But the gossips did not know how stifled this new lady would feel existing among this section of British society. What would they do to her when they discovered her brilliant mind and fiery spirit?

Worse, Lieutenant Abramson discovered that Corbeau worked for Miss Gray's new suitor. They had not determined what kind of work Corbeau was doing exactly as he had met with several people during his time in port who paid him, but the former cook had yet to actually do anything to make him worth the money that passed to his hands beyond maligning Thomas's good name to anyone who would listen.

His head hurt thinking of it all. He needed to retrieve his supply shipment and return to England.

It was time for everyone to move on.

He was late to the ball. Truth be told, he was almost always late to every social gathering. The local English considered his tardiness eccentric rather than rude. He felt their acceptance of him had more to do with the news and goods he brought from home than their actually being charmed with his habits, but he didn't care.

So when he showed up to Mrs. Whitehouse's ball while it was in its full splendor of color and music, he was in decent spirits. Corbeau was all threat and no bite. Thomas had received word that his supply train was in fine shape and on its way to him. And thoughts of Miss Gray would become a thing of the past once he was out to sea.

His elevated mood plummeted when he caught sight of Miss Gray dancing with Nicholas Barritt.

"The devil's luck," he murmured. The woman looked content on the surface to be in the arms of such a man, but she seemed strained, wounded somehow. But what did he know of her? "Who am I to judge?"

He hadn't realized he'd spoken out loud until someone behind him responded.

"I've heard it said that you're a fine judge of a great many things."

He turned. "Miss Cole. How nice to see you." His tone was cool, but not cold.

"How nice to see you as well. So much has happened since we arrived here. It feels it's been an age instead of mere weeks."

"What sorts of things have happened?" He guessed she would tell him about the many balls and dinners she had attended. He guessed she would tell him about her many marriage proposals.

So it surprised him when she spoke instead of the many new foods she had eaten, about the fever the woman she lived with had acquired, and how the entire household was quite distressed over whether the woman would live. She herself had worried she would come down with the fever, but she had been assured by the doctor that she was past the point of contagion.

"It's a great relief to not have fallen ill." She took a great breath as if to illustrate the point. "I feel completely healthy."

"And have you been to many balls or dinners?"

"A few," she admitted with less joy than he would have imagined from her. "Miss Luke is already married. Her husband picked her out while attending service as one might pluck a flower from a garden. At church! Who shops for a bride during worship? Very unseemly."

He suspected she felt it more unseemly that Miss Luke married before she had. "Your time will come, I'm sure."

"I do hope it doesn't come in such a manner as that. I expect more effort on the part of my future husband."

He wanted to laugh at such a statement but her sincerity kept him in check.

"And how do you fare?" She tossed a glance to the dancing couples in a way that made him sure she was prying into his feelings regarding Miss Gray and Barritt. So he brightened and told her all about the supplies he'd invested in and how they would soon be arriving in Mumbai. He hoped to bore her with enough business details to assure her that his mind was far from any thoughts of the lady in question.

She feigned interested with her wide eyes and her insistence that he tell her more, which made him chuckle. She was good, this one. A man who had not spent an entire voyage watching her manipulate the other passengers might mistake her attention for interest. He felt grateful he'd had the chance to discover her in an authentic setting instead of on a dance floor. That was the terrible truth of balls. They veiled a woman with the low light of candles and muffled her voice under the thrum of instruments. How could a man possibly hope to know a woman when they met under such false circumstances?

He was surprised that Miss Cole had not been matched up already. She knew how to flirt and use the opportunities a ball provided to her advantage. As he watched her watching the dance floor, he realized her own agenda had nothing to do with him. Her eyes did not stray much from one person in particular.

She had apparently taken an interest in Nicholas Barritt, proving the woman to be as foolish as he'd always imagined her to be. Not only was Barritt a man with a distasteful reputation, he was clearly already infatuated with Miss Gray. Out of the many men who were eligible and desirous to marry, why would Miss Cole set her sights on a man who was obviously already spoken for? Did she feel herself to be in some sort of competition with Miss Gray?

Unwilling to watch Miss Cole watch the one couple he felt most anxious to avoid, he excused himself to indulge in the refreshments. He might not care for societal engagement, but he did not mind the fresh fruits and vegetables available to him at such parties that were not available to him on his ship.

"Captain?"

He nearly lost his head at the sound of that one voice uttering that one word.

"Miss Gray."

He bowed. She curtsied.

He could not tell if she was pleased or vexed at his presence. He quickly realized she was not alone. He acknowledged Barritt with a nod.

He considered all the ways he might remove himself from their company when he found himself really looking at Miss Gray. Underneath her pleased demeanor, there *was* something else. He was sure of it.

"Are you well?"

She blinked at the question. "Quite well,

thank you." But the answer was given too quickly and too lightly to be believed.

"Are you really, Miss Gray?" He didn't care that Barritt stood listening and watching. He felt genuine concern for the lady and had to know.

She waved her fan in a way that indicated a dismissal. "There *was* some distressing trouble earlier in the day with a man in Mrs. Williams's employ, a guard I had grown quite fond of. I'm afraid it did hang a dark cloud over my mood, but Captain Barritt has been most helpful in sweeping that cloud away." She smiled appreciatively at the man next to her. He returned an indulgent smile that made Thomas feel like a seasick passenger during a storm.

Before he could excuse himself, Miss Gray's smile faded. "And you, Captain? Are you well?" The way her eyes narrowed with concern, revealing that tiny wrinkle above her nose that appeared when she was trying to puzzle out something, was nearly his undoing.

His tone softened without his permission. "I have had my own distresses these past few weeks. I've worried over Tom."

He had not meant to enter into such a serious conversation, not with her, and certainly not with Barritt present. But the information slipped out, and there was no calling it back.

Miss Gray's brow furrowed, and the fan in her hand snapped closed as she squeezed it in her grip. "Tom? Is something wrong with him? Is he ill?"

He softened, knowing of her very real concern for the boy — and for himself. He also enjoyed Barritt's very real concern over the way she looked at him.

Barritt's scowl and stiff posture proved he did not like that the lady on his arm dared to pay attention to any other man in the room.

Which, of course, made Thomas work harder to keep her attention.

"There were signs that his previous master might bring harm to him."

"Corbeau is an evil man. If he goes any-where near that boy, why I will . . ." She seemed to recall herself as she gave herself a slight shake and her smile reappeared. "Surely the boy is safe."

Thomas nodded. "Quite safe. I've seen to it."

She stopped twisting and strangling her fan. "Of course you have. I would expect nothing less from you." Her eyes watched him intently enough to make him wish to gather her up in his arms.

Barritt, likely sensing the tension crackling between them, interrupted. "So this Tom is a child? A passenger on the ship?"

Miss Gray shivered as though caught by the sudden, unwelcome reminder that they were not alone. "An apprentice," she said. "To the ship's cook." She explained how the man had so badly mistreated the boy, and what Thomas had done to rectify the problem.

Thomas wanted her to stop. She'd mentioned Corbeau's name, but he doubted she knew her companion had dealings with that man. There was no way to politely silence Miss Gray, especially since he'd brought up the subject in the first place.

The orchestra began a new song.

"Why, Captain Barritt!" Miss Cole had surreptitiously migrated to them during the conversation. "I have yet to dance with you this evening."

It was a bold statement, bordering on desperate. He had to give Barritt credit; the man had good enough breeding to extend his arm to Miss Cole and ask her to dance, though his tightened jaw showed he took no pleasure in the task. Nor in leaving the woman of his interest in the company of Thomas.

"And you?" Thomas asked Miss Gray.

"Would you care to dance? You do know how to waltz, do you not? It's not so scandalous as our mothers feared."

She laughed at his joke, but then faded to silence as she considered his proposition. "I do know how, but . . ." She hesitated before looking to where Miss Cole and Barritt were already dancing. "I suppose it cannot hurt."

She let him lead her out among the couples who were attempting the waltz and making clumsy work of it. He was gratified to see that Barritt was far from proficient. The fashion of that dance had apparently come more slowly to this part of the world.

As he placed a hand at Miss Gray's waist, excitement thrilled through him. It shouldn't have. She had an obligation to Barritt. But perhaps she'd already fulfilled it. Perhaps she was now free to make other choices. But if so, she had no reason to be here at this ball looking comfortable on the arm of that man. If she *was* free to make other choices, she didn't seem inclined to explore what those choices might be.

And hadn't he been the one to tell her he could never accept her?

How could he think differently now?

He knew the answer, of course. It was because she stood in his embrace, close enough to feel her warmth, smell the faint scent of jasmine on her, hear the swish of her skirt as he led her through the dance.

He had made a mistake in telling her he would not have her. He opened his mouth to tell her as much when she asked, "Is Tom truly safe?"

The change of subject changed his mind about voicing his thoughts. She was not thinking of him, but of the boy. And she was unlikely to welcome his inconsistencies when it came to his thoughts about their relationship. More, she would think him a fool.

"Yes, Tom is protected. Peterson keeps constant watch over him. Much like your Barritt keeps watch over you." He nodded to where Barritt kept turning his head to keep her within his sights.

He felt her hand tighten slightly at his shoulder. "Yes. He is very attentive."

He could not guess what she meant by her movement or her words, but she did not deny him being *her* Barritt.

She then abruptly asked, "If you were to have children, where would they go to school?"

He frowned at the strange question. "I don't really know. It depends on where their mother and I were situated. Somewhere close to wherever we were." He had hesitated when he said "their mother," because Caroline's face was the one he imagined when he thought of someone filling that role. "Why?"

"No reason."

"Are things going well then? Between you and Barritt?"

She tilted her head and arched a brow at him. "Does it matter?"

"We are still friends, are we not? I ask out of my desire for my friend's happiness."

She slid her gaze back to the other dancers. "Happiness is not a destination. But I believe my journey with happiness is well on its way."

He stretched his neck and wished his cravat didn't feel so tight against his throat. He wanted further details, but kept his teeth firmly together.

Don't ask questions to which you do not wish to know the answers, he chided himself.

"I am glad you are happy," he said when he felt in control of himself. He had so much he wanted to say. He wanted to apologize for being so abrupt in his decisions regarding her. He wanted to share his dreams and his thoughts and his heart with her.

They danced in silence until the song ended.

Barritt came to collect her before Thomas could think of any reason to keep her in his company further. He had no claim to her. And she seemed content to leave his side.

Miss Cole had been deposited where Miss Gray had been collected. Miss Cole's face was downcast. She had apparently not found what she'd sought in such a dance.

Miss Gray glanced his direction several times throughout the evening, but she never approached him again. And he was too ashamed of himself for calling her a liar, for telling her she was not a friend to the truth, for thrusting her to a future without him.

CHAPTER TWENTY-FIVE

Caroline requested to sit out for the next dance, and Captain Barritt obliged. She tried to focus on him sitting beside her. He did not deserve her negligence. Not after how he had helped her when he had come to pick her up for the ball earlier that night.

She had still felt a measure of distress at the thought of Balvan having been sent away, perhaps brutally so, and Captain Barritt had placed his arm around her as he led her toward his curricle. He'd seen her safely seated and then joined her. He listened as she explained how trying the previous weeks had been. He even offered his handkerchief for her tears when she confessed feeling that she had reached her breaking point.

Captain Barritt let her lean into him. His presence, strong and understanding, had given her some relief from all the frustrations she'd held inside.

People.

People were the problem.

She felt weary of the rules and strictures that kept them all in their place. She'd known a boy from her childhood who'd caught butterflies and stuck them with needles to pieces of wood. She'd felt like that butterfly, created to fly, but forced to be pinned in place.

She had found relief in confiding this small part of her distress to Captain Barritt. Though he had repeated many of the things Mrs. Williams had forced her to hear, his words felt bred from compassion and understanding rather than contempt and superiority.

His kindness in her moment of ache filled her with gratitude.

Perhaps that was the moment when she had decided to accept him, to make a life with him in this country.

But then at the ball, she had asked him where his children would go to school when such a time came. He had answered immediately and with finality. They would go to school in England.

And then she had danced with Thomas, felt his hand at her waist, felt him move with her like his ship moved with the ocean. They were a team, pushing and pulling in a way that ached but that also felt like it generated power and strength. He had given a much different answer to the question of children and school.

It was one of the many things she loved about Captain Thomas Scott.

She paused in her thoughts.

She *loved* him.

Even if he had told her she was no friend to the truth.

Yet she *was* truth's friend. If proving herself true to truth meant not marrying, she would do it. If it meant working to earn her passage back to England to reunite with her family as a spinster and be passed around like a parcel from cousin to aunt to sister, she would do it. If it meant never having a family of her own, she would do it still.

Because truth was something she believed in very much in spite of what Thomas said.

She had said happiness was not a destination, but surely happiness could be found in living each day honestly and fully.

Loving Thomas meant she could not marry another — not if she wanted to be true. Living in a loveless marriage and being a childless mother would not be true.

"You are far away from me," Captain Barritt said as the orchestra started another song.

"I am directly in front of you," she answered as she tried to find the important words she had to say.

"Your body might be here, but your mind is somewhere else entirely. Did that sailor say something to you? Has he upset you in some way?"

Yes, she thought.

"No," she said. It seemed everyone had said something that had upset her that day. "It was seeing Miss Cole and hearing of Miss Luke's marriage that has me thinking."

Captain Barritt's lips curved into a long, satisfied smile. "You needn't worry on that score, darling. You are not far from such celebrations."

She winced inwardly. That was not at all the direction she had wanted for the conversation. She had to be honest with him. "I am in no hurry for such a celebration to greet me."

The curve of his lips flattened. "I don't understand."

"I am sorry, Captain Barritt. I feel as though I have dreadfully misled you." Her hands were sweaty in her gloves. Why were any women required to wear gloves in this heat?

"Miss Gray, be clear. Are you saying that

371

were I to make you an offer of marriage, you would refuse it?"

She faltered. This was a moment she would not be able to reclaim in the future. Her answer to this one question would dictate every moment of her life thereafter. How could she know her heart? How could she be sure of herself and her decisions when her life was tossing her to-and-fro?

But she did not love Captain Nicholas Barritt. She knew that. She esteemed him, but she did not love him. And she could not marry one man when she loved another. Maybe sometime in the future, her heart would have healed from Thomas's rejection and be capable of opening to another, but that time was not now.

She felt her lips tremble, a tremor that furrowed its way through her body as she answered the question with words that would not please anyone. "I am not in a position to accept a marriage proposal from anyone at this time, Captain Barritt. My heart is not mine to give at the moment."

Captain Barritt's face was all hard lines from his eyebrows to his mouth to the set of his jaw. "So you *have* misled me."

"Yes," she whispered. "But I have misled myself as well. I falsely believed traveling to a new country would fundamentally change who I am. I have found you to be an exceptionally amiable man, but please do not consider me for a marriage choice. I am ill-prepared to take on the task of being someone's wife."

Captain Barritt finally tore his gaze from hers, which gave her a momentary relief, until she realized he was looking toward the door where Thomas was speaking to another man. Thomas nodded to the man and then took his leave.

Captain Barritt fixed her again with his steely eyes. "I see. Your heart is not yours because it is another's. Do you think his fortune to be greater than mine?"

The question surprised her. "His *fortune*, sir?"

He'd got to his feet, fists clenched. "He ferries a boat. Your life would neither be easy nor comfortable with such a man on such an income."

"Captain Barritt! That man's income is not open for our discussion. It has no bearing on either of us or our current situation. This decision is mine. It is not because of anyone else. There is no one to blame, it is I alone. Please do not seek out foes from the shadows."

"So you do not wish to marry. What will you do?" He threw his hands in the air.

"You are in a foreign land with foreign ways. You have no skills that I've been able to discern these past weeks that would earn you an income. How do you suppose to survive?

"You, as an unmarried woman, will no longer be a welcome guest in Mrs. Williams's home, though she has been quite generous to forebear your presence." He put his finger in her face. "Mark my words. She only took you in because of her great affections for my mother. Think hard, Miss Gray. Your next words could take the roof over your head and the food from your belly and leave you here with no way to return to England. Is that really what you want, when you could have the respectability of being my wife, of having a proper home with servants at your disposal?"

If he thought telling her that she had no skills would convince her to change her mind, he did not know her at all. But that was the problem. He didn't know her. How could he when she'd not dared show anything of herself to him? And what did she know of him?

The current conversation revealed more of him to her than any of the many hours they had previously spent in each other's company. A man who could threaten a woman with poverty and starvation in order to make marriage to him more attractive was not a man she wanted for herself. She had not been entirely confident in her decision to refuse him, but now she knew her instinct had been right.

"I believe you underestimate me, Captain Barritt. And now I see that I overestimated you. I apologize again for leading you to believe that there might be a future between us, but I believe we have nothing further to say to one another. Now, if you will excuse me."

She lifted her skirts and hurried away. Away from him. Away from the ballroom. Away from the smell of too many candles melting their way into the hours of the evening. Away from a future that could have been sure and secure — but where she would have been dismally unhappy.

She did not know what her future held, but it would be her choice. She had friends in this country. Miss Jeffries, who would soon be Mrs. Apsley, was situated in Mumbai. Miss James was also in Mumbai and living with a nice elderly woman. Miss Bronley had moved to Kolkata, but traveling there would not be so unmanageable if Miss Bronley would have her. She had options. There would not be a husband in her future, but there was friendship to be had here in India. That friendship was its own sort of sisterhood.

She moved to find the hostess of the ball and arrange for a carriage back to Mrs. Williams's home when she ran into Miss Cole.

"Why, Miss Gray! Are you ill?"

Miss Cole appeared to be genuinely concerned, but Miss Gray only shook her head. She would not share details with this woman who had already caused her heartache and interfered with her relationship with Thomas.

She left without a word, without hope, but with grim determination.

Captain Barritt's prediction of Mrs. Williams's reaction was exact. As soon as she'd had the news of Caroline's refusal of her friend's son, her fury blazed as fiery as India's heat.

She stood in Caroline's room and berated her for her empty-headed, senseless, and selfish decisions as Caroline packed her trunks. She wished the ills of all misfortunes to fall upon all of Caroline's future days. She threatened to pull her support from Caroline in every manner, including refusing to accept her in the society that would be able to help Caroline keep her footing

376

on this new continent.

She even spat out insults in Hindi — at least Caroline thought it was Hindi. She hadn't thought the lady cared enough to learn any of the language that surrounded her, least of all insults, which were the basest part of any language. And though Caroline didn't understand the words, she had no trouble comprehending the meaning from the underlying tone.

"You will have nothing!" Mrs. Williams concluded. "You will have no reputation to hold you up. You will have no inclusion among our people. You will have no friends here. Nothing."

Each word fell like a lash on her shoulders. She felt sorry for Mrs. Williams, trapped in a home and a life that gave her little to do to fill all the empty spaces. But she would not allow the woman to hold sway over her.

She squared her shoulders, determined to take ownership of her choices. "You misjudge me. I said goodbye to my father several years ago when he passed away. I said goodbye to my mother and my sister and her husband only a few short months ago. Losing their company pained me greatly. But while I think it unfortunate to lose the society of people I might have come to appreciate as friends, losing the associa-

377

tion of those barely known to me is much less distressing. I feel certain of my future happiness with or without them."

"You're a selfish girl, intruding on my home and my generosity and then refusing me the gratitude that is my due!" Mrs. Williams pursed her lips until her mouth became a pinpoint. Her cheeks were sucked in so deeply as to make her cheekbones cutting slashes under her skin.

Caroline stopped at the doors of the house. "You're wrong, Mrs. Williams. I am quite grateful. You were kind to take me in, and I do thank you for that kindness. I am sorry we are leaving one another on such terms, but I want you to know that I will always think well of you for the kindness you've shown me."

It was true. She did appreciate the woman, and while there was both good and ill in the woman, Caroline would choose to remember the good.

"I will not think well of you!" Mrs. Williams snarled in return.

"As you like." Caroline exited into the courtyard where a carriage waited for her. She found herself suddenly grateful she'd saved what bit of money she'd had. It would allow her a moment to catch her breath and make decisions regarding her future. She could pay for food and lodging for perhaps a month, if she was frugal. Maybe a week beyond that.

"What will my mother say when she discovers what I've done?" she murmured after settling herself into the carriage.

At least it would be some months before news of her current actions ever reached her mother's ears.

Find love, dearest, her mother had said.

I did what you asked, Mama, she thought.

But finding something and keeping something were not the same thing.

CHAPTER TWENTY-SIX

"I think your complacency will endanger your investments."

Abramson had spun Thomas through this conversation several times that evening, and he had long since wearied of it. Abramson still believed Corbeau was a threat despite having no evidence other than what he referred to as "a gut feeling."

"Fine." Thomas wished he could take his meal in peace. "What do you propose I do about it?"

"I believe the supply chain needs greater security."

"That will cut into profits." Profits mattered because each successful supply train would bring him that much closer to retiring from the shipping business altogether. The sooner he had appropriate funds saved, the sooner he would be able to settle down somewhere — in England — because he could not mingle in the same society as

Miss Gray and her new husband.

"Losing the entire supply train to sabotage, or worse, will cut into profits far more."

"We have no evidence of danger."

"Corbeau is up to something!" Abramson slammed his glass on the table.

"Yes, he very likely is, but what proof do we have that his business has anything to do with me?"

"He made threats against you."

"Yes, while locked up in one of the cells on my ship. Any man would threaten his jailor. But I am his jailor no longer. I do believe he has moved on."

"You are not a gambling man, yet you are willing to bet everything you have worked for on that one hope?"

"I have given you my decision. And that decision is final."

Abramson shook his head. "Your judgment has become cloudy, Captain. I do not know if you truly do not see this danger, or if your head is simply too full of Miss Gray and the loss of her from your life."

Thomas jabbed a finger into the table in front of his lieutenant. "You forget yourself." His friendship with the man notwithstanding, such insubordination among his crew could not be tolerated if he wished to remain at his post.

Abramson mumbled an apology but didn't look at all sorry. "Fine," he said. "Then there is no reason for me to be skulking about the city. I request permission to return to the ship."

Though the request was a surprise, Thomas did not feel up to another argument. He gave his lieutenant a quick nod of his head and a wave of his hand. "Permission granted. Keep watch over the cargo that has already been delivered and stowed. And make sure the crew is ready to leave as soon as the shipment is delivered. I will see to the needs here in the city for the next few days."

Thomas knew Corbeau had no prior intelligence of a personal supply that would be coming. Nor did the man know that Thomas had decided to dabble in trade beyond that of a courier. If he were to make a move against Thomas, he would do it at the ship, where he would find a formidable force waiting. To assume Corbeau would attack the supply train directly was to give the man far more credit than he deserved.

Thomas did not sleep well that night. The heat drove him from his bed, and he sat at the chair by the window. He thought a lot about young Tom, glad the boy was still under Peterson's care.

Of course, thoughts of the lad led to thoughts of the lady. She had looked beautiful at the ball, a vision too tempting. He should not have asked her to dance. Perhaps Abramson had been right to accuse Thomas of being willing to gamble it all simply because he had lost the girl.

Am I so foolish? he wondered. Peterson would have likely answered yes, which made him glad Peterson was on the ship and had no voice in the matter.

He replayed all that had happened that night in regards to Miss Gray, Barritt, and then Abramson. He tried to make sense of it all in his head, but found himself still awake when first light touched the sky.

He rubbed his eyes, and then readied himself for the day. He had meetings scheduled with several landowners over future indigo crops, and staring out his window pining over a woman would not help him with those meetings.

By the day's end, after successful meetings and amicable agreements with those landowners, he felt good. He would be keeping the coming seasons in a fashionable blue.

He had thought of Miss Gray throughout

the day, but he had managed to stay professional. It had not been easy.

The truth was, when he thought he heard her laughter from across the marketplace, he rushed to see if she was there. When he saw a little boy who looked like a darker-skinned version of young Tom, he turned to tell her, forgetting she wasn't by his side. When one of the landowners promised he could produce crops that would give consistent rich color and showed him a sheer scarf dyed with the richest blue he'd ever seen, he immediately asked to buy the scarf.

"Is this for your wife?" the landowner asked.

"Yes." The absentminded, wistful word came out in a reverent whisper. "No!" he quickly amended when he realized what he'd said. "It is for a memory."

He would never be able to give it to Miss Gray, but for reasons he could not explain, the scarf reminded him of her, reminded him of the color of the evening sky as she walked the length of the *Persistence* and stared out into the blue, star-speckled expanse.

"I will give it to my mother," he grumbled to himself as he left with the scarf folded and tucked into his pocket.

He didn't sleep that night either.

He realized he may never sleep again if he did not right a terrible wrong in the universe. He had accused an honest woman of deceit when he was guilty of the same thing. He had not told her the complete truth.

He had not told her he was sorry.

He had not begged for her forgiveness.

He had not told her he loved her and would die without her.

He suddenly could not wait another moment.

As he stuffed his feet into his boots to rush to the home where Miss Gray had been staying, he could almost see Lieutenant Peterson grinning at him.

Standing outside Mrs. Williams's house, Thomas pulled the bell rope. The moments waiting for one of the servants to answer were agony. Waiting for Miss Gray to appear was impossible. He glanced several times at the darkened windows of the house. Surely she would come down. Surely Miss Gray would not refuse to see him.

Instead of the woman he dreamed to see, it was Mrs. Williams who appeared at the door.

"I apologize for the late hour, madam, but I must speak to Miss Gray immediately."

Mrs. Williams narrowed her eyes. "The

girl is no longer here."

His heart stopped. "What do you mean?"

"I mean she is no longer welcomed at my home."

He frowned. "Where is she?"

Mrs. Williams's expression was one of arrogant dismissal. "I do not know. And furthermore, I have no *wish* to know. The girl has behaved most unseemly from the moment I met her. And you, sir, would be wise to set your interests elsewhere. Miss Gray is not fit to be included in our company."

Thomas nearly took a step back at Mrs. Williams's tone of righteous superiority. The woman must be out of her mind to think that Miss Gray was somehow unfit for polite society. Miss Gray deserved so much better than whatever society claimed Mrs. Williams as a member.

Against his better judgment, he asked, "Is she with Captain Barritt?"

Mrs. Williams's face became even more pinched. "I would never dream of discussing the personal reputation of a dear friend, sir. I must bid you good night."

She closed the door in Thomas's face.

Thomas waited for a moment as though Miss Gray might still somehow appear. But then Mrs. Williams's words truly sank in.

Miss Gray was not here, and it seemed unlikely that she was with Captain Barritt.

Something had changed between them, but Thomas didn't know what exactly. He knew what he *hoped* had changed — that whatever connection or obligation or possible engagement had been forming between Miss Gray and Captain Barritt had been called off.

If so, then that meant Miss Gray would be free. It meant he could proclaim his love, and, he hoped, have that love returned.

That spark of hope was quickly smothered by the cold realization that Miss Gray was missing. She had vanished into the night — alone — and he didn't have the first idea of where to look for her.

CHAPTER TWENTY-SEVEN

Caroline awoke the next morning in an inn, one of the cheaper ones. The noises from the tavern downstairs had kept her awake most of the night. She felt disoriented and had to remind herself that she was homeless and without friend or protector. At least for the moment.

There would be a cricket match at Colonel Eden's today. She had accepted the invitation long before she had left the Williamses' household, and she still planned to attend. Miss Jeffries would be there. She would be able to talk with her and get help.

She hoped.

Oh, how she hoped.

At Colonel Eden's home, she wound her way to the back gardens where the cricket match was being held. She tried to hold back her worry. Mrs. Williams wasn't a strong enough woman to turn her own friends against her, was she? Surely it was too soon for Mrs. Williams to have done any mischief. Surely.

She was wrong.

One of the ladies sniffed in disdain at seeing Caroline's approach. "The nerve!" the woman said with her nostrils flared and her lips puckered in obvious disgust. "You showing up here after what you did to poor Captain Barritt."

She swallowed hard but refused to duck her head in shame. Refusing a man was hardly reason to feel disgraced, yet the woman and those with her acted as though no greater crime had ever been committed.

She kept her head high even as her spirits plummeted further and further. She spotted Miss Jeffries — no, not Miss Jeffries. She had gotten married over the weekend and was Mrs. Apsley now. How many times would she need to remind herself of that? She quickened her step.

Mrs. Apsley turned and saw Caroline, and Caroline's heart stopped for fear of what would happen next.

When Mrs. Apsley immediately smiled and greeted her warmly with an embrace and kiss on the cheek, Caroline nearly cried. Other women looked perplexed by the friendly welcome, but they did nothing to stop the reunion.

Mrs. Apsley linked her arm through Caroline's and exclaimed, "My, but how good it is to see you!" She led Caroline toward a small duck pond at the far end of the green from where the cricket game had just started.

"Tell me you know of my situation, so I may accept your kindness without guilt."

Mrs. Apsley laughed. "I am sure all of India knows. Mrs. Williams is nothing if not a malicious and persistent gossip."

Caroline looked back to make certain no one was eavesdropping. She did not want her friend to suffer by her association.

Mrs. Apsley laughed at that as well. "No one else is of consequence. I am *your* friend. Just as you have been mine from the first moment. And how could I turn away from the woman who saved my life in that storm?"

"But are you not afraid the others will shun you?"

"What if they do? I have a kind husband who loves me. I am situated nicely, Miss Gray. I am not in fear for my standing simply because my husband's love is enough to make me feel secure. But beyond that, his rank is enough to make me important. Imagine that! Me! Important!"

Caroline laughed at the happiness in her

friend's voice. "You've always been important."

Mrs. Apsley looked content in a way Caroline had never seen. "You are one of the first in my life to think so. So, how true are the rumors?"

"Probably entirely true." Caroline kicked at a pebble on the walkway. "You would think no woman in this country ever refused a man."

"It's not that you refused a man. It's that you refused Captain Nicholas Barritt. Many women have either tried to catch him for themselves or for their daughters. They've taken your slight against him personally. But enough about him. Where are you living currently? If the rumors are true, then Mrs. Williams has tossed you from her home."

Caroline huffed. "In truth, I left of my own volition." She filled in her friend on all the details that rumor had left out. By the time she was done, Mrs. Apsley looked sorrowful.

"I wish I could offer you a place to stay, but Mr. Apsley has been moved to a new post. We are packing already."

"So soon?"

She shook her head. "I've been told it is useless to pack too much as most of it will break or be lost in the move. I have been

391

advised to leave most everything behind and buy afresh when we arrive. It is a good thing we are newly married and had so little to begin with, is it not? We'll be departing in only a few days. Miss James will also be moving. Mr. and Mrs. Keller, the people Miss James lives with, are also being moved to a new post. I had hoped we would travel to the same place, but it is not to be."

Caroline's heart fell at hearing that Miss James was moving as well. It made the idea of staying with her friend impossible — at least until she had settled. And would she even be able to say goodbye? The Kellers had not moved in the same circles as Mrs. Williams, so Caroline had not been able to see Miss James. She was also sorry to see Mrs. Apsley leaving but was at peace because her friend had found happiness.

"Does Miss James fare well here?" she asked.

Mrs. Apsley frowned slightly. "I do not know. She says she is happy, but so she always says. I do worry for her. But let us worry over you for the moment. She, at least, has a roof over her head."

Caroline could not argue that logic. They discussed other options and opportunities for Caroline, though there were few enough of both to make the discussion short.

"I wish there was something I could do for you," Mrs. Apsley lamented, taking her hand and squeezing fiercely.

"Ah, but see? You have done the very best thing for me. You have remained my friend though the rest of the world has turned from me."

A short time later, Mr. Apsley came to collect his wife as they had prior commitments. He was kind to Caroline, which the rest of the ladies and several of the gentlemen noted with interest. But once the Apsleys were gone, the crowd became cold in spite of the sun searing through the sky.

Caroline had determined to hire a carriage to take her back to the inn where she might work out new options. But in the front courtyard, Miss Cole appeared.

Caroline had been alone aside from the servants, who likely did not care that she had become a social outcast. She expected Miss Cole to turn her back and walk away toward the cricket match, but instead she initiated conversation.

"Miss Gray. It appears I was right when I said we were women of mystery. Well, I was right about you, anyway."

Caroline noted Miss Cole's unexpected tone and posture. Something was bothering the woman, an invisible burden that seemed to weigh on her shoulders.

"Imagine my surprise when you ignored Captain Scott at that first dinner, refusing to engage in conversation about Volta and his battery. And yet you also refused to indulge in flirtations and smiles at the ball the other day, which might have secured your relationship with Captain Barritt. It makes one wonder. Are you a lady pretending to be a bluestocking? Or are you a bluestocking pretending to be a lady?"

Caroline did not respond. Partly because she did not know the answer herself, but also because this was not at all the direction she expected the conversation to go with Miss Cole.

"Captain Barritt asked all about you at the ball. And now that I hear that relationship is over, I am sorry for my part in what I told him."

"What did you tell him?" The idea that Miss Cole had sabotaged her yet again was unsurprising, but it was surprising that she felt a need to apologize. Had she ever apologized to Caroline before?

"I told him all about Captain Scott and my certainty that you two had feelings for one another. I thought that by telling him that, he would somehow, oh, I don't know, choose me. But no one chooses me, you see.

Not even now. Not even here."

"The decision to end things with Captain Barritt was mine alone, so you have no need to apologize." Caroline felt it necessary to be clear on this point. Miss Cole should not feel burdened with some crime she had not really committed.

Miss Cole shifted her parasol as she frowned. "I know. I am not sorry for that. I am sorry for what else I told Captain Barritt."

"What else was there to tell?"

"I told him how Captain Scott was looking to get out of the shipping business and had made a large investment in a supply of goods coming from the subcontinent."

How Miss Cole knew of such a supply surprised Caroline since *she* had not known of any such investment. Unexpected fear pricked at Caroline's spine, making her shiver in spite of the heat. "Why would such a thing require an apology? It seems harmless enough."

"I thought that telling Captain Barritt such information would show him that you were taken, that Captain Scott was making, I don't know, preparations for a future with you. But Miss Gray, I swear to you I did not know the truth. I may not be a nice person, but I am not so wicked as that."

Caroline's patience thinned. "You didn't know what?"

"I didn't know Captain Barritt had" — she frowned as she searched for the word — "associations with those who want to do Captain Scott harm. And though Captain Scott never showed the attention I wished he had to me, he is not deserving of such malice."

"What associations do you mean? Please explain clearly, Miss Cole."

"I believe Captain Barritt has enlisted the help of Mr. Corbeau — the same Mr. Corbeau who had been the cook aboard the *Persistence*. And now both he and Captain Barritt know to expect a shipment. Interfering with the shipment would allow for Mr. Corbeau to take his revenge against Captain Scott, and for Captain Barritt to possibly injure you for your refusal of him."

Caroline dropped her parasol and grabbed Miss Cole by the shoulders. "Corbeau? The very same? Are you certain? Are you quite, quite certain?" She didn't care about Captain Barritt, but if Corbeau was planning something against Thomas, she had to know everything.

Miss Cole's eyes widened in shock, and she nodded with tears in her eyes. "They mean to cut off the supply, but worse, they mean to damage the ship as well. They said they would cut him at the knees."

"How can you know? Surely Captain Barritt did not reveal such plans to you." Caroline felt she was going to leap out of her skin with fear and dread. Cutting off the supply train was bad enough, but damaging the ship meant possible harm to those she loved. It meant danger for Captain Scott and for his crew and for young Tom.

"They did not have to tell me directly. I am a woman, which means to many that I am neither worthy of attention nor intelligent enough to matter. I was merely there when Captain Barritt relayed the information to a man I don't know. He told him to find Corbeau and gave him instructions on where to strike. I fear people will be hurt. It is all so horrid, and it is all my fault." Miss Cole was near hysteria, her eyes swimming with tears, her hands trembling violently as she swept her fingers over her cheeks. "I am not so wicked as to want a massacre."

"No. You are not so wicked." Caroline reached out and embraced the woman. Such physical affection was not necessarily the way of women in society, but the brief embrace was enough to calm some of Miss Cole's trembling.

"You are not wicked at all," Caroline

repeated, drawing away. "In fact, I would call you heroic for being brave enough to come to me with such news, for being brave enough to do something rather than stand aside and let terrible things happen."

Miss Cole sniffed and dabbed a handkerchief to her eyes. "What do we do?"

Caroline was surprised by the question. She had assumed Miss Cole would immediately depart after having unburdened herself of her information. But Miss Cole had said *we*. They were in this together.

"We do what all brave people do."

"And what is that?"

"We act."

Young Tom would not come to harm. Neither would Thomas or any of the rest of the crew. And that supply coming from the subcontinent would reach the ship safely if she had anything to say about it. Thomas might have decided he would not have her as a wife, but he would have her help whether he wanted it or not.

CHAPTER TWENTY-EIGHT

Thomas ground his teeth together as he looked up and down the street. He had lost count of how many inns he had checked, looking for Miss Gray, but she seemed to have been swallowed up by the vastness of India.

The only lead he had left was to ask Colonel Eden. He was hosting a cricket match; perhaps Miss Gray had made an appearance there?

By the time he reached Colonel Eden's home, his confidence had waned. He despaired of ever finding her. But he could not abandon her in this country. He had to tell her all that was in his heart.

He was escorted to the back lawn where tables and chairs had been set up under large canvas tents. The cricket match was nearly finished. Some ladies and gentlemen sat at tables where they could watch the games with as little effort as possible. Others were involved in the game itself. The colonel's hunting dogs played with a few of the colonel's children on the far side of the lawn under the watchful eye of the children's *ayah*.

Colonel Eden greeted Thomas warmly, and Thomas quickly made his way through the required small talk in order to ask the only question he cared about.

"Have you perhaps seen Miss Gray at all today?" Hope beat in his throat as he waited for the answer.

The colonel shifted in thought. "I believe I did see her earlier."

Thomas's heart raced. "Do you know where she is now?"

"She went off with that other woman — Miss Cole, I believe."

He heard the words but they didn't make sense. Caroline would never have left with Miss Cole, not unless someone held a knife to her throat. Colonel Eden must have been mistaken.

Still, he widened his search to include Miss Cole, just in case the women really were together. He searched through the day and long into the dark.

Eventually, he trudged back to his room at the inn. His supply train would arrive the next morning, and once it was loaded, he would be forced to leave for England.

And Caroline would never know how much he loved her.

He was in bed and staring at the ceiling when a savage knock nearly splintered his door. He jumped to his feet, slipped a shirt over his head, and threw the door open.

He wasn't sure what he expected to find, but it certainly wasn't a young Indian woman holding a note in her hands.

"*Sahib,*" she said. Then, without another word, she shoved the piece of paper at him.

Frowning, he took the note and hurried to light a lamp so he might read. He'd expected his midnight delivery woman to slip away once she'd handed off the note, but she followed him into the room. The note bore Abramson's seal. Frowning deeper, he broke open the letter and began to read.

Captain,

I've received intelligence that an attack on the supply train is imminent, as well as an attack on the ship. The woman who delivered this message to you — Charita — will bring you to where we are meeting to protect the caravan. Come quickly. Bring your revolver. It looks to be a long night.

The *Persistence* is ready. She is protected. Let us ensure she has a full cargo when we leave.

— Lieutenant Abramson

Before he could even process what he'd read, he'd reached for his revolver.

He swiftly readied himself to leave, and before long, he and Charita were out into the night. She hurried him along a back road and led him to where two horses waited. They mounted up, and before he could speak, she sped off, motioning for him to hurry and follow.

They rode for what felt like hours, and he worried the entire time about what might have transpired since the note had been sent to him. Eventually, Charita brought her horse to a stop, dismounted, and indicated they would walk the rest of the way.

He wanted to ask questions, but Charita cut the air with her hand to indicate he should be silent.

He obeyed.

Before they could step into a small clearing, he felt the hackles on the back of his neck rise. As he moved forward, the sharp end of a dagger pierced the top layer of his skin at his throat from someone behind him.

"Do not move if you value your life. Tell me your business or this little mosquito bite will become a gaping hole."

"Honestly, Abramson. I thought you could kill a man three different ways with your hands. Why are you bothering with blades?"

A breath of relief came from his lieutenant. "Captain. You're here."

Charita disappeared into the trees before he could thank her for bringing him directly to Abramson. "Yes. What is happening?"

"Corbeau is what's happening. But we've luckily acquired a little help." He turned to the man next to him. "This is Balvan. He is capable and brilliant and has my complete trust."

"Captain." Balvan nodded. "I have heard much of you."

Thomas nodded his own greeting and listened as the two men explained the situation and how they had decided to handle it.

The caravan had stopped for the night so the men could rest. The attack was meant to come at approximately two in the morning, giving Thomas and his crew just under an hour to implement the safety measures they'd put into place. Abramson had already strategically placed men along the route to stand as lookouts to give warning when the attackers were close.

As Abramson explained everything, Thomas realized that many of the shadows he had taken for trees were actually men.

Men he did not recognize. "Where did you find all this manpower?"

"It's a long story. One I will tell you in detail on our way to England."

They finished preparing and settled in to wait in the dark.

When the first calls came, sounding like night birds, Thomas knew it was time to fight for his future.

Chapter Twenty-Nine

Standing on the *Persistence,* Caroline felt exhaustion burrow straight to her bones. She'd spent the day locating Lieutenant Peterson and divulging the whole of her information to him. She'd hoped to find Captain Scott, but no one had seen him. In the meantime, she had been able to recommend the help of several Indians, including introducing Balvan to the lieutenant.

But now at the end of the day, when all the plans were to be finalized, when she should have been asleep, Caroline's heart felt like it might explode from her chest as she stared at Lieutenant Peterson. "I think I understand."

"You cannot just think. You must be certain. A gun in the hands of someone unsure is a gun that does no one on our side any good. The other side *will* be sure and *will* kill you before you can decide whether or not you are certain." His fierce gray eyebrows were quite frightening when he looked at her with such intensity.

"I'm certain." She had to be. The gun in her hand felt like an explosive that could go off at any moment. But she would use it if she had to. She would use it to protect young Tom, to protect herself, and to protect anyone else who might be in need. These attackers would know that English-women were not cowards.

"All right, then. It's time to go."

She took young Tom by the hand, and the three of them crept to the gangplank, keeping low to avoid being seen from the dock. They stopped there and waited until Lieutenant Peterson felt the danger minimal enough to allow them to move. The crew was scattered throughout the ship, keeping watch over weak spots — and over the three of them. There would have been four of them, but Clara had insisted she would stay and fight by Mr. Black's side.

The attack on the ship would come at any time, but preparing to protect the supply train had taken so much time, they had not been able to focus on the ship as much as they would have liked.

Though the *Persistence* was outfitted with cannons, Captain Scott had forbidden their use while in port. Lieutenant Peterson assured her that every member of the crew had several weapons at their disposal. And they all knew how to use them.

Do I know how to use the weapon in my hand? she asked herself. She had told Lieutenant Peterson that she did, but her mind roared with panic. Would she remember what to do in the moment? *Please let me remember!*

The lieutenant gave the signal and crept forward. She went last, keeping the boy between her and the lieutenant. They knew young Tom would be in danger no matter where they placed him on the ship. It was better to remove him entirely.

When they were off the gangplank, the lieutenant maneuvered them onto the docks, using the wooden crates as barriers to anyone who might be watching.

At the end of the dock where roads converged to carry goods to and from the ships, Caroline finally allowed herself to take a breath of relief. They had made it. She had done all she could for the ship and its captain, and now it would be up to them to fight for what they had.

She would take Tom to stay the night with Mrs. Apsley, who had immediately agreed to help as soon as she heard the tale. Caroline had assured her it would all be over by morning.

She assured herself of the same thing over and over as the trio slid in and out of the shadows, making their way to where an enclosed carriage waited. The lieutenant opened the carriage door and handed her up. Tom scrambled in after her.

"I'll come for you in the morning," he said. Though she knew he meant he would come for the boy, she wanted to beg him to take her as well.

"Be safe!" she said as the carriage driver clicked his tongue at his horses and they moved away from the docks. She wasn't sure if the lieutenant responded or not.

They drove into the night for much longer than expected. Caroline tossed a worrying frown out the window. They should have arrived already. Her worry deepened into alarm as she found herself in unfamiliar surroundings. She had not been in Mumbai long, but she had a sound sense of direction and a good memory for places. She had never been on this road before.

"What is it?" Tom whispered.

Smart boy. He understood it was not safe to speak aloud. "Tom," she said quietly. "I am going to tell you something that might be frightening, but I trust you to be brave and to do exactly as I tell you."

He nodded, his eyes wide and his lips pressed together so tightly they'd turned white.

"Someone we do not know, and do not trust, is driving this carriage. We need to get off and run into the trees as fast as we can. Do you understand?"

If his eyes had been wide before, they now looked like twin moons. But he nodded again. Her heart broke. No child should have had to endure all that this poor boy had endured.

She glanced back out the window. The lights of the city were gone. There was nothing but the wild landscape racing by and the calls of animals in the trees.

What should I do? She considered her options, which were few. Why, oh, why had she not inspected the driver of the carriage before getting in? What naïveté induced her to believe she was safe? Well, she may have been foolish then, but she had her wits now.

If she waited to see where the driver planned to take them, it would be too late. "Tom." She motioned him closer to the door. "I'm going to open the carriage door just a bit, enough for you to slip through, do you understand? Start running before your feet touch the ground. It'll help keep you from falling. And then keep running.

Do not look back to see if I am behind you. You must promise me. You must keep running. Do you promise?"

"I'm not leaving you alone." Tom lifted his chin in much the same way she did when people tried telling her what to do. She would have laughed if she'd had breath in her lungs and not fear.

"I have a gun," she told the boy. "And I'm a very good shot." So maybe the captain had been right about her being no friend to the truth since that was the most horrific lie she had ever told.

"You've never shot a gun before or the lieutenant wouldn't have had to show you how."

"All right, yes, that is true. But I still have the gun, and I *believe* I'm a good shot. You have your legs. We will use what weapons we have. I cannot protect us both with this one gun. You must do your part. Promise me."

He nodded. "I promise."

"Start running before your feet touch the ground," she said again before opening the carriage door. She glanced up to see if the driver noticed. No sound came from him, and the horses did not alter their current speed. She pushed the door open as much as possible to give Tom enough room while also allowing her to keep her grip on the door.

Tom lowered himself and started kicking his legs as though running. He jumped from the door and landed with a soft thud that made Caroline cringe. She looked up to the driver again, checking to see if he'd heard the noise. He hadn't, and Tom was free of the coach. Free and running.

She had only to do the same. She waited a moment to allow Tom to disappear into the trees before she started her descent after him.

The carriage wheel hit a rut in the road, making the whole carriage jolt. The door swung free of her grip and slammed hard into the side.

The driver looked down, and their eyes met for the briefest of seconds.

Corbeau.

She mouthed that one horrible name before she allowed herself to tumble out of the carriage. She rolled into herself to protect her head and thumped along the roadside until her body landed in a heap half on the dusty road and half in the grasses. She did not check to see if she'd broken any bones before she popped to her feet and did as she'd told Tom.

She ran.

She wanted to scream but dared not waste her breath. No one would come to save her even if she screamed. No one would even know she'd gone missing until morning.

The carriage halted a short distance from her. The thunder of someone's feet pounded after her.

"Where do you think you're going?" Corbeau called out. "That's the jungle you're running to!"

She slipped into the trees and kept going, hoping young Tom had found somewhere to hide, hoping he would stay hidden.

"There's snakes in those trees and grasses," Corbeau shouted. "Tigers too. Probably wild elephants who will grind you into the earth. You're safer with me. I'm not gonna do you no harm. Just keeping you for Barritt. See? No harm at all. The boy, though. He's mine. He owes me a debt, he does, and I'm gonna get it out of 'im."

She ducked behind a tree and pulled the gun from her reticule. She prepared herself to use it. She suddenly wished for trousers and sturdy boots like Captain Scott wore. Her skirts made her feel incredibly vulnerable to whatever wildlife hid in the grasses.

"I'll find him," Corbeau called. "I'll find ye both, and I won't be so nice as I would if you came willingly."

She was prepared to dive out from behind the tree and shoot when a low growl sounded close to her.

"Tigers! I told you!" Corbeau warned.

"I'll take my chances with the beast!" she yelled as she leapt from behind the tree and took aim.

The shot rang out into the night, startling birds from the trees. It was echoed closely by a snarling yowl. Then everything went quiet.

She ducked back behind the tree and breathed. It took several moments for the insects and animals to recover and stir back to life. She readied to fire the gun again.

It was terrible enough not knowing where Corbeau was, but not knowing where Tom was hiding filled her with dread. What if she accidentally shot Tom? What if she fired the gun and missed again and Corbeau over-powered her?

What if the tiger could hear her breathing and was slowly threading his way through the grasses to attack her?

The snap of a twig breaking came from her right. She twisted her head in time to see Corbeau's large shadow looming over her. She did not have time to scream as he barreled into her, knocking her head into the tree and scraping her arm against the bark as she tried to bring the gun up to shoot. He grabbed her arm just above her wrist and slammed it against the tree above her head.

She dropped the gun.

"Thought you were so clever!" he said, his breath hot and smelling of ale. Flecks of spit hit her cheek.

She held her breath and turned her head away. Her fingers touched something cold — her haircomb. She gently tugged it out of her hair and maneuvered it so she had a good grasp of it.

"Yes," she said. "I think I am very clever." She jabbed the teeth of the comb into his hand.

He cried out in pain and released her wrist. She landed a good kick, knocking him off balance and toppling him to the ground, but he reached for her and took her down with him before she had the chance to run.

They wrestled, their legs getting caught up in her skirts. He rolled on top of her and used his weight to pin her to the ground.

Something hard jabbed her shoulder from underneath. The gun.

Just then, the tiger roared from behind Corbeau. He jumped to his feet and whirled.

Caroline swept up her weapon and jump

to her feet as well. She took a few steps, thinking to flee rather than stay and fight. She did not want to shoot anyone — not even this horrible man.

Corbeau grabbed her shoulder and yanked her back his direction. The motion whipped her arm around and her finger pressed against the trigger as she tried to maintain her grip on the weapon.

It fired.

"My leg!" he yelled, releasing her.

She used the moment to flee as far as possible.

"You'll pay for that!" he snarled from behind her as the growl from the tiger ripped through the air. The blur of an animal raced past her and toward the wounded man.

She covered her ears against the shrieks and struck out farther into the jungle. "Tom!" she yelled, frantic to find him. "Tom!"

She worried another tiger or maybe a snake had gotten to her boy, but she kept looking, kept calling, kept listening for his voice beneath the sounds of the tiger and the other animals that were awake and prowling.

Caroline wept when she finally heard him call out, "I'm here!"

She reached him and hugged him fiercely, pulling back only to verify he was all right. Aside from being dirty and a little bruised on his arms, he seemed fine. "Are you all right? Has anything hurt you?"

"I'm all right," he said. He didn't ask what had happened to Corbeau, and she offered no explanations.

"We need to get out of here. This is much too much adventure!" she said, hoping to keep her voice calm. It wouldn't do either of them any good if she broke down into tears. Once she had his hand firmly in hers, they made their way to the road, back to the carriage.

"Do you know how to drive a carriage?" he asked when she put him inside the box.

"How hard can it be?" she responded, trying to add some lightness to her voice.

"Can I sit with you?"

She agreed. He had been so brave up until that point, but to leave him alone in the carriage without any comfort seemed unpardonable. He scrambled up next to her. They were both dirty and exhausted.

And alive.

CHAPTER THIRTY

Thomas rode his horse alongside the caravan of supplies. He had taken a blade to his left shoulder and another to his left arm, but he could hardly mind such injuries in light of everything he'd gained. His enemy had planned a surprise attack and were not prepared for a planned battle. They fell easily. Not one of Thomas's men was lost. No woman either.

He cast a sidelong glance to Charita, who rode behind Balvan on a horse. Abramson had promised to explain how he'd come by such incredible help. He promised to explain everything. When Thomas pressed him for information, the lieutenant scowled and said, "Ask me when I'm stitched together again."

The ship's surgeon would be busy with the wounded, but their wounds would heal.

Thomas didn't know what he would find when he got back to the dock. Maybe the ship would be burning or scuttled. What he didn't expect to see when he arrived was Peterson's relieved smile.

He slid off his horse and faced his lieutenant directly. "Tell me the damages."

Peterson's smile fell. "We lost two of our men. One to cowardice — he ran away before the fight even began — and one to a dagger."

"Who died?"

"Graham. He fought bravely. I couldn't save him, though I tried." The exhaustion and sorrow in his friend's voice pierced clear through to his own heart. Nathaniel Graham had been a good man.

"I know you did."

"Black cut down the man who took Graham from us. He was avenged properly. The authorities are here, gathering details of the attack and the perpetrators. They've already arrested Barritt and the others who helped plan and participate. The authorities wish to meet with you to offer their apologies for your troubles in their port."

"No apologies necessary. It was hardly their fault."

"We'll see to the cargo while you explain that to them." Peterson saluted and left to tend to his task.

Thomas was tired and his left arm ached

from his wounds, but he made his way to where the Indian authorities waited for him. They had enough of their own work to do. They did not deserve to be kept waiting.

By the time he made it back to his cabin, he felt entirely wrung out. With the lamp lit, his eyes fell on the drawing on his desk. It was one Miss Gray had done of him early in the voyage, before he had known how much he could feel for her. The drawing was a side portrait of him standing at the railing, looking off to a horizon he felt he was always chasing.

She had surprised him with it when they were just beginning their friendship. She truly was talented at making a page look like a mirror of reality. Had he ever told her that? Had he ever told her how much he admired the depth and vitality in her art? No. He didn't think so. And now, he would never have that chance.

He put out the lamp. He would be needed again on deck in only a few hours.

He fell heavily into his cot and closed his eyes.

He was tired of chasing the horizon.

The next day, Thomas was again at the railing, looking out toward land as it grew smaller and smaller. In all the chaos, he'd not been able to find Miss Gray, to say he was sorry, to say goodbye, to say anything at all.

Peterson and Abramson had informed him that the intelligence of the two planned attacks had come from Miss Cole — a person he had underestimated. Young Tom was asleep when Thomas checked on him. He had not received details on how the boy fared through the combat aboard the ship. He would have been devastated if he'd returned and found that the boy had come to harm.

He grunted with the pain of leaning too heavily on the railing and stood to relieve the pressure from his shoulder. The cut had been deep and would take a while to heal.

Peterson stood next to him. "I think Balvan is going to work well with the crew. And Charita and Clara are already best friends, but Black wants it to made known that taking another woman aboard the *Persistence* is asking for a torrent of bad luck."

"Even though one of those women is his wife?"

Peterson shrugged. "I don't pretend to understand his superstitions or the rules that govern them."

The two men laughed.

After a moment of silence, both men staring at the tiny strip of land on the horizon, Thomas asked, "What do you think she thinks of me?"

"You tell me who, and I will tell you what."

Thomas sighed and shook his head. "Miss Gray. She likely regrets the day she met the likes of me, wouldn't you agree?"

"You can always ask her the next time you see her. We'll be back to Mumbai soon enough," Peterson said before moving away from the railing. "Apologies, sir, but it's time to collect a debt from a little wager with the helmsman."

Thomas knew there was work to be done but could not force himself from his melancholy mood to see to any of it. Not yet. Not until the land was entirely gone from his sight.

"What is it you are looking at with such intensity?"

He sucked in a breath that seemed to carry no oxygen. He turned slowly, blinking in case the woman who stood at his shoulder was a mirage or illusion. "Miss Gray?"

"Hello, Captain Scott. I do hope we will continue our lessons regarding distance and travel on a ship. That strip of land is barely visible. It must be at least forty nautical miles considering how high we are above sea level. The land is a fairly decent elevation as well, wouldn't you say?"

It was her. Not a phantom, not a hope, but her! She stood before him in her white dress, the one she'd worn the first day of the voyage that had brought her into his life. She had a scrape on her cheek and a bruise on her forehead. Her single braid was threaded with blue ribbons, reminding him that he'd purchased a blue scarf for her.

"Miss Gray . . ."

"Yes. Hello. Am I right about the nautical miles? I do so love being right."

"I — Where have you been hiding this whole time?"

She lifted her shoulders. "In my cabin. Lieutenant Peterson locked me in, saying that his actions were under your orders and that I was to take any grievances to you directly."

"He locked you — ? Wait." He was going mad. And why did it feel like he was not breathing? "How are you here?"

"It is a long story." Her voice lowered, losing the playful tone. "And I will tell you the whole of it. But it started when I realized I could not marry a man I did not love, not if I wanted to prove myself honest to the one man whom I did love. I am sorry I was not truthful to you when I ought to have been." Tears filled her eyes as she slid next to him and faced him directly.

She took a deep breath. "I understand if you do not want me still, if your feelings are unchanged. But I am hoping you will forgive me. You once told young Tom that to forgive is the most honest way to accept an apology. Please accept my apology."

He reached up and brushed away the tear that had slid down over her scraped cheek to her jaw. She closed her eyes at his touch, and a small, shuddering whimper left her lips. He let the backs of his fingers trace up her jawline until his fingers smoothed back her hair. He pulled at one of the ribbons that kept her hair fastened and watched as the wind untangled the braid until her hair flowed around her.

As her hair unraveled, so did he, and he found tears in his own eyes. "Forgive you? It is I who must beg your forgiveness. It is I who stubbornly clung to my pride and foolishness until I let things become quite lost." The lump in his throat choked off his ability to speak. "I thought I had lost you."

She made a soft shushing sound and placed her cool hands against his cheeks and looked into his eyes. "My mother told me to find love, and I found you. It has been a long journey, but I think we've finally come to the proper destination. Do you agree? Please say you agree."

"Oh, Caroline," he breathed as he pulled her to him and kissed her.

He didn't care if any of his crew or new passengers might be watching. He didn't care that there was so much left unsaid between them. They would have time for conversation later. But with the wind and his fingers tangled in her hair, all he wanted was the communication they were having, the one in which he told her again and again with each kiss traced over her lips that he loved her.

That he was hers.

EPILOGUE

Caroline lifted her face to the morning light of her beloved England and closed her eyes. She still felt the sway of the *Persistence* under her feet though they had landed in port days earlier. She was almost sad to be on land. Almost, but not quite.

She stood on the front steps of her uncle's house in Salisbury. It felt good to be in surroundings that were at once familiar to her and foreign. She'd grown so used to the ship, to life on the sea, she almost wanted to turn to Thomas and tell him to abandon this thought of settling on land. But she would not do any such thing.

She would see her mother — only a few short minutes away. It would be a wonderful reunion and a wonderful surprise for her mother as Caroline had had no way to send word of her arrival ahead of time.

At least, she hoped it would be wonderful. Caroline worried that Nicholas Barritt's mother might have prematurely spread news of Caroline's supposed engagement and marriage to her son since there was no way for Mrs. Barritt to have had news to the contrary. Such a rumor would certainly create a stir. When she'd asked Thomas if he feared being the center of such scandal, he had laughed. He'd then given her a wolfish grin and told her a little scandal of their own making might be more interesting. She'd blushed and laughed and scolded him.

Caroline hoped her mother would find Thomas so enchanting and be so glad for Caroline that she would not mind the rumblings of gossip.

"You're stalling, darling," Thomas said.

"Yes."

"Are you all right? You're not rethinking our plans now that you're home?"

She turned to him, surprised that after so many months together he still harbored such worry. "*You* are my home. No matter where we are standing, if we are together, then I am home. I've never been so sure about anything or anyone than I am of you."

He straightened under her words. When she'd first met him, she thought him arrogant and starchy. Since then, she'd found all the ways he was gentle, compassionate, accepting. She'd also found he had insecurities stemming from his father's demanding method of upbringing.

She laced her arm through his and leaned into him. "Being here in Salisbury again has brought me a joy that borders on ache. You here with me has made this place a perfection I cannot quite comprehend."

He pressed a soft kiss to her head. "Yet you hesitate on the doorstep of your relations almost as if you've done something wrong."

She closed her eyes at the brief kiss, loving how he made her feel safe and strong. "I believe I hesitate because I am at the edge of things. Beginnings and endings. I'm not explaining it well because I'm not sure how it all works."

"Is that worry I see in the brazen woman I am to marry?"

She lifted her eyes to his, and they both smiled. He lifted her hand and gave her knuckles a lingering kiss.

"I will not be the woman you are to marry if we do not go inside where you can speak with my uncle." She gazed up at the rough stone exterior of the house.

"Then, by all means, let us not wait another moment longer. Unless you're not ready?" Thomas squeezed her arm slightly in encouragement.

"I'm ready," she said and knocked on her uncle's door.

Though it had been a long time since she'd seen any of the servants in her uncle's household, she was recognized and ushered in immediately. A look of surprise passed between the housekeeper and her uncle's valet as she and Thomas were led to the parlor. Clearly, no one expected her arrival.

Thomas and Caroline hadn't been waiting long in the parlor before her mother arrived in the doorway, looking white as death.

"Caroline." The word came in a gust of air, a breath of disbelief.

"Mama!" Caroline crossed to her, only wanting the feel of her mother's arms around her.

The embrace was quick. Her mother pulled away. "How are you here? What has happened? Are you well?" The questions spilled out in quick succession as her mother touched Caroline's face as if verifying that Caroline was real and really in front of her.

"I am well, Mama. I am home! And I would very much like to introduce you to someone dear to me — Captain Thomas Scott." She released her mother and stepped back to allow Thomas the space to bow for her mother.

He did so, looking every bit the well-bred gentleman in his captain's uniform — a man her mother would be pleased to have as a son-in-law.

"Thomas," Caroline said, "allow me to introduce you to my mother. Mrs. Gray."

"A pleasure, ma'am."

"He is the captain of the *Persistence*, Mama. We met on the voyage to India and became fast friends."

Thomas gave her a look that indicated he found humor in her words. While there had been fast emotions between them, friendliness hadn't been one of the initial feelings.

"Yes," Thomas said. "Our friendship has led us to fonder feelings, the likes of which lead me to ask to speak to Caroline's uncle."

"Of course." Her mother's eyes widened and her mouth opened for the briefest of seconds upon hearing and understanding the implications of such a request before she recovered herself and rang for the housekeeper, who then took Thomas to meet with Caroline's uncle.

Her mother blew out a breath as if she intended to fill the sails of the *Persistence*. She pulled Caroline to the settee. "Explain to me everything, and be quick, before he returns."

Caroline did as asked, trying to fit in as

much information as possible. She talked of the journey, the pain of not knowing herself or how to act, and the home she had found in Captain Scott.

"He is handsome to be sure," her mother said. "Odd how I always thought all sea captains wore beards."

Caroline laughed. "As did I!"

Her mother shook her head. "But Mrs. Barritt has told the whole of the world that she sent you to meet her son and that it is very likely that her son is already married to you. There will be gossip."

Caroline stood and walked over the braided rug in front of the fireplace. "A little gossip is worth avoiding the misfortune of being married to Nicholas Barritt." She then explained the treachery and low character of the man who'd had her abducted and nearly murdered in the jungle. "I will go to Mrs. Barritt and apologize that her son and I found no compatibility. Though I would imagine that she's now received a letter from her friend, Mrs. Williams. We brought many letters over from India."

"Oh, my darling! I am so sorry. I had no idea Mrs. Barritt's son was such a man."

Caroline returned to the settee and took her mother's hands in her own. "How could you have known? But do not be uneasy. Had

I not undertaken this journey, I would not have this wonderful man at my side. I told you that when I returned, we would have wonderful adventures to discuss. And so we do."

Her mother glanced to the door and squeezed Caroline's fingers. "And this Captain Scott? He makes you happy?"

Caroline felt happiness swell in her. "Deliriously so. Thomas accepts me as myself in the same way Father accepted you."

"And his prospects? You would be happy married to a man who is on the sea for many months of each year?" Her mother inspected her face to verify Caroline's sincerity.

"Isn't that the lovely part? He has one more voyage to complete before he can shift his focus to other business, and I, as his wife, will accompany him on that journey. I find I quite like the sea, and I am taken with the crew as well as with India, and I wish to see it again. Then, when we return, we will settle here, close to you, close to Josephine. We wish to marry as soon as possible. We've waited long enough."

Her mother tightened her grip on Caroline's hand. "You did it then, dearest. You found love."

Tears formed in Caroline's eyes. She felt a

wave of emotion greater than any swell of sea during a storm. "Yes, Mama. I found love. I found him."

ACKNOWLEDGMENTS

Working on this book required a lot of nautical know-how. My naval-captain father, Walter Peterson (who plays the character of Lieutenant Peterson), was only too happy to impart his knowledge on a grateful daughter. Anything that might be wrong in regards to the ship is not the fault of the captain, but of the author. Thanks, Daddy. I love you.

So much love goes to Heidi Taylor Gordon and Lisa Mangum. I love our brainstorming sessions and your brilliant editorial advice, and I love laughing with you two so much! To the entire Shadow Mountain team, I can never be grateful enough. You are all such a huge part of every page. Thank you!

A big thanks to my agent, Lane Heymont, for everything! Working with you is such a pleasure.

Writing is a solitary business, but writing

friends make it less so. Heather Moore is one of those friends. With a spot-on edit that helped me smooth out scenes that were needing some love, she allowed me to hand in this book with confidence. Also, she makes my life better because she's in it.

I have a huge writing family who encourage me, champion me, and take care of me. You all know who you are. Thank you all for being my friends. It matters. So much.

I am lucky enough to have an incredibly supportive and amazing mom and dad. Let's be real. Without them, I wouldn't even be here.

I am *always* grateful for my children — McKenna, Dwight, Merrik, and Chandler (and grandbaby Theo) — for putting up with all the ways their lives were altered by having a mom (and mom-in-law) who decided to be a writer rather than a professional dishwasher.

And as a strange little side note, my middle name is Caroline. My husband's name is Scott. It is interesting that this fictitious love story is far more believable than our real one. Thank you, *min kärlek,* for always believing in me, for always supporting me, and for always holding my hand through the hard stuff. *Du är min lyckliga någonsin efter. Du är min alltid.*

AUTHOR'S NOTE

The Fishing Fleet began at the end of the seventeenth century when the East India Company began shipping women from England to India to marry their officers. The title of "Fishing Fleet women" is not kindly meant as it was used to refer to women who had to go out "fishing" for husbands.

By the time of this fictional setting of 1820, the East India Company had removed itself from the business of finding husbands for their officers, but women still made the journey when their prospects at home were slim. I first heard of this phenomenon from fellow authors Josi Kilpack and Jennifer Moore while we were on a writing retreat together, and it made me wonder how bad a woman's prospects would have to be to convince someone to try her luck on another continent, leaving behind family, friends, and a country she loved, all with the knowledge that she may never see any of it again.

While this method of finding a husband may seem extreme, I see courage and strength in the choices these women made. I don't know that my spirit is adventurous enough to have made such a journey.

During my research for this novel, I discovered the book *Women of the Raj* by Margaret MacMillan. It helped me understand what colonial India might have been like for both the English and the Indians. I patterned the fictional Mrs. Williams after some of the real-life women of the time and drew inspiration from some of their actual thoughts and language to give voice to that character. While I changed the quotes to fit the conversational needs of my story, the general ideas remain. I thank Margaret Macmillan for the thorough and intense amount of research she must have undertaken in order to bring to light the thoughts, journal entries, and letters of many women of the Raj.

I took a small amount of creative license regarding the timeline. During the voyage, the characters discuss a protest at Manchester (known as the Peterloo Massacre), where innocent people were wounded and killed by their own government who saw them as a threat. Percy Shelley wrote a poem about that event entitled "The Mask of Anarchy," a line of which Caroline quotes in the story. While the poem was written during the time period of the book, it was not actually published until 1832 after Shelley died.

Finally, during the time period of this book, Mumbai was referred to by the English as "Bombay." Since this is a work of fiction and not a history book, I decided to respect the choice of modern-day Indians who saw the name Bombay as a legacy of British colonialism rather than a reflection of their own heritage.

DISCUSSION QUESTIONS

1. The Fishing Fleet women left their homes to venture to new lands in the hopes of finding a husband. For what would you be willing to leave home and country, even if you knew you would likely never be able to return?

2. Caroline visits public lectures in an effort to learn as much as she can. How would attending these educational discourses form a mindset that is different from the other women of her era? In spite of those differences, in what ways is she similar to those same women?

3. Captain Scott tells young Tom that to forgive is the most honest way to accept an apology. He then withholds his forgiveness from Caroline when she tries to apologize and explain. Is his action hypocritical? In what ways can we balance apologies and forgiveness when working toward our own personal and relationship

growth?

4. Caroline wants to fit in with the other ladies on the ship and also with her new acquaintances in India. She even tries to change her own personality. What dangers might be found in working too hard to fit in?

5. Caroline uses her art as a means to escape from society. How does her art draw her closer to other people?

6. Captain Scott feels disdain for the Fishing Fleet women because he feels they are making poor life choices. What are ways he unfairly judges his passengers without understanding their histories and reasons? How can we avoid doing the same thing to people we meet?

ABOUT THE AUTHOR

Julie Wright was born in Salt Lake City, Utah. She's lived in LA, Boston, and the literal middle of nowhere (don't ask). She wrote her first book when she was fifteen. Since then, she's written twenty-five novels and coauthored three. Julie is a two-time winner of the Whitney Award for best romance with her books *Cross My Heart* and *Lies Jane Austen Told Me* and is a Crown Heart recipient. Her book *Death Thieves* was a Whitney finalist.

She has one husband, three kids, one grandbaby, one dog, and a varying amount of houseplants (depending on attrition).

She loves writing, reading, traveling, hiking, snorkeling, playing with her family on the beach, and watching her husband make dinner.

The employees of Thorndike Press hope you have enjoyed this Large Print book. All our Thorndike, Wheeler, and Kennebec Large Print titles are designed for easy reading, and all our books are made to last. Other Thorndike Press Large Print books are available at your library, through selected bookstores, or directly from us.

For information about titles, please call:
(800) 223-1244

or visit our website at:
gale.com/thorndike

To share your comments, please write:
Publisher
Thorndike Press
10 Water St., Suite 310
Waterville, ME 04901